On The

Market

—.—

The Chalkewood Tales - Book 1

Saphel Rose

Searchmatix

Wonderlust, Book 2 in The Chalkewood Tales Series.

This edition is published in 2022 by Searchmatix , 71 – 75 Shelton Street, London, WC2H 9JQ.

Editing: Katrina Harvey, Athena Copy

Book Cover Design: Graham Addison, Addison Design. Copyright owned by Searchmatix

Authors website address: saphelrose.com

Published 2022. Printed in the United States of America unless otherwise stated. A catalogue record for this book is available from the British Library

ISBN: 978-1-915733-03-0   paperback

CONTENTS

Your FREE Book Is Waiting   V

1. Park Run   1

2. The Last Days of Chalkewood   14

3. We've Just Been Taxed   31

4. I'm Monica McStrachan   51

5. Miss Adventure   64

6. Pigs in a Blanket   75

7. The Female of the Species   96

8. A Whiter Shade of Pale   108

9. Under Offer!   124

10. Secret Garden   155

11. Friends to Lovers   189

12. Conducted Tour   211

13. A Fete Worse than Death   234

14. Chalkewood Festival   256

15. Valley of Love   278

16. Tuscany   296

17. The Torture Garden   309

18. Final Reckonings   328

19. Solo-man   344

A Request To Review On The Market   356

Preview Book 2 The Chalkewood Tales -   358
Wonderlust

Wonderlust Chapter 1 - The Power of   360
Love

Moving On (The Prequel) - FREE Book   369

Preview Your Free Book - Moving On (The   371
Prequel)

About Author   372

More About Saphel Rose   374

— • —

Your FREE Book Is Waiting

 Meet Laura, independent woman of independent means. Living the life in New York as a management consultant. Laura works hard and plays hard but is hoping that Mr Right will catch her eye. She has decisions to make as she is heiress to the family estate, Chalkewood. Where will life take her? What decisions does she need to make? Moving On is the prequel to On The Market and will have you laughing out loud as she makes friends and influences people from all walks of life.

Download Moving On Here – FREE BOOK
https://saphelrose.com/download-moving-on/
Preview Moving On Here
https://saphelrose.com/book/moving-on

Chapter One

Park Run

Saturday, 1 January.

Flushed with the success of graduating from her 'Couch to 5K' running programme, Laura turned up for her first ever Park Run. It was all part of her new quest for a better way of life and an attempt to lose weight... once again. The ultimate goal was to get fit, get herself out there and, hopefully, put an end to being a singleton.

The notice on the website said this week's Park Run was starting an hour later than usual, at 10.00. Laura hadn't noticed this. The change had been made to give people an extra hour to metabolise last night's New Year's Eve alcohol.

Turning into the car park, she noticed that she was still being tailed by a white van that had been following her almost since she left Chalkewood. Damn it! She had even taken the wrong lane coming in and almost bumped into him. Thinking smart, she decided to drive down to the end of the lot, hoping he'd soon forget about her. Peering closer in her rear-view mirror, she felt a slight flush of embarrassment – it appeared to be one of the organisers, as he was now unloading Park Run paraphernalia from the van.

Reversing into a bay gave her a better view of him, and it allowed her to people-watch as others parked up to unload. Curiously, he was quite a bit overweight, and he walked with a limp. A thick-set guy with salt-and pepper-hair, he wore shorts, like many larger men seemed to do, even in the winter.

As she was so early, Laura decided to wait a while, keeping a low profile. She reached for her phone. Nobody she knew was up yet, so she scrolled through the previous night's messages wishing her a happy New Year. Mostly couples.

Time at last to make her way over to the sign-in desk, where any hopes that white-van man might have forgotten all about her were quickly dashed.

"Hi, you're from Chalkewood, aren't you? I'm Trev," said Trev. "I followed you in. Saw you pull out of Fanhams Lane. I know your father from when I did work experience for him in the late nineties. Bet you don't remember me, though! Them was good old days! I ended up joining the forces after that, though, and picked up this injury in Iraq. So, it's just volunteering for me now."

Volunteering lay at the heart of Park Run, and other volunteers were just getting into their stride.

'Event Day Course Checkers' Heather Warden and Aiden Corseley were laying out the route markers. Pete Checkley joined them. "Whoever wrote this risk assessment needs bloody shooting," he said, in a slightly nasal voice, whilst crossing something out on his clipboard and amending it.

Laura had often driven past the park on a Saturday morning and seen the colourful, Lycra-clad 'stick-insect people' in there, darting in and out amongst the trees. It had built up a real fear of missing out, or FOMO, as that feeling was now called. She had driven past and longed to be one of them, but had continually put it off, thinking she might be too fat to take part. Now she was there with them. One of them. She had earnt her place. It was thrilling, but she was still nervous of failure. Looking around and closely studying the other runners, she was partially reassured to see that some were fatter than her.

At 09.45, 'Senior Marshal and Warm-up Leader' Thelma Hardwich started yelling out instructions. "If you're a new runner, over there to the flag for your First-Timers Briefing, please." Most people were on site now and doing a variety of casual warm-up routines. Heather Warden, the 'Run Director' picked up her radio mic. "One two, two one. It's okay, Pete, it's working now – I just wasn't close enough to the amp... So, people," there was a slight pause whilst the hubbub died down. "So, for those of you who don't know me, I'm Heather and I'm your Run Director for today. So, can you all hear me? Okay, good," she said, laughing nervously. She then went on to disseminate all the usual information and reminders like 'this isn't a race' and 'we're all in this together'. Finally, there was a cheer for all the volunteers.

Laura took her place at the back and then noticed she had a shoelace undone. Great start! By the time she had re-tied it, the claxon had sounded, and everyone was surging forwards. The Tail Walkers in their fun costumes were standing by her, their dinosaur tails wagging, but soon she and they were off. Before long, she was starting to pass the elderly Brisk Walkers and those with knee braces. A little further still, and she was graduating through the spectrum of running abilities.

The pack headed onto the long straight by the river, the rising sun reflecting gloriously off the water as the mist began to lift. It was a delightful scene to behold. "Run on the left, please. Express runners coming through." Laura and others obeyed the marshal's instructions and shifted to the left to allow themselves the mild indignity of being lapped. Even worse, though: the front runner was some guy pushing a pushchair with a kid in it. Same with the number two runner. They were actually racing each other. Laura tried hard not to think what an utter piss-take this was, but fair do's. It was very impressive and a great way to celebrate human health and fitness. Plus, the toddlers must have been getting a real buzz out of the ride. What a dad...! What a dad indeed, thought Laura. But that was just the problem: they were dads.

Next, up ahead in the distance, was a lady Laura had seen in the car park earlier. She had a big chunky bottom, looked anxious and was sweating profusely, and that had all been true even before the run started. She was now making slow, awkward progress then suddenly she ground to a halt and sank to her knees with runners passing either side of her.

Laura stopped and crouched down beside her, almost too out of breath to speak. "Are you... okay?" She shook her head. Laura held her hand and said, "It's okay, everything's going to be okay. What's your name, sweetie?"

"Patz," gasped the woman.

"Hi, Patz." Laura then negotiated getting her arm around Patz's shoulder and managed to get her a few yards off the track and onto a park bench. Patz was no longer red-faced but was now complaining of indigestion. Looking up, Laura saw a man in a pink marshal's vest making quick progress towards them across the grass with a wheelchair. One of the fast runners had apparently alerted a marshal.

"Hello..." He turned from Patz and looked at Laura questioningly.

"Patz," she said.

"Hello, Patz, my name is Jim Singh. I'm medically trained, and I can help you. Just relax, I'm here now and we're going to get you all sorted very soon." He was very slick and professional, and after he'd radioed ahead and dispensed some treatment, Laura abandoned her run and helped by carrying Jim's kit bag, whilst he pushed the wheelchair. The local hospital was very close by, and an ambulance arrived within moments. By this time, the run was finishing and people were catching their breath, warming down and talking about PBs and going off to Café D'Souza for a coffee.

"How about I buy you a coffee then, Laura?" suggested Jim. She agreed that this sounded like a fabulous idea, and they wandered off to the café. Soon the place was rammed with runners. There was a wonderful energetic atmosphere, but you wouldn't want to be there during this most frenetic hour if you were a non-runner. Pushchair man crashed in through the door, folded pushchair on one arm and child in the other. He seemed to be able to simultaneously drink coffee, bottle feed the toddler and pick at a Danish Pastry, and that was just with his left hand. Laura wondered what his wife was like. Probably even better at multitasking, for sure.

Laura realised she had let her attention drift. She turned back to Jim, who was telling her how often people think his name sounds like a health care additive. "What? Jim?"

"No, Jim Singh, they always think it sounds like ginseng."

Laura's first impression of the Park Run volunteers was that they were a bit of a cross-section. For some, it provided an opportunity to stand up in front of a crowd and express themselves and test their banter. For a few, it seemed like they might be compensating for a lack of fulfilment in the day job – finally, a chance to be 'in charge'. Jim, however, like the majority, was in neither of those camps. Maybe he was a pure altruist? He had a nice, easy way about him and could be quick-acting, yet without over-reacting.

"I've seen you before, Jim. Haven't I? Shopping at the indoor farmer's market?"

"Ahh, yes, no, well, kind of. I'm a supplier. Health food products and no, not ginseng."

"Well, Jim, you look very athletic, so I could easily believe that. It's kind of interesting though, because..."

Zus-zus, Jim's phone buzzed on the table with a PM. "Aww no, no... that's so sad... really sad... Patz won't be running with us again, I'm afraid. She didn't make it. Heart attack apparently. I suspected as much."

Laura said, "So ironic, because Patz was trying so hard to improve..." then the reality hit her. Her bottom lip went. She pulled her neck tube up over her mouth and started to cry.

Jim took her hand across the table. "It's okay, it's okay. I'm afraid that nature can be mysterious in its ways, sometimes. All we can do is do our personal best, as it were."

It was a strange situation – bitter-sweet, in deep despair yet surrounded by positive, glowing people, all exuberant and happy. Laura watched over her neck tube. The windows were now running with condensation and a small group had started to sing the Park Run song that they had learnt off YouTube, 'See You at the Finish Line'. It seemed impossible to believe that, amid all this, the runner she had held hands with earlier had now reached her own 'finish line' and was now trading in her sneakers for a harp.

The seated crowd had now thinned out considerably. Still a few people left, though. Many trying to download their run from apps and doing the social media thing, or simply waiting for a lift home. One or two were nursing their feet. Nobody seemed to care much about bare feet in the café on run day.

"Jim, under any other set of circumstances, it would have been a pleasure to have come here with you. Thanks for the coffee. I guess I'll see you down the Farm Shop."

"Okay, Laura. Thank you for being the one who cared enough to put people before PBs. I wish you the very best and hope to see you soon."

Laura got into her 'Chelsea Tractor' – as her father had loved to call it – and took a deep breath. Her Land Rover was a big old diesel vehicle, a bit at odds with Laura's vision of leading an environmentally responsible lifestyle. It had, however, been indispensable on a number of occasions – towing heavy estate machinery, horse boxes, and other trailers. Probably not ideal for the Park Run, though – it had hardly fitted through the gateposts of the park entrance and looked well out of place amongst all the other more minimalist vehicles. Many people chose to cycle, which was a really clever alternative because it meant that you could turn up having already done your warm-up.

Driving out of the park, it seemed an even tighter fit than on the way in, but soon she was away, and Chalkewood bound. Laura put the music on. As she turned off onto the long country road, the sun began to shine, and her mind drifted back to the earlier sad events of the morning. 'We're All Runners' started playing on the radio, and she listened to the words. They made her quite emotional and she had to pull off into a layby and close her eyes for a while.

Regaining her composure was a longer process than she'd expected. It was one thing being strong in the face of adversity, but this was one of those times, when being strong wasn't enough and only time itself could ease the intensity of the moment.

Laura woke with a start. The engine was still ticking over; the car was now boiling hot. Her mouth was dry, she wanted a wee and was starving all at the same time. She wiped her eyes and pulled out onto the road. Winding down the window cooled the car down pretty quickly. She passed the sign saying Hampden 1¼ miles and then joined the private road leading to the heart of the Chalkewood estate.

Gordon Peasley, the estate manager, was out with a trailer-load of clients on a bird shoot. Laura always regarded them as gross, rich old men, with hip flasks, all out robbing defenceless birds of their lives, just for fun. Mind you, pheasants were pretty mindless birds, as Laura was immediately reminded when one dived straight under the car, escaping miraculously. She waved as she passed Peasley, and he tugged the wide brim of his wax cotton hat in response. Making sure his clients saw him.

As Laura drove up to Chalkewood, her hierarchy of human needs desperately vied for position, so the last thing she wanted to see was bloody estate horticulturist Guy Pengersick changing direction to come over and chat with her. Luckily, he seemed to be carrying a huge, heavy coil of galvanised steel wire over his shoulder, which ought to at least guarantee he'd soon bugger off. Winding down the window, she brought the car almost to a halt, but not quite. "Hello, Guy, what gives? Everything okay?" she asked, slightly riding the clutch.

"Sure, good. How was Park Run?"

"Also good, in fact dead good. Look I must dash."

"Sure. Look, before you go," he said, shrugging the coil of steel back up onto his shoulder as if it were weightless, whilst Laura grimaced. "A few of us are getting together tonight for a game of Nine Men's Morris. Garth and Gren are up for it. Fancy it? We're doing snacks, beers and—"

"Guy, look, I'm so sorry. It's been a strange day. I have to dash." She wound up the window and pulled away briskly.

Once through the door. Loo first. Desperate for it. She was almost wetting herself. Laura sat there panting as she disgorged what felt like a whole gallon of pee. Still seated, she kicked off her running shoes and knickers. Now she felt cold though, as the heating wasn't on yet. Stumbling into the drawing room, she slumped onto the sofa and covered herself with a large throw. Time at last to gather her composure and think about what should come next. She reckoned it had to be food or a hot shower. Or perhaps a small appetiser to start with and then the shower, followed by soup?

The fridge was well-stocked, mainly with leftovers, as Laura had a real thing about not wasting food.

Sadly, every item in there contained at least enough calories to cancel out a Park Run, let alone just part of one. She went instead for a couple of slices of lean ham and a crispbread. Ideal. The hot shower that followed was heavenly bliss. It could have been a bath, but getting an early night beat any thoughts of a few hours soak in the tub. Feeling almost human again after her ablutions, she wandered into the kitchen and poured a glass of iced elderflower cordial, which she took up to bed with her.

And there she lay, alone, in the empty mansion, feeling restless. She wanted to think through the day's events and make sense of them, but she was far too drowsy, and sleep came up to claim her.

****

The day broke with a grey sky and some light drizzle. Laura woke at about ten o'clock, having slept monstrously well. By putting on two dressing gowns, she was able to insulate herself enough to lie over the hot radiator and prise open the large sash window. Raising it a few inches, she rested her chin on the windowsill and watched the world below.

The sound of the crows cawing high in their nests was only punctuated by the sound of a tractor working in the fields below. The cold air soon nipped a bit, though, so Laura closed the window again and went back to the luxury of her sumptuous bed. She wanted someone to talk to, ideally someone who was in bed with her.

Reaching for her phone for a spot of social media, Laura realised it must be buried somewhere in the folds of the duvet. She could see the familiar Chalkewood Crest phone case reflecting in the bedside mirror, but where was it? Even when she had solved her hall-of-mirrors puzzle, it didn't help her much, because – surprise, surprise: there was no signal. Oh bother!

Laura wished she had accepted Guy's invitation last night. Both he, Garth and Gren would have been superb company. Was his car still there? Scrambling back over to the window, she could see that it had gone. The parking space was as empty as her diary for the day ahead, but it looked like he had only just left because the gravel was still dry where the car had been. That was a shame. His presence might just have motivated her to throw on some clothes and dash down, at the very least, to apologise for being so brusque the day before.

Chapter Two

The Last Days of Chalkewood

These were the last days of Chalkewood – its fading glory hanging in the balance, ever since Laura's parents had put the estate up for sale as part of their grand retirement plan. One overcast August day, they had left for France, just like they did every summer. Except this time, they weren't coming back.

Their grand plan had various consequences, not least leaving Laura to facilitate the decampment to France from the British side, although it was beginning to look like her new role might be perfectly timed. She was approaching the end of her current contract with Hauptmann Vyse, for whom she had largely been working from home in her capacity as a freelance management consultant. She could easily go forwards on a reduced contract, working just a day or so a week, and then concentrate on the whole Chalkewood thing.

The ancient Chalkewood estate had been greatly extended by Laura's grandfather, John Jacob Arthur Stanhope, 'Lord of the Manor'. His many new land acquisitions had been largely funded by profits from the family business, Royal Hanbury Porcelain. Upon his demise in 1995, the estate and title had passed to Laura's father, Edward (Teddy) Barnabus St. Leger Stanhope. He and his wife, Teucia (Tice) Jean Stanhope, were of a rather more liberal mindset than the old man. They were artistic people and a bit bohemian, but whilst they shunned much of what had landed in their laps, they did want to try to strike a balance for the sake of the community and the estate tenants. They had previously felt they should preserve an option for Laura to take up her future title of Lady of the Manor, as they felt it was never theirs to give away in the first place. Laura now held the burden of that title, but without a husband or children, she was hugely reticent about taking it on, and she very much shared her parents' view that enmeshing oneself in the English landed gentry wasn't a good thing. Also, she had some concerns about the estate being very close to making a loss. A loss which she herself would have to fund.

Laura was entirely self-supporting with a well-remunerated career – quite a contrast to women of her mother's era when the only career considered respectable for a 'lady' back then would have been marriage. Laura could, however, under the right set of circumstances retain the estate and also her new manorial title. Without an estate attached to it, it wouldn't, however, be worth keeping. You can't be Lady of the Manor if you don't have a manor.

****

Inside Chalkewood Manor House, dust lines marked the walls where the old masters used to hang. Many had been removed and put into secure storage. Some of the less financially valuable examples had gone to France with Teddy and Tice. It all just added to the increasing sense of emptiness. The paintings were gone, the furniture gone, her family gone. What was left worth staying for, apart from the memories?

Laura stood over the kitchen bin with a huge armful of mail. Scooting all the junk items directly into the bin, she found a package from Slater Scotton & Emery, the selling agents. Searching for the letter opener she realised that even that had been taken to France.

Prising open the envelope, she removed what appeared to be the anticipated complimentary copy of the estate sale prospectus. Flicking through, Laura was delighted with the rich colour photography. They really had done an amazing job. The opening page read:

The Manor House consists partly of a remnant of the original medieval castle. It was later extended with the addition of a substantial two-storey, Georgian brick extension. A later 1950s addition to the rear is well-proportioned and sympathetic to the existing architecture and features a half-rotunda supporting a semi-circular balcony. The Georgian and mock-Georgian additions all have parapet roofs. Sash windows predominate, and on the 1950s extension, are dressed with faux French shutters.

Turning over the page, it continued:

A settlement since AD 488 and the reign of King Fobbe, Chalkewood, was rebuilt in AD 1147. The extant castle portion is complete with battlements and there is evidence that there was once a moat. Until 1957, the property had resident peacocks, and it still has a secret garden containing a small medieval chapel. All in all, the estate is set in 662 acres of mixed farmland, mainly arable. It includes twelve dwellings but also one working dairy farm.

"Blimey, I'd buy it," Laura said to herself, only half-joking. Reading the brochure just reminded her she still had feelings for Chalkewood. In truth, she was torn between keeping it and letting her parents sell it.

The estate sounded idyllic in the brochure, but even the heavenly world she had grown up in had its downsides. Chalkewood had totally spoilt Laura.

It had always been so easy to lean against it, instead of going out and grabbing all the gritty chances life had to offer. Why take risks if she didn't have to? Chalkewood provided for her every need. Her burning desire to prove herself, had been her saving grace, prove that she had what it took to contribute towards making the world a better place.

With the estate on the market, Teddy and Tice had taken all of their preliminaries with them and, off the back of the recent dividend payout from Royal Hanbury Porcelain, purchased a château in the Ardeche region of France set within a large tract of land and also containing a hamlet with several dilapidated and abandoned former dwellings within its curtilage. All for an absolute snip of a price and less than you would pay for a terraced townhouse in London.

Laura's younger sister, and only sibling, Daisy, had little interest in Chalkewood. Blonde and petite, she looked just like her mother and shared her artistic traits. When asked her opinion on the imminent seismic changes within the family, Daisy's only comments had been, "London is stupid," and, "Who's going to look after the cats?" All Daisy was interested in was being given one of the smaller, dilapidated houses within the château's grounds. She had also declared she would not 'spoil' it by renovating it. She'd be perfectly happy to just paint flowers on pebbles all day, look after stray animals and go wild swimming in the nude. It was unlikely Daisy would even get as far as organising her own meals; she'd expect to survive by eating wild berries all day. She was talented and bright, but inhabited an alternative reality. When Daisy had moved from Paris to join her parents in the wild countryside, Laura had half joked that she wanted her sister to carry a tracking device, worrying for her sister's safety in the unfamiliar terrain around the château that was riddled with hazardous caves, cliffs and fast-flowing rivers. It was all in huge contrast to southern England with its green and pleasant pastures. Having said that, Daisy had now lived in France for nearly fifteen years. Inspired whilst on a school trip, she had enrolled herself at the Sorbonne and sent Teddy the bill. She later naturalised as a French citizen and took up with a Parisienne boyfriend, rarely returning to the UK.

****

August Lodge was the third largest house on the Chalkewood estate, after the Manor House itself and Chalkewood House. It was the closest dwelling to the Manor House, and it was where Laura and Daisy grew up. But in 1995, when her grandfather, John Jacob Arthur Stanhope had abdicated as Lord of the Manor after an illness, he had moved into August Lodge, and Laura and her family had swapped to the Manor House.

Following her grandfather's death in 2004, the place had been rented to an elderly couple who had recently left and moved into sheltered accommodation. Peasley was keen to get the property relet, but Laura had blocked that, as she wanted it updated first. It also contained a room that had been left sealed up for eighteen years and which contained family mementos.

On this day, Guy Pengersick was not out and about, carrying his usual coil of steel wire. In fact, he was nowhere to be seen – which was annoying because Laura needed a word. In his role as estate horticulturist, Pengersick was principally employed to make informed horticultural decisions for the estate, independently of Peasley, the estate manager. Pengersick wasn't too demanding when it came to salary, so Teddy and Tice had ended up using him for just about everything. He was especially busy right now, what with all the imminent changes.

Laura never quite knew how to say his name. It read like Penguin Sick. Her parents had confused things even further by always pronouncing it differently. Maybe Penga-sick? Or Pen-gessick? Pen-gairsik? Or Pen-gursek, to use the local accent? Technically, Laura was his boss now, although Teddy and Tice still seemed to keep him busy.

He finally pulled onto the drive early afternoon, just after Laura had arrived home after taking

Honey her Haflinger mare out for a hack to Hamden and back. Grabbing a chance to pin him down, she strolled over, still in her riding gear and pushing her hair back off her face.

"I was just thinking earlier. How exactly do you pronounce your name? I really ought to know by now…"

"Penwick," he replied earnestly.

"Oh! Well, no. Really? Oh!" She noted a very slight smirk.

"You should know, Laura – we went to the same school."

"Hey, mister, you'll have to pronounce my name differently now, too. I wasn't called Lady of the Manor back then, but I am now… though, m'lady or my lady will suffice – so mind your cheek," she said, the corners of her mouth twitching as she too suppressed a smile.

He laughed. "Ha. Touché."

"Oh, and let's not forget I'm also your boss, now," she added earnestly, regarding him through narrowed eyes. "Anyway, what I wanted to ask you was… Look, I need you to do something." She paused expecting one of his usual offhand responses, accompanied by a sharp intake of breath, but none was forthcoming, because he genuinely wanted to work with her – for no other reason than he just liked how she was. Guy Pengersick was a straight-up, self-effacing type and a born optimist. "Guy, you're using August at the moment, aren't you? Peasley's after reletting it, but I'm saying it needs an update. First off though, there's that sealed back room. I want it opened and cleared."

"Well, that's assuming you have a key?"

"No, obviously I don't. Any chance you could just ease the frame a bit or drill the lock? Don't damage anything, though."

"Okay, I'll give it a try."

"And Guy, if you get in there, just clear it all out. Any old tat, I want it burnt. I'll leave it entirely at your discretion – I just don't have the time for going through it all. Thanks, and it is Pengessik, isn't it?"

"The more someone annoys me, the crazier the pronunciation I give them. You got off quite lightly with Penwick," he said, winking.

****

Wednesday dawned remarkably unremarkable. Laura was up and ready for her 09.30 face-to-face with Peasley. The meeting would be in the kitchen this time as the study furniture had already gone. The drawing room wasn't an option, either, as one doesn't entertain business guests in there and Peasley would know that. To make matters worse, the key to the front door had gone missing so she couldn't open it. Bonus point for Peasley; she would be starting the meeting already looking totally incompetent.

"Good morning, Gordon. Please, come in."

He tipped his hat to her and then removed it, walking in the back door, wiping his feet on the mat first. His opening greeting of, "My, the place is looking very different," was Peasley speak for 'it's not really a functioning Manor House that you are in charge of' and 'you aren't really the boss'.

"Please, take a seat, Gordon."

Some polite preamble ensued.

"Now, Laura," he said eventually, unzipping his leather document wallet and upping the volume of his tuneful voice to add authority. "August Lodge, vacant now, although I am given to understand that Guy has been using the place somewhat."

"Yes, Gordon. Mr Pengersick is staying there whilst he does some work on it for me."

"Who? Pen-ger-who? N-n-n-noooo," he said in descending scales. "That's not how one pronounces it. It's Penchildersley. He told me so."

Laura managed not to spit her tea out, before taking another opportunity to air her new title. "Yes, and speaking of names, my name is different now...!"

"Ye-e-e-es," he replied slowly, screwing his face up with a conceited smirk.

Laura waited. No, he wasn't going to do it. He just couldn't bring himself to say 'm'lady', not once, not even bloody once. Not even to be polite. He still saw her as a child. All in complete contrast to when he dealt with her mother. Oh, m'lady this, oh m'lady that. He was all over her like a rash. How radiant you're looking today, your ladyship.

There had been that time when her mother had been standing on the kitchen stool in her tight white Rayon slacks, reaching up for some silverware, when Peasley had entered.

"Ooh, no, Mrs S, we can't have that. You could slip and fall. Would you like me to steady you?"

Laura couldn't fathom what had made her mother say yes, but he was straight in there with both hands, grabbing her mother's bottom.

Then it was: "Ready to come down? Hold tight, Mrs S." Thumbs right under her bum cheeks. "Wheeee, off we go. Look, she flies like a bird."

It had crippled her mother with laughter. She so adored hanging a fool out to dry.

"Laura, Laura," said Gordon, as he drew her attention back to the present. "So, I shall speak with Penchildersley and advise him that he needs to remove himself, tout de suite." He zipped up the leather wallet with a satisfied flourish. Job done.

Oh dear. What a day. Pretty much on a par for a typical Peasefest. Why couldn't he just retire? Old git must be getting on for sixty-five. So, what next? A wee, followed by strong coffee. She hadn't offered Peasley anything. Why would she? If you had a plant you didn't like, you wouldn't water it, would you?

Coffee... ahh... so soothing. Laura's thoughts solidified. She needed to catch Pengersick asap, but no luck there. Once again, he was nowhere to be found.

****

The following day, Laura saw flames and black smoke coming from outside August. She felt a pang of guilt – Guy was probably burning up things she really should have kept.

It was evening before Guy appeared at the kitchen door. He was black from head to foot. Opening the door, she beckoned him in, excited to know what he'd found in the sealed room.

Guy was reticent to enter, "Laura, I'm really, really filthy."

"Well, that's as maybe, but I don't think I want to know about your personal life." It went completely over his head.

He came in holding a box, which he put by the door. "Okay, so I got in the back room, but bad – very bad. The lock itself was quite old. It's a single lever wooden Rim lock. I just put a small screwdriver in, tipped the tumbler, and straight in I went. Or rather, I didn't, because there was something big up against the door stopping me. Turned out to be four old mattresses, rank as hell. Something, I don't know what, has been nesting inside them, droppings everywhere. Hazardous too, spores in the air. My lungs got all tight, and I had to take a break and get a dust mask. Anyway, I got the mattresses out and burnt them straight off."

"Did you burn anything else?"

"No. Look, Laura, there's a lot of personal stuff in there. I'm not burning your family mementos – you need to check them over first. I don't mind helping. Oh, and then there was the wardrobe – a disaster. I opened it, and... whoom! Out flew a storm of bats, Pipistrelles. You know that's serious, don't you? Protected and all that. Jail for those who disturb them. They have been getting into the wardrobe through its vent holes and using it as a roosting box. There were about six inches of droppings in there, so probably been going on for a while now."

Laura was ecstatic. "Guy, that's awesome! Peasley's stuffed, then. Hey, you know he wants you out of August? Can't now though, eh?"

Guy picked up the box. "I found this. Not sure. Is it anything?" Placing the box on the table, he lifted the lid. Inside was a teddy bear. Laura couldn't hold back the tears that suddenly spilled over.

"It's Roary! I thought he was a gonner."

Guy gently lifted him out of the box and held the bear's nose to his ear.

"I have great news! He's still breathing!"

He carefully handed Roary to Laura. She smelt him and hugged him.

"Okay, well, I'm going to leave you two to enjoy your reunion. I'm not sleeping in August tonight, what with all the dust, so I'm going to get the keys and drive down to Keeper's Cottage and have a bath and a beer there."

"Thanks, Guy." Laura winked appreciatively and opened the kitchen door to let him out. She watched him as he walked off shaking more dust out of his bushy hair as he went.

What an asset, thought Laura. Perfect man for the moment. Good company, nice and easy to deal with, and apparently on her side, despite Peasley being his immediate line manager for most things.

Previously, they had led parallel lives. Laura had never engaged with him, most likely because it came under her mother's umbrella rule: One does not fraternise with the staff. Simple pragmatic advice, wisdom learnt over the years, but now Chalkewood was going up for sale, maybe it was time for Laura to integrate more with those around her.

****

Most people have favoured places within their homes that are especially conducive to developing deep thoughts and solving problems. Laura had a couple. One was standing with her bum pressing against the warm Aga in the kitchen, the other was the bath. Her 'think tank'.

Chalkewood had a rather fabulous and generously proportioned roll-top slipper bath in the main bathroom opposite her parents' old room, which she now occupied. She often wondered if she was the only person in the world who took a notepad and pen with them when having a bath. With the water just about as hot as she could stand, she dropped in a cedarwood bath bomb, and as it dissipated, she slid gently down into the water.

Her life, having just tipped over into dangerous-muddy-slope phase, was the focus for today's deliberations. It was that point where, if she didn't slow things right down, life would gather uncontrollable speed and she'd become little more than a passenger on a runaway train to destination potluck.

The infernal biological-clock issue was undoubtedly her key governing factor. She detested the cliché and all of its wretched implications, but she had decided that she wanted not just a husband but a family, too. In this pivotal moment Laura realised that it wasn't just the estate that was actively on the market, it was her too. She had tried looking at some dating apps, but making choices always seemed to play into the very prejudices she was trying hard to rehabilitate herself from. She felt considerable disquiet about judging people in the casual manner in which the apps were encouraging her to.

By the time the bathwater needed a hot top-up, the only decision written in Laura's notebook was get back control from Peasley and slow down break-neck speed he's pursuing sale of the estate. It was a mystery why he was so driven to expedite the disposal of the estate. He would stay on with the new people, for a while anyway, and her parents didn't need the money, as the dividends from Royal Hanbury Porcelain more than underpinned family finances. Her mother and father were due to come back for a meetup with Peasley within the next few months, anyway. "Why the urgency?" she wondered. Drying her hands, Laura called Guy. "Hello, only me."

"Haha, you sound echoey. You in the bath, or something? Must be urgent. Got your toe stuck in the tap? I can hear the water sloshing around."

Bloody embarrassing. Was it really that obvious? "Look, Pengersick, shut up, will you, and let me do the talking. Do you want your ass kicked out of August? I'm guessing not. Well, I don't want it relet either, so best you and I collaborate a little on this, eh? Okay. I want you to contact the council and report that bat roost. That way the room will have to be resealed and the reletting will have to be delayed, okay?"

"No way, miss... sorry, m'lady," said Guy. "Peasley will go mental, you know it. There's no way on this planet that I am incurring the wrath of that man again. You do it."

"You're no bloody use, are you, Pengersick? Looks like it's up to me, then."

"Sorry, Laura, I want to help, but I need to be careful. I don't want any trouble with Gordon."

Chapter Three

We've Just Been Taxed

Laura had fallen asleep on the sofa. It was after midnight on quite a mild night when she awoke. The moon was big and bright and partially illuminated the drawing room through the imposing eighteenth-century French doors. She drew herself wearily to her feet and headed, a little unsteadily, towards the stairs. Once in her room, she changed into her long, flowing white nightdress, ready to hop into bed for another night alone in the empty mansion.

Her mouth was dry, and it pained her to realise that she now had to put on a dressing gown and go back downstairs again to get some filtered water from the fridge dispenser. The moon was doing a good job lighting the house, though, so no need for the full glare of electric lights.

The refrigerator hummed away as she approached it. She dispensed a drink and added a slice of lemon and some ice, just to lift it a bit. Taking a sip, she closed the fridge door, but as she did so, she noticed something outside.

There was light flashing under the curtains, and she could hear some whispering. Putting the glass down, she crept across the floor, took hold of the curtains and, yanking them apart, came face-to-face with two hooded men wearing head torches. She ran straight up the stairs, through the bedroom and out onto the balcony. Panting, she looked down.

"Get off my estate. Do you hear me"? All she could see were two head torches, so she decided to change her tack. "Hey, you two, get over here. Get over here right now." They slowly walked towards her.

"Sorry, miss, we thought the place was abandoned. We just wanted to shoot a vid and get it on our YouTube channel." This lowered the tension considerably. Chalkewood wasn't a particularly private place. There had always been functions on site which had led to people blurring the boundaries between invited guests and trespassers in the past.

"Right, I want your names."

"We're the Blue Ninjas. YouTubers."

"No, I want your proper names."

"Can't do that, your ladyship. If we disclose our real identities, then we lose our secret powers."

"Ah, so you know who I am. You must be local, then."

"Yeah, Hampden," they shouted back.

This changed matters somewhat. As Lady of the Manor, the notion of noblesse oblige made it incumbent upon her to bestow a patronly attitude towards 'commoners', especially if they were also local, even if it was nearly one in the morning.

"Miss, could we come back and do a 'with permission'?"

"Sorry, boys, I can't grant that. There are some legal reasons which I shan't go into, and I also don't want to encourage any YouTube tourism."

There was some whispering and then one of them – his name appeared to be Tommo – said, "Okay, yeah, fair do's. Look, could we film a 'caught in action', instead?"

Laura had to think quickly and act intelligently here. They no doubt already had some footage, so the best option was to cooperate and negotiate her own terms. "Hmm, I might be up for that, but on the very strict understanding that neither I, nor the estate, are to be identified in the production. Does that work?"

"Aw, miss, that would be beyond awesome."

The arrangement was that the Ninjas would signal with their torches when they were ready, and Laura would flash the bedroom lights to signal she was ready too. Then the cameras would roll and the action would start. Just to add a bit of pizazz, Laura thought she might use her mother's shotgun as a prop. One of a pair – the other having gone to

France – it was a rather elegant Purdey side-by-side, which she kept under her bed.

She loaded the gun with two cartridges and, with it broken over her forearm, stood waiting. There was a brief pause, then a clear signal came from the field. Laura flung open the doors, marched up to the balustrade, slammed the gun shut, and yelled out, "Get off my estate!" Pointing the muzzle skywards, she let off two successive shots.

There was a moment's silence. Then, "Woohooo! Way to go m'lady. That was epic." Tommo was jubilant. "Wasn't expecting that! Beyond brilliant and... well... yes, thank you again."

Laura reminded them of their agreement and wished them goodnight.

****

Lying back on her bed, Laura couldn't quite believe what had just happened. She walked over to the curtains and parted them. Would you believe it! The cheeky pair of sods were now over at the pergola, sitting in there, their faces lit up by their laptops. Next, and somewhat bizarrely, they started running around the pergola, then filming each other. Laura was baffled. She dragged her laptop out and sat up in bed. Who exactly were these Ninja kids?

Forty-three million views and three hundred thousand subscribers, that's who they were. They had a back catalogue of several hundred videos dating back over seven years. Doing a bit of research and making some calculations, it became apparent that they were earning something like a quarter of a million a year. Pretty much the same as Laura, if not more. Suddenly, a live feed flashed up on their channel. Laura clicked it…

Out of breath Tommo was on there, saying, "We're at a secret new location. Never will we ever disclose it. Benji and I have only just escaped with our lives. This is our last video. We will never do this again after what just happened. We were exploring this abandoned mansion when this fat, mad witch came flying out of the building and tried to kill us. We're not sure if she was a zombie or a poltergeist. What do you think? Hit the button and enjoy the clip…"

"Get… off… my… estate!" Blam! Blam!

They had manipulated Laura's image and had her levitating, her face looking ghostly pale. It was an absolute work of art.

"This is Tommo and Benji signing out. Possibly for ever. Don't forget to like, subscribe and share."

Still in just her nightie, Laura ran over to the window. Seeing their torches moving away, she flung open the sash and yelled at them to come back. They came over to beneath her window. "Guys, I've just been on your channel. I have to admit, that live feed was very impressive. So which am I, "zombie or poltergeist"? And… do you really think I'm fat?"

Tommo had the good grace to look embarrassed. "Oh no, that was all just for theatrical effect. Artistic licence, y'know?"

"Tommo, I hope you won't think me impertinent or inappropriate, but may I ask you what kind of money you're making?"

Tommo and Benji put their heads together and started giggling and whispering. "No, miss, we're just poor people."

"Well, Tommo, I have it at around the 250k mark. Am I right?"

"Well, miss, you might possibly be right." Laura was now smarting with some irritation and perhaps a momentary flash of jealousy, but she still wanted to help.

"Firstly, may I congratulate you on such an achievement? It kind of makes you one of Hampden's most significant businesses, and I, for one, would like to fully support you in that. I have to ask you, though – do you have any arrangements in place for managing your taxes?"

"Yeah, we can run fast, haha."

"Boys, look, don't you think that everyone in business thinks the way you do? But you have to pay tax, or you'll end up losing the lot."

Benji spoke up, "We were thinking, perhaps, Cayman Islands? YouTube is international, so it could pay direct into an account there, and we'd just draw dividends?"

This caught Laura out a bit, as she was not a taxation specialist and didn't really have a clue. "Sure, okay, well, erm, I'd have to look into that. I'm not sure that an offshore arrangement might necessarily be the most tax-efficient model." She leant forwards to talk to them better and, just at that moment, her left breast popped out. Very, very carefully, she covered herself, hoping she'd got away with it. "Look, I'd like to introduce my company Hauptman Vyse to you. We're business consultants and accountants, and we look after clients with portfolios of your size. Would you like to pop round for coffee in the morning for a chat?"

"Nah, not tomorrow, love. We've got another at around dawn in Staffordshire – just popping down the Co-op fuel station now to fill up and get some steak bakes and a bag of Cream Eggs and some Red Bull, and then we're off," enthused Tommo.

"Really? Well, look, it's been a pleasure, and I look forward to hearing from you when you're back this way. Drive safely on that long journey."

Laura leant on the windowsill as they started to walk away. The wind was gently blowing towards her, so she could overhear their conversation.

"Benji man, what a result. This one's flying already. We're gonna get minted. She was a star, though, wasn't she?"

"Yeah and her tit popped out at the end, did you see that?"

"Yeah, I did. I tell you, she's a right filthy MILF. I'd love to have a go on that. Plump or not, I would."

Laura gave them one last wave as they briefly turned towards her. She picked at some loose flakes of paint on the downpipe just outside the window. "Plump...! Plump...? You horrible pair of little bastards," she whispered to herself. "Steak bakes, Creme Eggs and Red Bull. You pair of assholes.". Both had been wearing baggy jeans with something like a 30″ waist.

****

02.33

Laura slumped back into bed and let her thoughts run through her mind. Gradually, she became aware of a sound coming from the adjoining suite; she'd gone and left the gun in that room too, so that was far from ideal. She crept out of bed and stopped to listen. There it was again – clearly not her imagination.

She walked towards the doorway to the suite, gently opened one of the double doors and slid her hand up to the light switch. Bam! The light flared. And then she saw it. On the curtain. It was a bat. It took off, flying around the room in circles. Suddenly, it landed on her nightdress, its little claws just piercing through to her bare skin. She and the bat looked one another in the eye. It was a Pipistrelle, probably one of the ones Guy had disturbed.

"Hello, little friend. Us humans have a lot to answer for, don't we, my little flying mouse? I'm so sorry. Let me show you how to get home."

Out on the balcony, Laura took a pinch of her nightdress on either side and flipped the bat into the air. It was gone in an instant.

It was an unusually warm May night and, captured by the moment, Laura spontaneously took off her nightdress and stood naked in the breeze, enjoying a moment of complete freedom. The wind had picked up a bit, and it carried the fragrance of burning wood with it. Curious, Laura got dressed again and went out into the garden and over to the edge of the ha-ha. Looking down towards Hamden, she could clearly see a small fire. It might even be on Chalkewood land. It clearly was a fire, though. She couldn't ignore it, so she got in the Land Rover and headed down to Hampden, still wearing the zombie-apocalypse acting ensemble from earlier.

****

02.55

Close to the river, and it was confirmed: someone had lit a fire. Eight people, men and women, but all naked, were circling the flames and chanting in rising and falling tones. Checking the date on her phone, Laura decided it was probably a Beltane celebration. She wasn't a supporter of the occult, but this seemed safe enough. She could hardly knock it – hadn't she been naked herself just moments earlier? Technically, where they were having their celebration was on estate property, but why be churlish? Her parents certainly wouldn't have objected or intervened in this type of situation.

Just then, she saw someone dressed in black coming her way. Probably someone who had drawn the short straw and been posted on lookout duty. Laura tiptoed to the car and slipped away discreetly, letting the Land Rover roll silently down the track in the darkness.

As she headed back towards Chalkewood. A group of night hikers came into view. Head torches twinkling, they drifted to the side of the road as she approached. One, however, was waving her down. Pulling level, she wound down the window to hear them say, "Hello, you might have a problem up ahead. There's a tree down across the road."

One young lad piped up, "Yeah, it was awesome – we saw it go right in front of us."

"Well, I don't think this lady thinks it's very 'awesome', Josh," admonished the lead adult.

Laura smiled. "Guys, thanks for letting me know."

A few moments later, she saw it for herself. A single trunk of about eight inches in diameter – a young tree.

Laura jumped out to take a look. She noticed it was still rooted in a chalky root ball. Not wishing to go through all the palaver of having to call out the fire brigade, Laura wanted a quick solution, but one that wouldn't damage the car or injure her. After a great deal of thought and pacing around, she went to the car to see what she had. She found a pruning saw in the boot, still in its packet. It was devilishly sharp. That should do it, though she was going to have to watch the tension with the heavy chalk encrusted root ball up-ended and literally weighing a ton.

She had no doubts about the saw's ability to cut through the trunk, but what if it went wrong? She stood there in her nightdress, saw in hand, car dutifully ticking over and the lights shining on her dilemma. What are you waiting for?

The devil saw was amazing. In less than four minutes, it was halfway through, but Laura's sense of foreboding increased with each draw. She persevered regardless. Suddenly, there was a massive crack. The root ball shook, and the cut gaped. It looked perilous. She changed tack and judiciously started cutting away from the underside. A second crack, and the trunk violently burst in two. The root ball yanked the tree back up, and it went back in the ground like it had always been there, whilst the bushy top section overbalanced and rolled away down the steep slope on the other side of the road. It was now 04.19. Everything was still, just the sounds of nature and the car dutifully waiting.

"It's 4.19 in the morning, and I've just pollarded a tree. How surreal is that?" Shaking her head, she got back in the car and was almost at the Chalkewood House junction where now she was looking ahead at a dark, shadowy figure in the middle of the road. This was just routine now after the night she'd been having. Laura stopped about 25 yards short and got out.

"Who goes there?" she bellowed. No answer. The figure was staggering, looking like they might be drunk. Peering around, Laura couldn't see any accomplices, so she approached the man. Up close, she could see he was an elderly gentleman, very much the worse for wear. "Who are you? What are you doing here?"

"Name's Roy, Roy Turner, miss. I've been at the Huntsman."

"Which closed six hours ago. What was it then, a lock-in?" She stood in front of him, feet apart, hands clasped behind her back.

"No, just my retirement do," he said.

"What? And nobody saw you home? Oh wait, they were drunk too, I suppose. Where are you going?"

"Hampden, miss."

"Hampden! My, you have taken the long way round. How long have you been walking?"

"Hours and hours." He sounded like he was almost in tears.

"Right, mister, in the car. You will be coming home with me."

Poor old Roy had become quite weak, and she had to help him into the Land Rover.

"If you feel ill. You tell me immediately, understand? You're a Brookwoodie, aren't you?"

"Yes miss. Working the Brookwood estate forty-nine years, man and boy."

"In what capacity?"

"Dairy assistant then Head Herdsman." That was all the conversation that they could fit into the short drive to the house.

Laura sat him down at the kitchen table and put a plastic bucket in his lap. "You look pretty wobbly. Would you like a nice warm cocoa?" Roy leant forwards with a pained expression, shaking his head vigorously. "Oops, sorry. Okay, look, you need something... Iced water?"

Roy nodded. In fact, it was actually a glass of weak sugary elderflower that she gave him, which he gulped down.

"I noticed you were limping, Mr Turner. Let's have those boots off."

He was wearing cheap, stiff leather boots, and he nearly cried when she removed them. She was presented with a real mess of blisters and white skin, as it turned out, for some reason, his feet were soaking wet. Laura spent twenty minutes cleaning, medicating and dressing his feet, plus giving him a quick pedicure. That was a bit of an overreach, but she just couldn't resist it. She then put some complimentary Chalkewood branded slippers on his feet and his boots into a plastic merchandise bag. "Right, on your feet, Mr Turner, let's get you home."

****

05.12

A misty morning was now dawning. Laura, still wearing her flowing white ensemble, stopped just short of The Maltings and walked Roy the few yards to his door. He stopped, looked her in the eye and said, "We have always loved your family. God bless you, my lady". He then bowed elegantly, took her hand and kissed it. A streetlight came on at that moment, and a puff of breeze blew Laura's nightgown out behind her like a bridal train, as she swept away down the path in the misty early morning half-light.

Vikki Tweedy, living opposite, was just about to walk her dog and captured the whole thing on her phone from her balcony. It's always the early morning dog walkers who get to see the most interesting things.

****

05.58

Finally, bed. Sitting up with a camomile tea, Laura wasn't really sure if she even felt tired anymore. The night had passed, lost to a village that seemed to never sleep.

Meanwhile, Vikki Tweedy had just arrived back home and was looking at her earlier phone footage. It was totally amazing. The angelic figure appearing out of the mist, taking Roy to his door. His gracious bow and kissing of her hand. Then, at the exact moment Laura had turned to leave, the streetlight coming on and casting a column of light onto her. In the mist, it created a glorious rainbow halo of refracted light that silhouetted her angelic appearance. The light then momentarily dazzled the camera because of the new angle, and then when the glare receded... the angel had vanished! Vikki played it over again.

"Wow, what a fluke. How brilliant! This is too good not to share."

****

The midday sun tracked across the open sky. Inch by inch, its rays finding new paths. At just after twelve o'clock, a chink of sunlight fell through the curtains and onto Laura's face. She drew a deep breath and woke feeling wonderfully refreshed. The memories of the previous evening came flooding back.

It was almost like people didn't sleep anymore. The night had been full of people doing things: Roy, Laura, the hikers, the pagan dancers, Vikki Tweedy and the Ninjas. Yes, the Ninjas. How were they doing? Laura was desperate to know, but first and foremost, she was starving and needed a bacon roll backed up by a solid mug of English breakfast tea.

Bacon roll and tea beside her, she opened her laptop and went to the Ninja's page.

"Get… off… my… estate!" Blam! Blam!

Hilarious! She played it over and over. She was incredulous to note, though, that in less than twelve hours the clip had already attracted nearly seventy-two thousand views. There was also their new video from Staffordshire. Tommo and Benji running through the mist, out of breath, and screaming that they had 'seen' a poltergeist. Laura thought it was a brilliant production and just a little piece of her felt envious of their wonderful lifestyle.

Her thoughts drifted over the events of the previous night. Chalkewood had never been the easiest of places to keep secure. There were public rights of way running through it, and it was not uncommon for things to get stolen. Teddy had always been philosophical, though. He'd come in and say, "Looks like we've been taxed again." He held the belief that the perpetrators were not entirely bad people and it could be argued that they were just levelling up the difference between rich and poor. These days, though, the estate assets were kept in very secure buildings.

Back in the day, the 'poor' would take physical assets from the estate, causing damage to property in the process. Now it seemed they were more likely to be richer than the owners and be taking just video footage... and leaving nothing but footprints. They might even end up employing you as their tax consultant!

****

Laura was trimming the wisteria when Guy walked up the drive.

"Morning, I see you're a media star now!"

"Oh, have you been on YouTube?"

"No, I didn't realise it was on there as well."

"They're calling you the Angel of Hampden."

Laura was confused. "Angel? How?"

Guy took his phone out. "Look, here. Wait... Look, here we go."

There, on Facebook, was a video of Laura delivering Roy home in the misty dawn. From the angle, it looked like it had been taken from across the street, and from the Facebook name, the poster was a woman called Vikki Tweedy. From the number of shares, likes and comments, Facebook and the entire world seemed to be going crazy for the Angel of Hampden.

Laura found the whole thing very amusing, but was relieved that it didn't reveal her identity. Whether she wanted it or not, her family had a long-standing reputation in the community for proper behaviour and people wouldn't expect to see her running around the place at all hours in her nightgown.

"Guy, quick question? How did you know it was me?"

"That's for me to know and for you to guess."

Taking a quick tea and biscuit break from the pruning, Laura flicked the kitchen TV on to catch up on the main news. The national round-up had just finished and West Today was covering the local stories. One of which Laura wasn't quite prepared for.

She listened to the presenter's words and watched in disbelief, "...And finally, villagers in the sleepy village of Hampden have recorded seeing what they believe to be an angelic apparition. A villager recorded the whole event in which an Angel appears to guide a villager home before turning and vanishing into thin air. Some are calling her the Angel of Hampden. Tamara Lundquvist has the story...."

"Yes, thank you, Fiona. I am speaking to you live from the village of Hampden. Where one villager has filmed this mysterious clip. Take a look at this."

They played the clip and then interviewed Vikki Tweedy. Next, they interviewed Roy. This was an unnerving moment, but wow, he had sobered up suspiciously well. Clearly someone had had a word in his ear.

"The gracious Angel saved my life and led me home. I've never seen her before. Not ever."

He looked nervously at the reporter, clearly checking to see if she appeared to believe him.

Laura's relief that this frivolous bit of fun would now be drawing to a close was instantly shattered by the arrival of a large, white outside-broadcast unit on the drive. Furiously scrolling through her contacts on her phone, Laura reached Guy. "On the drive now. Get rid of them." She ended the call and hid upstairs behind the curtains of an open window directly above them.

A quick glance was enough to show her Tamara Lundquvist with her cameraman and sound girl making her way towards the front door whilst Guy ambled round the corner of the house. Laura heard the crunch of gravel as he strolled across and greeted them in a very affable and confident manner. After explaining that the lady whom they sought had been ill in bed all night and couldn't possibly be this 'Angel', he went on to ask if West Today might be interested in doing a feature on Chalkewood. He even offered to show them around, but no surprise, they crunched back across the gravel to their van and vanished just as quickly as they had arrived.

"Cheerio," he called to them.

Laura gazed through the gap in the curtains, struck by the consummate way in which Guy had dealt with the situation in such a gentlemanly manner. She looked down as her phone alerted her to a message: Done. Guy then ambled away, back to whatever it was that he had been doing before.

"Thank you," she called softly, but he didn't hear.

Chapter Four

— · —

I'm Monica McStrachan

After leaving Clarice Rutherford, the local minor public school, Laura moved to London. She wanted it to be her great escape from a domesticated lifestyle at Chalkewood, and she really wanted to see how 'common people' lived, to be part of it and lose some of her entitled behaviours in the way that her parents had tried to do back in the 1960s.

She had no idea how to go about it, but she had heard some song lyrics that had mentioned her college, Central St. Martin's School of Art and Design. The song had resonated with her, so she enrolled on a BA Honours degree course there in Jewellery Design. It was as simple as that and seemed like the logical course to take. She thought that jewellery had a kudos commensurate with her background. That kudos would appeal to her father. It was arty, so that would please her mother, and most important of all, it would please Laura – not because she had any great interest in jewellery, but because just being at college would enable her to mix with 'common people', as the song lyrics described them. Monica was one such person.

At the age of eighteen, Laura was chirpy and confident, but she was not streetwise about... well, pretty much any subject under the sun. Her first encounter with Monica came whilst walking down a corridor towards a set of double fire doors. They suddenly flew open with such force that Laura was knocked backwards, hitting her head against the wall. The perpetrator of this deliberate act was a tall, powerful barbarian of a woman who, rather than apologise, just stood there shrieking with laughter. Then she swept away, her faux mammoth-wool trench coat swirling around her as she went.

At Laura's first plenary meeting. A faculty member started with a few 'admin items'. "We need one Student Union rep from this course. Roll up, any takers? None, obviously..." The lecturer paused then swung round to look at Laura. "Hey, you'll do it, won't you?" he said, winking.

Laura grinned and nodded. She cluelessly accepted an envelope that was handed to her containing details of the first meeting. At least it would get her involved with other students.

Laura's heart sank as she approached the Student Union meeting room for the first time. She could see the other reps in there, but amongst them was the barbarian woman, all jet-black hair and

Amy Winehouse beehive. Some guy was holding a sofa cushion against his chest whilst she practised roundhouse kicks on him with the others cheering her on. Laura tried hard not to catch her eye, but...

"Oh! It's you, bellboy. Slow at opening doors, aren't you? You need to fix that." She was wearing a black sweatshirt with, I'M MONICA MCSTRACHAN emblazoned across it. She was terrifying, and that was intentional.

Monica opened the meeting. Holding the agenda, that the admin office had helpfully prepared, in one hand and her Zippo lighter in the other, she set light to it and threw it in the fireplace. "That's the starting point – Freedom!" she shouted. "Anyone got anything?"

A rather geeky-looking guy from Industrial Design had raised his hand. "The canteen. No vegan options," he called out.

Monica squeezed the bridge of her nose between her thumb and index finger, "Yeah, vegan. Vegan-schmeegan. Let's go with that then, for starters."

The meeting went on like that, and people gradually drifted away. There was no real structure or democracy; it just turned into the Monica show until there were only three people left. When the vegan chap picked up his bag and left, it was just Monica and Laura. Laura got up to leave, but Monica blocked her exit. Laura looked up at the barbarian

Amy Winehouse lookalike, who simply stared back down at her with massive, dark eyes. She gripped Laura by the forearm, and Laura felt a little bit of wee trickle out. Looking at her captive's flowery dress, Monica whispered, "What are you? From the wallpaper department, or something? Look, my mouth's dryer than a nun's chough. Let's go to Dixie's and get wankered. There might even be some buff dick in there." Laura was crapping it by then, so she obeyed, not daring to argue.

Dixies was dead, but they found a great place to sit – some deep upholstered red seats in a corner. Monica had calmed down by this time and was almost being girly... except, rather oddly, when the barman delivered the drinks to the table. When he innocently put a pint of Guinness in front of her, she had kind of hissed like a giant black panther. Her issues seemed to revolve around men in general.

"Anyone banged you yet?" Laura was just too shocked and embarrassed to answer such an intimate question. "Nah, nor me. I wanna get banged, then wankered and then shpongled. Plus, I want to die before the end of the course."

Laura was new to Monica and hadn't yet tuned into the fact that this was just how she spoke. It wasn't meant to be taken too seriously and was just her nineteen-year-old way of conditioning peers to fit in with her world – it was devastatingly effective. Laura peeped over the top of her drink and grinned whilst listening to the tirade. It was just so rock and roll – exactly what she had come to London to find.

"So, Laura Stanhope, where are your digs?"

"Leytonstone."

"Leytonstone?" Monica sneered.

"Yes, I moved there six months before term started, as accommodation was in such short supply. It's inexpensive, but it's lovely. It's where the Wanstead Flats meet the ancient woodlands of Epping Forest. We even have cows there, and they sometimes get out on the road and stop the London traffic. I once saw a city trader get out of his Porsche and herd them back off the road." Monica looked a bit surprised. Laura relaxed and opened up. "I've got a crazy flat-share with five others, including the landlord, Bruce. He's the same age as us. He works for the railways and sells bootleg tapes and tells me about his adventures, like getting stuck down a cave for three days. He has a sideline in residential property and sometimes takes me along when he goes to view new properties. We pretend to be husband and wife, and some of the places have to be seen to be believed. We went to one in Stratford once, and the vendor had turned it into a love palace, full of zebra stripe fabrics and all that. We just couldn't look each other in the eye. When we got outside, we were crying with laughter."

"You're banging him, aren't you...?" responded Monica. "Yes, you are! You filthy little mare, and

there's me still haven't busted my duck here yet."
Laura went bright red. She was aware that she
was considered pretty, her looks boosted further by
being young and honey-blonde, but men seemed to
find that intimidating and rarely had the courage to
approach her. "So, this dirty git, Bruce, seduced you,
did he?"

"No, quite the reverse. I said I wanted to live
like 'common people', and he just looked up from
stirring his hot chocolate that evening and said, 'I'll
see what I can do,' and we just went to bed. That's
about it, really."

Feeling much more relaxed by then, Laura
decided it was time to play her ace card. She told
Monica that she was landed gentry and teased her
new friend by saying that one day she would have
to address her as 'my lady'. It had the desired effect;
Monica was seriously impressed. The imbalance
between them instantly resolved and their bond
locked tight. They went on to visit a couple of bars
familiar to Monica as they moved closer to her flat
in Camden.

"I must be getting back to Leytonstone, now."

"No, Laura, it's too late. Come back to mine. It's
only one stop away on the Northern Line from
here."

Monica had a first-floor flat in a Victorian Terrace
on Camden High Street. They turned the key and
walked in. It was past midnight, and they both

had lectures in the morning. Monica handed Laura a gothic-looking black nightie, and they both got ready for bed and climbed into Monica's massive bed.

The light off the High Street spilling past the blinds illuminated the flat with a continuous ambient glow. The two girls snuggled up under the great heavy duvet and Laura was filled with a tremendous sense of well-being. It had been a stunning night and boded really well for the future.

"Monica, if you're so cool, then why are you a Student Union rep?"

Monica was quiet for a moment, clearly caught out a bit. "Well, mate, if I told you that I'd have to kill you," she said, grabbing Laura round the neck and pretending to strangle her. "You can tell I'm up to something, can't you? Damn it. Alright, fair do's, I am. I play a bit of bass guitar – my brothers taught me. My master plan is to book bands for the Student Union that will let me perform with them. Last night was about frightening off any reps who might want to compete for the job of Entertainments Officer, and this is our little secret, missy – okay? And if you betray me, I will take you into the bogs with a length of rope and hang you." Monica's faint Irish accent gave some credence to that threat.

****

That summer Monica had The Crystal Nobodys headlining at the Student Union. They were an experienced cover band that had an impressive repertoire. However, they lacked a tenor singer, and the bass player was unreliable, so Monica had managed to work her way in with them. She wasn't up to speed with many of the songs, but arguably her finest hour came when they allowed her to take the lead, singing and playing the iconic base line in Bon Jovi's 'Livin' On A Prayer'.

Laura would never forget it...

The second half of the set was about to begin, and Laura and a few others looked up at the big stage as the lights came on and the band took their places amidst the cheering and the whistling of the well warmed-up crowd. The keyboard began to whine with the opening minor chord arrangement. The rhythmic triple chink of the tambourine sequence started, then the first drum burst crashed through, and Dave came in on cue with the "Wha-oo-wah-oo-wah-ooh" talk-box vocal bars. Monica edged forwards, driving the pounding bass line. She put her lips to the mic and began to sing.

A massive deafening cheer went up, and Monica was immortalised in the hearts and minds of everyone present. The hairs on Laura's arms stood on end and her heart soared.

Back at Monica's, they lay in bed together. They had wrung the evening and the contents of a bottle of Southern Comfort dry. Laura picked at Monica's hair. It was all stuck up with some terrible gunk that she had used to make her hair three foot wide. Monica was snoring. Laura kissed her shoulder, sad that she would have to tell her that her time at St. Martin's college was coming to an end. After just one year, they would be going their separate ways.

Laura's landlord had been sowing thoughts in her mind and they had taken root. He had astutely pointed out to her that she didn't have a creative bone in her body and asked why she was 'piddling around' with jewellery when she should be expanding her massive left-brain propensity for analytical and logical thought. She ought to be getting out there, becoming a captain of industry, he told her and so it was that she now had just two weeks left at college before switching to join Imperial College London, where she would start over on a business degree course.

****

Monica cried the day Laura told her. They were never lovers, in the physical sense, but they had formed a strong reciprocal bond based upon their contrasting attributes and mutual respect.

Laura and Monica briefly went their separate ways when Laura moved to the university. The change had hurt them both, but they needed to have some separation for a while, just to resettle themselves and find their new directions.

They still socialised after Laura left St. Martin's. Monica introduced Laura to the whole dubstep scene that was happening in South London at the time. They would pop pills, smear menthol gel on each other and go dancing all night at the Fridge in Brixton until chucking out time at 6.30 a.m.

Monica had become an increasingly regular guest at Chalkewood, often for events like the last of the hunt balls – that was before Teddy, Laura's father, finally managed to get his way and banish the event from his house and his life for what he hoped would be forever. Grandfather John Jacob had established the Wainthrop Hunt and its foxhound pack. He had always wanted Teddy to inherit the mantle of Master of the Foxhounds, but Teddy had steadfastly refused to have any part of it. Both he and Tice, and Laura, were absolute in their resistance to anything involving animal cruelty. The hunt, however, was a part of the estate and also the wider community, so ending it entirely was, unfortunately, unthinkable.

It was always fun trying to dovetail Monica into the lifestyle of the British landed gentry. She spoke with a slightly strange, yet far from unattractive accent – the result of taking elocution lessons in a botched and misguided attempt to remove her Irish brogue.

Monica always behaved impeccably at Chalkewood – Laura taught her all the correct airs and graces, and she loved dressing Monica up in extravagant ball gowns and her mother's expensive jewellery. However, whilst her own parents had no interest in the hierarchical, aristocratic lifestyle into which they had been born, the family knew it brought out the worst in some of those on the fringes, people who desperately aspired to the lifestyle and inappropriately elbowed their way into it. Teddy used to call them greasers. Ironically, whilst the Stanhope family were doing everything in their power to escape the privileged world and carve out a life with more virtue and meaning, a number of people in the community were travelling in the opposite direction, or trying to, which meant the Stanhopes had to constantly assess whether people were genuine friends, or just greasers on the make.

Teddy and Tice would never escape their inherited world entirely; it had been far too formally ingrained in them from such a young age, mainly by Teddy's father, John Jacob Arthur Stanhope. Laura was living in more enlightened and meritocratic times, and she relished any opportunity to engage with that.

For Monica, it was just one huge game. She was very perceptive and adored playing with all the nuances. In front of non-family members, she would often ham it up with her mawkish renditions of the upper-class condition. She'd use her theatrical-looking face to full effect: perfecting the ironic asymmetric smile, the enquiring look and the sardonic lip.

At one reception, Tice came into the kitchen with her hand on her forehead and said to Laura and Teddy, "I've just witnessed Monica introducing herself to one of our tenants as 'the Duchess Scrivener-Blowberg' or something." Monica had put together the full repertoire: the fake German accent, the absurd laugh. Her titles would become more outlandish as the evening wore on. Lady Felatio-Hornblower was one of her favourites for testing the guests' attention and patience.

The following morning over breakfast, Monica would regale the family with impressions of some of the people she had met the previous evening, repeating some of the outrageous things they had said – much to the chagrin of Teddy and Tice, who were unfortunately lumbered with these people as age-old acquaintances. It brought the truth home to roost, and Teddy and Tice were left to reflect that their quest to move away from their roots had not yet been fulfilled.

That being said, there was always the contrasting beauty that these events brought to their lives. The glorious live renditions at the grand piano in the ballroom and string quartets in the hall; the flamboyant costumes; the exciting, upbeat hubbub; the traditions; the beauty of the house, both inside and out. There were romantic encounters lying on the Camomile Lawn. Misty sunrises, and ladies in ballgowns playing croquet at 5 a.m.

The stakes were high, and they were complex, and nobody was quite sure what the outcome should be, or whether they were making the right decisions.

CHAPTER FIVE

MISS ADVENTURE

Laura loved the business course. She instinctively knew that this was her vocation. It was more black-and-white, with a strong focus and clear sense of purpose. Her family experience of running the estate and the family business, Royal Hanbury Porcelain, meant Laura was at the forefront of her cohort when it came to understanding commerce. Unexpectedly, she found that she had a real talent for giving persuasive and well-crafted presentations. This, coupled with her strong sense of justice made her wonder, briefly, if the law might have been a better career choice, but she quickly decided greater things could be achieved through industrial reform.

Having sated her initial desire to immerse herself in the world of commerce, the somewhat dryness of the academic and social life by her third year gave Laura time to think about how much she missed Monica and the heady days of Central St. Martin's past. She reached out to arrange a meetup and got quite the big surprise!

Monica, now graduated, had embraced the artistic scene full-on. She had linked her fashion course to her liking for London's burgeoning fetish scene. Working with glass-fibre moulded corsetry and latex fashions, Monica had fully embraced the Zeitgeist of this subculture and had discovered that, although it was a smaller market, it was a much less competitive one, and you could become a big fish in a small pond quite quickly.

Although Monica was very tall at 5'11" in bare feet, she had the kind of voluptuous, hourglass figure that made her an automatic sexual icon in this fashion genre. It had taken her all of two seconds to realise that she could model her own fashion creations and become something of a celebrity in the process. The subculture had strong links to space-age, sci-fi and fantasy costumery, and specialist fetish fashion houses were often the go-to sources for film and TV stylists. All of this had combined to create an explosively successful lifestyle for Monica. She would design and make costumes, model them for magazine covers, give edgy late-night interviews on radio and then take to the stage in fetish nightclubs. She really was living the dream.

On the downside, to keep it all going and remain competitive, Monica had had to acquire a certain level of notoriety, which had led her down a path that had the potential to get dangerous. Her chosen fashion niche overlapped with the BDSM community, and this provided lots of opportunities for Monica to 'have sex in colour' as she often described it. She was by no means a misandrist, but she loved hurting men for pleasure, and there was no shortage of men who got their kicks from being hurt by women. She got off on the energy she drew from the power games her high-octane lifestyle bestowed upon her, and she had embraced it to the max.

When Laura texted Monica, it became clear they had a lot of catching up to do. Monica's life had moved on so much she was worried it would be impossible to put it all into words, so she chose, rather clumsily, to invite Laura and a couple of friends to a massive scene party that she had in her diary. In retrospect, it was probably not the greatest idea.

Of course, she explained the gist of it all to Laura and told her to turn up wearing something that gave at least a nod towards the risqué. Otherwise, they would stand out a bit. Laura, hungry for some contrast to her studious third-year of uni life, enthusiastically invited her friends, Beth and Martha, to come along.

****

An address off The Strand in London seemed an odd place for a party. When Laura and her friends arrived, they found themselves looking up at an empty four-storey office block, its front door and windows blacked out. Inside, there was a reception podium, the sound of pulsating music, lots of atmospheric neon lighting and a couple of door supervisors standing to the side. A constant flow of people trickled in. Feeling slightly underdressed, Laura, Beth and Martha gave their names at the reception podium and made their way up the crowded stairs. They spent the first twenty minutes with their mouths open, as they visited the various themed areas and all that they contained. Arriving on the top floor, the dance floor, they looked on in amazement.

Suddenly Monica appeared. With her beehive and six-inch heels, she stood at about 6'10". Her voluptuous figure was squeezed into a sci-fi outfit that was both scary and revealing. Beside her stood a man: gorgeous, fit, tanned, muscle-bound and blond. He was all but naked except for a black harness and a chunky diamante collar which had a dog lead attached to it. Monica was pulling him along by it. Everyone cheered as they paraded.

Laura turned to her mates. "Remember me telling you about my pal? The one who invited us here… Yeah? That's her." A not inconsiderable degree of terror set in with business students Beth and

Martha, who only moments earlier had been more focussed on puzzling over the economics governing the commercial property housing the event – why it was vacant, whether it had D2 planning consent for a nightclub, that kind of thing.

Spotting her old friend in the crowd, Monica strode towards them, dragging her submissive companion with her by his leash as she went. Laura's friends were trying not to cry with fear. In her spare hand, Monica held a long cigarette holder, a pale blue Balkan Sobranie cigarette trailing smoke as she moved through the crowd. Her theatrical-looking face, heavily made-up, wore a faraway expression, like she had transcended into a parallel universe and metamorphosed into some kind of hedonistic mentalist of a female goddess.

"Look! These days I have sex in colour. Isn't it simply divine?" she said. Half-turning to the crowd, she yelled, "Repent, and turn your back on the world of vanilla!" She was wearing a set of Dracula costume teeth, and Beth flinched, her eyes wide, when Monica grinned at her, flashing the fangs. But worse was to come. Right in front of them, she reeled her companion in by his lead. Pulling his head back, she leant over and gently bit into his neck with the fangs. As she withdrew, there was blood on her teeth and running down her submissive's neck.

Laura, somewhat aghast, speedily withdrew her business cohort pals and whisked them off to a nice, cosy corner at the end of the bar. Whereupon they promptly ordered three straight Red Bulls with no alcohol. Laura's eyes widened when she looked over the bar; she couldn't quite believe what she was seeing. "That's disgusting," she affirmed in a whisper, nodding towards the barman. In between serving drinks, the busy, butt-naked barman was enjoying the odd moment of self-abuse.

"I don't want another drink," said Beth, and they drank up and headed back into the pulsating darkness. In the corner of one room, Beth saw something so peculiar, or disturbing, or both, that she had to run off to the loos to be sick.

Mortified, Laura apologised to her friends and tried to recover the situation. "Let's go – I think we've seen enough. Look, why don't we go to Dunkin Donuts, or something?" Upon hearing that, Beth dashed away to the loo again, but when she returned, they decided they would go and have a drink somewhere nearby.

They found a rather nice café bar. It was pretty quiet, and they soon settled down for a fair few rounds of strong alcohol. Feeling somewhat responsible for her friends' state of shock, Laura tried to think of how she could make up for it. Beth had her hankie out, and Laura wasn't sure if she was still feeling sick or whether she was crying. She refused to say what had seen in the backroom, and Laura didn't want to press her on the matter for fear of inducing more vomiting. Martha was simply grumpy.

"What kind of man works behind a bar, naked, and them attempts to 'knock one out' whilst still on duty? All in front of female clientele. The guy is a complete horse's arse, if you ask me."

Laura nodded in token disapproval, but her mind had drifted back to Monica. She must have felt fabulous – the grand empress of all she surveyed, and when she had bitten that guy's neck... it was so wild. What might have calmed the ensuing shock and outrage somewhat was the knowledge that Monica hadn't really bitten anyone; she had simply had a capsule of Kensington Gore in her mouth which she bit down on when she pretended to bite Rupert.

"And your friend biting that guy's neck. Is she insane? She could have punctured an artery. Bloody fool," added Martha.

What the group of friends hadn't taken into account, was that they were all still dressed rather provocatively and had attracted the attention of a group of guys who were pretty much the only other people in the bar.

One good-looking fellow sauntered over, his rather less confident mate trailing a few paces behind him. "Well, girls, you look like you're going to, or coming from, some kind of party."

Martha was a couple of years older than Laura and Beth. She was on the master's course and was very striking to look at. With her big bush of auburn hair and green retro glasses, she carried some considerable gravitas. Martha had truly had enough of having her shockability levels challenged. "Fella, I'll be plain with you. We're fetishists and we're looking for a man who is willing to have a lubricated steel ball slowly pushed up his arse."

The chap leant in closer. "Ladies, you have yourselves a wonderful evening." He smiled and retired, his terrified-looking friend trotting along behind him.

Martha may have been a little too quick off the mark in dealing with that guy, though, as their paths were destined to cross again in just a couple of days.

****

Mondays were always a good day on the Master's business course, especially after lunch, when the college usually invited in a local business practitioner to deliver a lecture designed to inspire the students. On this occasion, the speaker was a man called James Batchley. Martha took one look at him and her heart sank. "Flip my luck. I told this guy where to get off in a bar on Saturday night," Martha confided to the classmate sitting beside her.

After his presentation on business ethics, the class took a short refreshment break, and Martha walked right into him in the corridor.

"Hey, I know you, don't I?"

Martha tried to be evasive. "Maybe we met at the Guild of Commerce?"

"No... don't worry – I'm sure it will come to me."

Martha prayed heavily that it wouldn't.

When all students were re-seated, James delivered an even better second half to his presentation, and everyone was really engrossed. For his conclusion, he said, "So, in the final reckoning, it will only ever be down to you to make the moral judgement... And sometimes that really does take... balls of steel." He looked across at Martha and winked.

There was a standing ovation, which gave Martha the ideal opportunity to reverse unobtrusively out of the lecture theatre in the midst of the rapture.

****

Laura had been incredibly close to Monica, but sometimes you can get a bit too close to a person, and sometimes the only option is to let them go. Maybe for the best. They will still be there in your heart, but what was inspirational once, might be destructive now.

As for Monica, she was learning the consequences of an addictive lifestyle. The human mind has to have lows as well as highs, otherwise the highs cease to be highs anymore – they just becomes the new normal. Monica had failed to understand that. Her life had no contrast, and she just ploughed on, stacking one experience on top of another, and she did so to the detriment of her well-being. Monica, it seemed, had no 'off-button'.

Although she had graduated well with a sensible degree, her focus was now on fame and notoriety. Her remaining virtue was her physical fitness levels, and she had been successful in getting to second dan level in karate and in developing her kick-boxing to a high level.

Professionally, she was wavering. The BDSM scene was heavily populated with professional dominatrices and she had become fixated on them. It just seemed unbelievable to her that you could get fantastically well paid for doing nothing more than torturing men. The pull was irresistible, yet the proposition was full of paradoxes. Although not defined as prostitution, her strong Catholic guilt would never allow her to accept money in exchange for any kind of personal services. She was, however, desperate for some hands-on experience... and she wasn't prepared to give her time away for free. As a compromise, she started acting as a guest assistant for some of her fashion-buying dominatrices, who regularly spent lots of money with her.

However, one cold November afternoon, one of her friends inadvertently killed a customer by way of pure misadventure. Monica turned up at the house, for what she thought was going to be some edifying interaction, only to discover her distraught friend standing over a dead body and the police on their way.

Monica was so traumatised by seeing the poor, glassy-eyed man lying there on the floor that day, she dismantled her whole life and engineered a new direction. In so doing, she found a wonderful new world of lower key adventure in the more mildly erotic world of gothic fashion.

All of her skills were directly transferrable, the dynamics were similar, and from the day she first picked up a stick of black lipstick, she was on the path to a new life in Belgium where she immersed herself in the New Wave Spooky-Beth scene. It even had links to her electronica music tastes – a logical progression on from her dubstep days. That same year, she met a guy called Gaston at Summer Darkness, just over the border in Utrecht and they ended up living together and developing a successful fashion brand as a joint venture.

Chapter Six

—·—

Pigs in a Blanket

Teddy and Tice's formative years were never as complicated. They had occupied a very binary world, one chiefly comprising of 'the haves' and 'the have-nots', and they were very much the former.

This life of privilege had left them painfully riven by guilt. Constantly reminded that their lifestyle hadn't been earnt, made them feel like takers, rather than givers. They were also aware that the 'having' part wasn't just about money; it was also about health, freedom from work, influence, respect and education, and that was just the shortlist.

Critically, their world lacked any challenging diversity. It lacked contact with those outside of it, or with different cultures. Theirs had been the modern era – a binary culture that carried many assumptions had since been displaced by the ambiguity of the new postmodern, global-village era. Sure, they understood what went on elsewhere, but the unwritten 'rules' of their world diverted them from engaging with anything considered part of the undesirable non-standard minority zone. One thing was undeniable though: once they set aside their guilt, they were fabulously fun, kind and entertaining people to be with.

They would make their apologies to God at church every Christmas and Easter, but back home, they'd whoop it up in a spirit of perpetual thanksgiving. And then they made the move to France. It had been a whimsical leap in the dark, laden with expectation of a simpler life. They had hoped to cut out 'all the noise' and to live off the land, but a healthy bank balance and a factory business back home, churning out porcelain would forever confine them in their gilded cage.

****

Teddy and Tice were due back at Chalkewood for a month. Business needed attending to, not least the sale of the estate, but also the management and future of Royal Hanbury Porcelain.

Nothing much had moved forwards with the sale of Chalkewood since Guy had discovered the wardrobe full of bats at August Lodge. The time it had taken to get a legal steer on the bat situation had put a pause on advertising the sale, and although this had given Laura more thinking time, she still hadn't come up with any answers to either her Chalkewood or biological clock dilemmas.

After legal advice from local government, Laura had called in bat specialist, Dr Timothy Diament, to conduct a survey. His report said that all the rooms at the end of the top floor at August must be left untouched for three months until the bats had resettled in their chosen home of the old wardrobe. This meant the property couldn't be relet. Peasley had made a huge fuss about how that could delay the sale of the entire estate – yet Laura still couldn't figure out why exactly that should be a personal concern for him.

In the week leading up to Tice and Teddy's arrival, an advanced wave of their presence was felt, which made Laura feel both happy and excited. Tuesday saw a courier van full of clothes and cases arrive. It even included a casket containing three of their favourite paintings to be re-hung on the walls for the duration of their stay. On the Wednesday, the cleaners arrived for the day. Next were the deliveries of drinks and comestibles from Waitrose and Fortnum & Mason. Finally, on the Friday a van load of flowers and plants were brought in.

The most curious arrival of all, though, turned up at around Friday lunchtime in the form of two furry visitors. Prior to leaving for France, Tice had given Hansel and Gretel, the family cats, away to the residents at Chalkewood House. This had given rise to the most amazing phenomenon, whereby, whenever Teddy and Tice were due to come home, this pair of tabby cats would somehow sense it, and they would come home too.

Friday night, and Laura had vacated her parents' bedroom and was now back in her old room, lying there, alone in bed, in the empty mansion, as usual. Just resting and thinking about her life, as usual. She asked herself, if a fairy godmother suddenly appeared and granted her three wishes, what would they be? Laura closed her eyes and imagined a glowing pantomime fairy godmother floating in the bedroom.

The first two wishes were always the same. Laura wanted family life: she wanted a husband and children. With two wishes used up, it was the third that always eluded her. Outside of domestic bliss, what exactly was her want or need in life? Was it to preserve or modernise Chalkewood? Was it to make a name for herself in industry? Unlikely, because she just couldn't focus intensely enough on developing a full-on career because of the constant time-pressured distraction of the finding a husband. Tick-tock.

****

Saturday turned out to be a beautiful June day, and her parents were prepared and dressed for it. Stepping down from the courtesy coach with the rest of their luggage and presents in tow, they looked very European and elegant. Tice was wearing a multicoloured dress of broad vertical stripes, gathered at the waist by an elegant cinch belt. Teddy wore white chinos, a dark blue, short-sleeved shirt and a grey cravat. No mistaking they were fresh in from the South of France.

Laura breathed in the familiar fragrance of Teddy's cologne, as she threw her arms around him. Tice simply did the usual two kiss thing – she wasn't being cold, she was just in a rush to get indoors to have a wee. Once relieved, Tice dried her hands on the soft, clean towel.

Back in the kitchen, Tice began her 'piggy' routine. Ever since Laura was a toddler, Tice had gone through the routine of pretending they were 'piggies'. It had started as an incentive for Laura to not be a fussy eater, to be more enthusiastic and embracing of new taste sensations. The premise being that piggies never turn down food.

Laura was thirty-four now, but her mother still loved the piggie routine. She led Laura over to the fridge. "Let's take a peek, shall we, and see what the farmer delivered, eh...? Oooh, what's this, Baby Piggie...? Hoo hoo, lots of scrummy swill for Mummy and Baby Piggy to chomp on." Lots of schnorking noises of approval then followed with the discovery of each new item, and Laura played along to please her mother.

Tice had perfected a schnork rating scale. Mere veg would just get a kind of grunt of disdain. Quality items like pies and favourite cheeses would get a sumptuous schnorking noise and enthusiastic facial approval to go with it. Laura knew when Tice had spotted the ultimate item: a tray of gourmet pigs-in-blankets. Turning to look at Laura with eyes wide, she started a frantic squealing noise. This was accompanied by a lot of excited wiggling whilst snuffling Laura's ticklish neck. And then the finale: a great phat, long lick on Laura's face to gross her out to the max. Tice then grabbed her round the waist saying, "Who's a lucky piggy then? Who's a lucky piggy then?"

Laura endured all of it for as long as possible, before managing to lure Tice away, using some gooseberry gin as bait. Now all Tice wanted to do was get pissed and talk loudly for hours. Laura loved the sound of her mother's voice and couldn't wait to get the drinks poured and light the blue touchpaper.

"Where the bloody hell's your father?" said Tice.

Laura knew her mother didn't really care what the answer was, already benefitting from the initial and welcome anaesthetic effect of the alcohol after a long day's travelling.

****

Teddy, meanwhile, had gone off on house inspection. His motivation was complex. It wasn't really an onerous chore – more an enjoyable and nostalgic reassurance. First and foremost, it would remove him from the intense pigfest in the kitchen. When Laura was little, he had once tried to join in, but was so useless at being a pig that he had had Tice and Laura crying with laughter and they still hadn't forgotten about it.

Teddy's house-inspection ritual involved walking every corridor and passage in the extensive building, examining as he went – a bit like an airline pilot doing a pre-flight visual check on a plane's exterior. Teddy relished the formality of the procedure. He approached it like a detective, being all cautious, prepared for any horror that he might meet along the way.

It was an old building, substantial and large. In practical terms he'd be looking out for things like plumbing leaks, ingress of rainwater, pest activity, signs of attempted forced entry, radiators left on in empty rooms, unusual smells and sounds, new cracks in the plasterwork, fire exits that wouldn't open. On the upper floors, he would use the vantage to get an initial overview of the grounds immediately outside – missing items, fallen trees, damaged fences. He went into the gloriously warm Plant & Equipment room to look at the heating and water treatment systems. All control lights were showing green and there were no apparent leaks.

He was enjoying the good memories of Chalkewood that came with all its sounds, smells and sights. So much so that, just before re-entering the kitchen, he was momentarily pierced by the realisation that he still loved the place. He stopped

and rested his forehead against the wall whilst
he gathered his composure and reminded himself
that, without doubt, before it was time to return to
France, someone would surely have said or done
something to remind him of why he and Tice had
left for France in the first place.

"Papa, he say yay!" Teddy made a flamboyant
kitchen re-entry in a loud and very random Spanish
accent, whilst doing a crazy kind of dance jiggle
truly befitting a seasoned dad. The two women
completely ignored him. Tice now had Laura sitting
down on a kitchen chair and was brushing her hair.
It was clear no one was going to offer Teddy a
drink, so he opened the drinks cabinet himself and
was delighted to find that someone had partially
restocked it. He poured himself an island single malt
whisky. Putting it to his nose, he wondered if maybe
his tastes had changed, perhaps becoming slightly
more continental? – what with all the Cognac,
Armagnac and Calvados he had been drinking
recently. One sip of the malt put him right on that
question, though.

****

The canapes were a delight, and Laura assembled
a cheese board and put out some savoury biscuits
together with pickles and chutneys from the local
indoor farmers' market. This was it – finally, a
moment of quiet and tranquillity. Laura opened
proceedings with a summary of all that had taken

place recently. Her parents were saddened to hear about her Park Run experience. They were shocked to hear about the Blue Ninjas creeping around at night, but utterly in awe of Laura's 'admirable sang-froid' under such testing circumstances.

Laura then had to broach the subject of the bats at August. Her parents took this revelation surprisingly well, and Teddy was fully supportive of her chosen line of action. Laura had made sure to be highly complimentary about Guy's contribution as she knew her parents never questioned his judgement and, as usual, they were super enthusiastic about his versatility. Laura went on to say how much she liked him as a friend, but that brought the somewhat predictably sharp rebuke from Tice.

"Noo, noo, nooo, darling. Remember, Guy is staff, and we must keep it that way. He lives in his world, and we live in ours, and never the twain shall mix, my dear."

Spotting an inconsistency here, Laura said, "Oh yes, Mummy, of course. But... not quite the way we treat the Peasley's though, is it?"

Tice didn't have an answer for that and looked to Teddy for help, but then said, "Yes, I know, Piggy, but there is a subtle distinction. You see, Gordon Peasley is 'senior management'; he is our land agent, our eyes and our ears, and whilst he is technically staff, your father and I both feel that he has a certain je ne sais quoi when it comes to representing Chalkewood in the community."

Je ne sais quoi? Pah! That phrase had such a spooky double entendre when applied to Peasley, thought Laura.

Tice got up to top up the cafetiere. "Oh, darling." Both Laura and Teddy looked up, not sure which darling she was referring to – both as it turned out. "I have invited the Peasleys for dinner on Friday. We need all their help and cooperation right now, so a bit of conviviality is just what the doctor ordered, I think."

Laura was stunned, but she didn't think now was the time to speak out – Peasleys aside, it was so lovely to have her mother and father home, and it was turning out to be such a warm and cosy evening. Whilst handing out the port, Laura remembered she had something for her father. Laura leant over the back of his chair. "Here, Daddy, go for it," she said, handing him an expensive cigar she had bought the previous week. It was always so lovely to have the scent of cigar smoke in the house, a strong reminder of her father.

"Ooh... oh, no, darling. It's very sweet of you, but you see, I gave them up. No, I never touch them anymore. My personal trainer would have a fit if he knew. But hey, look, I know a man who does partake: Gordon. I'll pop it on the side, and give it to him on Friday evening."

Laura slumped back in her chair. Several internet memes had just sprung to mind which would have perfectly expressed how she was feeling right now.

****

The following morning was a bit of a late start, but it was a Sunday, and everything was right with the world. Teddy was an early riser, especially as he was still an hour ahead on French time, so he was already up and out for a walk around the estate. Tice was awake and still in bed and on her laptop.

"Morning, Mumsie!"

Tice held out her arms for a nice, big porky snuggle with Laura.

Laura offered to make breakfast in bed for them both and it wasn't long before the place was awash with croissant pastry flakes. The conversation then drifted round to what direction Laura's life was taking.

"Mummy, I just want a bloody husband. Is that really so much to ask for?"

"Don't you start on that one; you know my feelings on the subject. You had a perfectly good partner in Mike, and then you let him go. What's to say?"

She was referring to Mike Hopgood. Everyone had loved him. He had fitted in perfectly with the estate with his sense of country style and his great conversation and wit. The word 'charisma' is often overused and very few people actually have it, but Mike was one of the rare examples of one who genuinely did. The problem was he and Laura didn't share any goals or interests. He had loved the estate and Laura just wanted to escape from it. He had wanted to keep bringing her back to it – hunting, shooting, fishing and all that.

"Mummy, Mike was a bore."

"Then he should bloody well suit you then... Piggy!" said Tice, roaring with laughter. "Piggies always marry boars, don't they? You, my girl, need to get your finger out."

"But that's what I've been trying to do. Mummy, look," Laura took her phone out and activated the online dating app. She showed her mother a few examples, swiping left and right.

"What the damn hell are you doing on that?" Tice's face dropped. "How on earth are you ever going to explain to people on there who you are and what you come with? It's fantastical. You're kidding yourself. You'll end up attracting a gold-digger. Put it away; it's making me feel ill just looking at it. My advice? Go and speak to Pru at Tatler magazine. Get her to let you run a lifestyle and work/life balance business article, slip it in somewhere that you are unattached, but then say you are setting up a business discussion blog and see what contacts come from that."

Laura lay back and reflected. Maybe something like that might work.

"What about Cowes Week? Get in with the yachting brigade. Plenty of 'our sort' amongst that lot." The use of the phrase 'our sort' in that sentence pretty much ruled that out for Laura. Tice rolled onto her side, facing Laura. "Shame they don't have Pig's Week, instead of Cowes Week, isn't it? Cor, just imagine that – every rich swine in the country turning up. All snaffeling around looking for rich truffles like you, my sweetie," she said, tickling Laura.

"Yep, cheerio, Mummy. That's enough of that. I'm off to get a shower."

****

Friday arrived, and Laura woke to the realisation that the Peasleys were coming for dinner that evening, and there was no way of escaping that tragic fact. In her half-awake state, she was rather confused though, because she could hear Peasley's voice downstairs already. Like, he was twelve hours early. She wondered if she was dreaming, having a nightmare, or something. There it was again, Gordon mansplaining away to her mother at full volume. It turned out that he had just arrived back from a fishing trip and had brought a couple of trout for Tice to cook. Not Laura's favourite fish, but never mind.

Laura went downstairs after she heard him leave and found Tice in her element. The poaching tin was out, and she was making a list of items to buy from Waitrose. Fruit, rocket, endive, watercress, fennel, radicchio, lemon – all written down in her familiar handwriting. Laura knew what the rush was all about: her mother had to get this nailed quickly, because the minute Teddy came in and saw the fish, he would want to have a go at smoking them. Not acceptable. Tice would be wanting to show off to Gordon, show him she was the perfect kitchen angel. She had every right to claim that title too: she was Cordon Bleu trained from her time at the Institut Chateau Mont-Cedre – the Swiss finishing school she had attended.

****

The Peasleys were due shortly. Tice had everything in place in the kitchen, and she looked immaculate. Laura had been fully instructed on what was expected of her, and it soon became apparent that she, as the fifth person at the table, would be consigned to waitressing duties for the evening, just like when she was sixteen.

Teddy was nowhere to be found. Laura eventually found him in the bedroom, rummaging through the drawers, grumbling away to himself. He had managed to get a thorn in his finger, fiddling with something on the estate earlier, and now he was looking for a pair of tweezers. "All I want is a bloody pair of tweezers, and all I can find are ruddy jam rags, face-cake and clown paint."

"Hey, Daddy, is there something I can do to help?"

Teddy swung round, an anguished look on his face and clutching his finger. "Look, a splinter and no tweezers."

Laura suppressed a smirk – you'd have thought he'd lost an arm or something. It even looked like he might be feigning a slight limp as he shuffled about.

"Daddy, the Peasleys will be here soon, so look sharp." That said, it sounded like they had actually arrived.

Hurrying downstairs, Laura saw Tice was there, taking their coats and greeting them. They managed to spare a nod and a smile for her.

Margaret Peasley had brought with her all of her glum glory. Laura kept it a secret that she thought the woman looked like a serial killer's apprentice. Her face could easily have served time as part of the nation's coastal sea defences. The woman had pretty much given up on her appearance; Laura guessed she'd thought her personality would win through and make up for it.

Teddy swaggered down the grand spiral staircase with everyone waiting below. His mischievous yet humble expression made him look like he was just about to make an acceptance speech. He didn't bother soiling his repertoire with any such dry verbiage, though. Instead, he greeted them with a series of gestures, rather like a conductor introducing his orchestra. To be fair, it did look rather cool. He swung round off the bottom step and did a bit more hand jive voguing, before entering into a routine of kiss-and-shake.

As Laura led the Peasleys through to the reception room, she noticed how Teddy's finger had made a miraculous recovery as he was now using it to pinch Tice hard on her bottom. "You look ravishing, sweet pea," he whispered in her ear. The face-cake and clown paint clearly having served some purpose.

Laura took everyone's order for Martinis and set herself to that task, out of the way in the kitchen. Swishing through later, silver salver in hand, she served the two couples with their drinks. Back in the kitchen, Laura took the generous amount left in the cocktail shaker and poured it into a half-pint glass. Bum warming against the Aga, she was good to go until next summoned. Except not. Teddy appeared from nowhere.

"Hey what are you up to? You've got to come and join in. How else are you going to know what's required of you once we go back to France?"

Laura tipped some of her drink into a Martini glass, necked the rest and followed Teddy back through.

With everyone seated, it fell to Laura to bring out the starter course of watercress and mint soup, with goat's cheese crostini. Deserved compliments to Tice, though, because it was unbelievably delicious.

The evening wore on reasonably quickly. Margaret was never really allowed much input.

In between keeping an ear out for key points, Laura pretty much looked after the older woman. Margaret had worked on the estate longer than Gordon, having started out age sixteen as a clerical assistant. Over the years she had risen to become Chief Financial Officer, just shortly after she and Gordon were married.

Finally, it was time for the 'gentlemen you may smoke now' moment – although not so common or popular in today's post-smoking era. Teddy reached behind him. "Here, Gordon, try this," he said, handing him the cigar that Laura had bought earlier in the week.

"Ooh, very nice. Ambassador Maduro, hmm, don't mind if I do. Impeccable choice, as per usual, Teddy old chap." Having trimmed it, Gordon lit the cigar in an ostentatious kind of way before taking a huge puff. Not wanting to blow it in his host's face, he blew it more in Laura's direction.

If this was what being Lady of the Manor was all about, then Laura truly wanted to come back in her next life as a Johnny no-stars down at Maccy D's.

Gordon then went on to make a withering complaint about how Guy and Laura had handled the bat situation at August, and Teddy just patted him on the back and ushered him away to the drawing room for a bit of men-only talk.

Laura was just about to slip away when her mother called out. "Ahem! Laura, why don't you come through and have a chat with Margaret."

Using the door as a shield, Laura looked her mother in the eye, gave her the middle finger, blew her a kiss and walked off, saying, "Sure, I'll be back in just one moment," whilst muttering, "Not," under her breath. Tice tried to look annoyed but couldn't stop herself from laughing a bit.

****

It was a Sunday. The month's visit had come to an end, and Teddy and Tice were gone now. Laura sat up in bed. It was Groundhog Day for her. Empty house, again. Life not moved on, again. Everything was okay, though. Apparently, she still had two arms and two legs. The central heating had come on, on time. The fridge had plenty to eat in it. No lack of cash, or anything like that. She was simply a whole month older than the last time she lay here, having the exact same conversation with herself.

Maybe she could just lie in stasis for a few decades? Maybe get out of bed around the year AD 2082, look in the mirror and see a wizened old lady looking back at her. Book a quick slot at the crematorium and that would be it, job done. Excellent, cheerio, Roger and out.

Today was what she called a recalibration day. A kind of 'today is the first day of the rest of my life' moment. She did a quick status check. Yep, nothing had changed. Life goals all still the same. She had had a great idea, though. She would go on the net right now and order a whiteboard. She'd put it up somewhere reasonably private and list on it some intermediate goals.

Ideas were entering her head already, and she needed to get them down quick. Her phone hadn't charged, so she couldn't use Notepad. Looking around for something to write on, there was an empty pizza box lying by the bed. Why had she even done that? Pizza? What an idiotic and self-destructive life choice it had been ordering and eating that. Trying to write on the lid with an old eyeliner pen was even more pitiful, especially as it wouldn't write on a greasy surface.

Laura took a deep breath and leapt out of bed. Downstairs she went. Pizza box in the bin, wash hands, pen and notepad from the bureau, back up to bed with a coffee, phone on charge. Control had been regained. When the going gets tough, the tough get going.

First. Fitness. She had achieved a personal miracle recently when she made the journey from Couch to 5K to Park Run. She took a sip of her coffee and reminded herself how glorious her body had felt after each run. She had also trimmed up and lost a little bit of fat. Goal one, she wrote. Maintain Park Run. Then: Goal two – get down to dress size 12 (remember, size 8 if buying from US). She was still about two sizes above that right now.

Problem, huge vast problem. The fridge was still utterly rammed with about a quarter of a million calories of leftovers from her parents' visit. She couldn't ever countenance throwing that lot in the bin. She should do, but it would be impossible for her. What about all the starving people in the world? What an utter disgrace it would be? Worst still – all those meat products. Throwing meat in the bin after an animal had died for it just didn't seem right. You bought the meat, but oh dear, you're on a diet now, so just pop it in the bin, eh? Although maybe some could be frozen? Maybe the puss cats might like a bit? That was if they hadn't already jogged on back to their new real home at Chalkewood Lodge. Laura thought maybe she could try becoming vegetarian again. At that thought she could hear Tice's voice in her head shrieking with laughter and saying, "Piggies don't approve of any of that kind of nonsense." She was right – it would just be unachievable for Laura.

Goal three. No, there was no way ever that she was going to write Get a man on her whiteboard. Even if it was kept somewhere private it would just be such a pathetically sad thing to do. Maybe she could write it in code? Like a capital M with a circle around it? No, that's all too ridiculous. In any case, she had already decided it was a subject that needed a brainstorming session all of its own.

Fourth and final for right now. Work. She needed to re-engage with it. Potentially, she could end up having a career instead of a family, so she really needed to get in and preserve that as an option.

Chapter Seven

— · —

The Female of the Species

Laura had always stuck to her own career, and she strenuously avoided any involvement with Royal Hanbury Porcelain. Teddy oversaw that side of things, and RHP had done just fine keeping the Stanhope family in clover for generations. Whereas in recent years, for reasons unknown, the Chalkewood estate only ever broken even.

For Laura, having an independent career was not about money – it was about self-fulfilment and contributing towards making the world a better place. This drive was also what had earnt her a reputation for being a real stickler in the fight against corporate corruption. On one operation she'd headed up, she'd had the police come in and arrest several people at their desks.

Some while after that, she was in a bar with a construction guy who used to work for her company. She was bragging to him about her police operation, when he took a sip of his beer and said to her, "Alright for you though, eh? What's your title? Honourable Lady Stanhope, or something? No worries for you, eh? Some guys grew up with their single mother dying on her arse and just living off Universal Credit. Things like that can make a man desperate, but yeah, good job on your corruption bust and all that," he said, raising an ironic toast to her.

Reflecting on his remarks, she replied, "Yeah, but there's a fine line between want and need, though, isn't there, eh?"

****

Laura was loading the car with her laptop and overnight bag, ready to drive to the station. She was quite early, so the plan was to get a coffee and a pastry at the station before the train arrived. Then she suddenly remembered: No! It wouldn't be a pastry; it would be a cereal bar. Start as we mean to go on.

Distracted by the sight of Pengersick kissing some woman goodbye, Laura just couldn't help herself. "Guy," she called out, waving her hand. Walking over, she asked him how the bat thing was going. She didn't even listen to his reply, far too focussed on stopping herself asking what she really wanted to know... which was none of her business, really. She walked away, none the wiser, and drove off to the station. Good luck to him. At least someone was getting on with their life. Perfectly delighted for him, she told herself.

Her train drew into the station. The carriage was quite empty now rush hour was over, but Laura wanted a forward-facing seat at a completely empty table, so she continued walking through the train. Then, right there, it was the girl Guy had been saying goodbye to earlier. Laura paused. Just as she had passed, the girl pulled her bag open to get something. A black ladies leatherette bag with a name tag on it, Pengersick.

Entering first class, Laura took a seat. "Tickets, please." The efficient conductor was already there. Laura handed him her ticket. "Erm, this is for second class, ma'am."

"Right, upgrade it, then," said Laura, handing him her credit card, without so much as looking him in the eye.

****

The imposing sight of the Hauptmann Vyse building came into view as Laura turned the corner into London's Shoe Lane. It's imposing synergistic façade of glass and steel demonstrated both its strength and dominance on this expensive plot of city land. Laura had felt a real sense of achievement at having penetrated its corporate world, rising up through its ranks without, yet, having bumped her head on the glass ceiling in this male-dominated sector.

HV was by no stretch of the imagination a benign organisation, but it had, through the passage of time, moved on from a cancerous workplace culture where people would be told they could work any hours they wanted – when that was just a cynical ploy to create a competitive environment where in actuality, the person who dared to be the first to get up to go home each day got flagged up as being the weak link and was sacked.

Niall Frazer would head up that morning's meeting of the Performance Improvement Steering Group. It used to be called the Performance Improvement Steering Team, but that spelt PIST, so they had to change it.

The agenda was always somewhat circuitous in content and mainly comprised of a rolling review of ongoing projects. Niall Frazer's delivery of it, however, always had something of the night about it. Rather than 'point and evidence, point and evidence' it tended to be 'point and consequence, point and consequence'.

Despite almost three months out of the office, when it came to Laura's turn to speak, she was thoroughly relaxed, thanks to having been briefed by the devastatingly efficient, Miss Dolly Deloitte, the diligent and committed sub-director who was famous for once having delivered a winning pitch to a client whilst standing there in soaking wet knickers because her waters had just broken, due to the imminent arrival of her fourth child.

Laura drew her report to a close. She knew she had a great way with words and had been complimented on her ability to deliver her presentations in a polished, old-money style. Typically, she would thank someone for something, then include a moral message and then always end on a note offering a positive course of action. She was happy to speak prophetically, with vision and with cautionary wisdom, but the delivery was always genial. Quietly confident this had been a top-notch example, her thoughts were corroborated when Gaby Parsons, sitting opposite, went to clap, but when she realised none of the men had any intention of clapping she quickly converted the clap into a bizarre holding her hands together in the praying position whilst looking thoughtful kind of a gesture.

Niall Frazer thanked Laura in an almost inaudible voice, but Laura had already made her mind up about him long ago. He was a misogynist, hiding in plain sight, masquerading as a enabler of women.

Mr Frazer went on to the last item. "Folks, just a little heads-up. Following on from the excellent progress on improving workplace culture by Richard Sopel, the board wants to conclude the work by asking a firm of change consultants to come in and present to us at the next meeting, subject to, hopefully, awarding them the contract. That's it then, folks, you're all done," he said, with one last glance around the room.

The meeting broke up into small groups. Gaby went straight over to Laura. She rubbed her arm gently as a discreet signal of female solidarity. Laura chatted expansively and asked her if her mother was recovering well from her recent operation.

Laura did a button up on her jacket. It was a tailor-made, double-breasted, woollen Saville Row suit. Its straight lines helped to cancel out her curvy figure. Sadly, this choice of suit was a by-product of previous experiences. She had once given a presentation wearing a lovely feminine suit, but some smirking lad, slouching in the front row and chewing his pencil, had gawked at her tits. She had had to stand for nearly forty minutes clutching a document wallet to her chest to obscure his view. She did nail him at the end, though, during Any Questions, when he failed to answer a not-too-difficult question, thus demonstrating that hadn't listened to a word she'd said.

****

It was an unusual day, thanks to a work trip south of the river. The HV steering group had been summoned to the Young Vic theatre to watch a play, a performance organised by the recently appointed change management company, Dexter Newhouse. They had, for some weeks, been studying staff members in the workplace. The Young Vic had been specifically been hired for its theatre-in-the-round stage layout, allowing team members to be spaced out around the 360-degree central acting space, so they couldn't confer with one other.

Change consultant, Anna Le Pley-Dougall stepped up onto the stage and welcomed everyone. "True success comes when tiny changes occur. A wise man changes his mind, a fool never does. The people who are crazy enough to think they can change the world are the ones who do. The question is, are you one of them? I want you to enjoy the play, but we will be pausing occasionally, so I can come on and ask you questions."

The action started: clearly an office setting. It all seemed quite routine. Then suddenly the awful truth dawned. The company had hired actors to act out the working lives of all the individual members of staff. Laura realised and put her hand to her mouth. Oh... my... word.

In that moment, the actors all froze, and Anna Le Pley-Dougall stepped forwards. "If you think you know what this is all about yet, please would you just raise your hand in the air?" Only Laura responded. "Okay, let's watch some more, shall we?"

At the interval, Anna came on again. By this time, all but a few young men had worked out what the deal was. When Anna explained it to them, they thought it was 'really brilliant' that an actor was playing them in a play.

Anna asked, "So, the actors are based upon our observations of you all in the office, but what do you think will happen in the second half of the play?"

One of the team asked, "Are you going to do it again, but this time, show us how you think we should have done it?"

"That's a common response, but actually, no. So, let's see what does happen, shall we?" Anna took a step back. The lights came up, and the action began. It was an exact repeat of the first half, but this time there was one difference: the actors were now wearing clothes attributed to their opposite gender.

When the action restarted, the male actors were still playing the parts of male employees, but they were now dressed as women and talking about the game at the weekend, again. A couple of others joined the group, and the conversation, as was seen in the first half. Then a woman, dressed as a man, approached the group, but she got totally excluded. It was a bit of an ouch moment, but more was to come.

Group Leader Niall Frazer's character, now dressed as a woman, came on. There was a bit of a hushed cheer of support from the male members of the staff audience. He approached Dolly, now dressed as a man. "Hey, Dolly, I hear you pissed your knickers on stage. Brilliant, that's commitment! Still, at least you're off now with your feet up, playing babies. Good for you." The real Niall, visible to all staff was seated in the circular pattern facing everyone, as had been intended. To recover the situation, he put both thumbs up, swinging his hands from one side to the other as if to say, yes, this feedback is good. The gesture didn't really cut it and the indictment stood.

Anna came on, and the full blaze of the house lights returned everyone to real life, and the inquest began. The session then wrapped up with question time.

"Any questions then?"

Nick Cleverly went first. Looking around the circle for a bit of eye contact with other male colleagues, he asked, "So, is it possible to have workplace sexism caused by women?"

Some oaf whispered, "Nice one, Nick," but despite the bright lighting, Anna didn't manage to catch who said it.

She responded with the standard stock reply. "It applies to all genders. Thank you for that. Next question?"

Billy Smart, the new intern, spoke up. He had the least to lose by saying the wrong thing. "Can I have a selfie with the tranny person who's playing me dressed as a chick?" Niall Frazer looked across at him in a way that subtly signalled that he may have just won a permanent appointment.

"Nope," was Anna's response. "Okay, let's have a question from one of the women here."

Norma Baron, from Support Services, had a go.

"I think I get it. Is it like 'Wear a Skirt to School' day? You know, where those transwotsit people, like your actors here, have a day of action?" Niall wasted no opportunity here to offer the wrong kind of support via a gentle ripple of applause.

"Okay, anyone else?" When there was no response, Anna tried to bring everything to a conclusion, but by now people were chit-chatting and going on their phones, so she had to speak in an extra loud voice as she read from the pre-prepared autocue slides.

Laura was not the kind of person to get angry. She was good at gaining the grand overarching view of affairs, and she never went in for hand-to-hand combat. She grabbed Anna the second she came offstage. "Meet me outside, we'll take a taxi back together."

Anna was surprisingly sanguine about how the session had gone. She explained that it really was just another routine day at the office for her. "Clearly Frazer is the root of the problem. Don't let that concern you. As you know, I report directly to the CEO on all this. I am, however, critically low on evidence, so our main objective is going to be evidence-gathering, and I would be happy to allow a carefully measured amount of entrapment if you were to feel comfortable with that."

Laura indicated she was prepared to move a little in that direction, in order to achieve the desired outcome.

****

As the train left London, Laura closed her eyes and her laptop to allow herself some reflection on the day's events. She was still on a first-class ticket and the carriage was nice and quiet which was very conducive to a bit of deep thought whilst occasionally dozing.

Laura was too tired to think constructively, so instead she fantasised about what it would be like if Monica had a senior position at the company. She would be deliciously unemployable in that environment – within a nano second, there would be issues.

Although Monica enjoyed having a man between her legs, it was only ever subject to a raft of strict caveats. Her tolerance levels of men were always in the minus figures, and she was a highly committed sadist as far as men were concerned.

Billy Smart probably wouldn't be alert enough to see the first lightning-fast drop-kick coming. Cleverly and all the rest of the loose jumble of hyenas would probably all be lined up along the glass partition in the corridor, and then she'd walk down the line, delivering a hefty punch in the stomach to each one. By lunchtime, who knows? Most likely in the men's executive washroom, she'd have Niall Frazer's arm wrenched up behind his back and his face held underwater in the sink, seeing how long he could hold his breath for.

Any remaining super tough intransigents might then be subject to a mis-adventurous trip to one of her friend's dungeons. A trip that they might fail to ever return from. Monica was the archetypal human scorpion. She even had a tiny, discreet yellow warning triangle tattoo, and she represented the notion of the female of the species rather well.

CHAPTER EIGHT

— · —

A WHITER SHADE OF PALE

Park Run had just finished, and Laura was leaning back against her car, just cooling off. Thirty-three minutes twenty-two seconds: getting very close now to reaching that iconic sub-thirty-minute time. The endorphins had definitely kicked in today. She could feel them coursing through her veins. Nature's natural high, the antidote to the trauma of running, trauma which was almost non-existent now that she had reduced her weight right down and was pretty much at her target.

She was sure her new kit had helped massively – new running shoes, new Lycra sprint pants that felt like a second skin, but best of all, a new high-impact sports bra that was heavenly bliss, as she no longer felt like she was carrying the world on her chest.

Laura was looking out for Jim Singh. She liked him and wanted to chat, but it didn't look like he was there this week. She thought about going over to Café Desouza to soak up the atmosphere, but then decided it would be best to just make tracks for home and get a few things done. In reality, there was nothing pressing that needed doing anyway, but she felt a nagging unease that there were so many unresolved things still going on in her mind. Maybe the short journey back would initiate some solutions? Then again, maybe the clarity and stillness of her own home would be better for that, so she put on 'We're All Runners', enjoying the powerful feeling that came from listening to its tune and lyrics.

Living on her own in a twenty-bed mansion was something she had got used to. It was beyond brilliant for times like this when clarity was needed. With a great guzunder of fresh coffee in hand, Laura stood in front of the grandfather clock, listening to its soft, slow ticking. Its face was so big, and she could see the big hand move slightly with each tick.

Agenda item one. The corporate world. Could she make a difference? She certainly didn't need the money. However, she had just embarked on a mission of justice supporting Anna, so at the very least, she would be sticking with it until that was finished.

Having virtually killed herself to lose weight, and get trim and fit, there was now nothing stopping her from embarking on her quest to find a member of the male species whom she could capture, pin down and make into a dad. She already had a few irons in the fire, so that agenda item was well in order.

****

Laura had been playing a bit of text-tennis with Monica over the last few days, and it seemed her old friend was keen to catch up, so she was next on the list.

"Hello, moosh, how are you? Long-time no-speak, managing to stay out of prison, are we?"

"Shut it, you posh cow. Look, yeah, lovely to hear from you after such a while. You okay?"

"I might be. What are you up to? You want something, don't you? I can tell."

"Wow, am I that transparent? Aw, no, look, I just want to run something past you. Okay, so I'm done with Gaston. Yeah, all too much really. Got to hand it to the guy, though – Goth to the core, really faithful to the culture, and he was good to me, too. We had some truly amazing times with all the parties and our fashion design business. We were constantly dressed-up and in the vibe, and the business side has been great, and we still own the company together."

"Sounds good. What's the problem?"

"It's just got too much, too extreme. I thought I was the only one who didn't have an off-button, but he's out-peaked me. I came home one day, and he was naked on the bed. Lying there, on one of our best latex bed sheets... and covered in leeches."

"Oh heavens, Monica, no."

"Well, I knew he did all that stuff. He was passionate about bloodletting. It staves off cancer, reduces the hardening of arteries and it burns calories. See, yeah, you're even thinking about it now, aren't you? Well, it's not good; you end up covered in bruises. It's time-consuming and, to be honest – want to give blood? Well, do the world a favour and give it to the hospitals instead.

"He'd lie there for hours, going an ever-whiter shade of pale." Monica started singing the song down the phone. She started laughing. "I have to laugh. That's what it always reminded me of. That song. He used to keep jars of the things, all swizzling around. Also, even more disgusting, once they've sucked the blood and swollen up to ten times their size or whatever, you have to dispose of them. Not nice – he'd drop them in a bucket of salt to dissolve them. Fricking disgusting, and it stinks!"

"Right, okay. Well, if I was hearing this from anyone else, I'd be utterly shocked by now, but okay, please continue."

"Yeah, I wanted to be one of the sixteen vestal virgins and piss off to the coast, but he wouldn't have it," she said, shrieking with laughter. "Alright, Laura, look, I want to come and live in Hampden."

Utter silence... "No, you damn stupid bitch. Are you out of your mind? I won't have it. I'll call the army in to stop you. I don't want you anywhere near here.

I don't want anyone seeing you anywhere near me. I have a fifty-mile Monica exclusion zone in place, and you are not allowed within it unless I have issued you with a written warrant."

"Pretty please?"

"No, hun. It wouldn't work. Why can't you keep it simple and just come down here occasionally for snuggles and cocoa... in disguise... in the dead of night?"

"Mate, I'm all burnt out; I need to live a quieter life."

"Yeah, well, you just spoilt that by putting 'er' on the end of 'quiet'. Plus, I don't think you've thought things through. Firstly, there isn't anything here for you. Secondly, I won't acknowledge you in public, here in Hampden. Thirdly, there aren't any suitable properties in the village, and you ain't renting anything on my estate."

"Okay, one last shot. Look, how about if we just have a strict rule that, in public, we pretend we don't know each other? I'll just walk past you in the street?"

"Firstly, that kind of shows that you are expecting to be a social catastrophe when you get here, but yeah, okay, I'll try to visualise it, do the 'what ifs' and give it my full consideration, but then, and only then, will I let you know if you have my permission to enter the county."

****

Within an impossibly short space of time, Laura received a text saying, Just moved in. Let's catch up soon.

She was furious. Hitting the 'dial' button straightaway, she yelled, "I never gave you my permission."

Monica didn't miss a beat. "I don't need your permission."

"You jolly well do, missy, if you want to remain friends."

"Oh, look, hun, it's been difficult. Can't you just come down here – incognito, if you want to – and celebrate with me?"

****

Laura had driven down there within the hour. It turned out to be a property she knew quite well. Hampden Lodge sat back from the road at the east end of the village. It had been dilapidated for years and was a rather unusual building, comprising of a Victorian façade just one room deep, like it had the back missing. "How the hell did you afford this?" demanded Laura.

"Oh, it wasn't expensive. I bought it cheap at auction. My brother came over and did the bidding. He checked the place out for me, too."

The front part of the long garden to the rear had recently been bulldozed and there appeared to be trenches, footings and services laid in for what looked like a massive extension. "You've been here for ages, haven't you? How did you get a mortgage on this place? Who's been paying for all this work?" Laura stared in disbelief. "Right. Indoors. Now!" She pointed to the house.

"Why, what's up?"

"You're a lying little minx, and I want to shout at you – that's what's up."

"No, no. Laura, don't do that. You'll disturb the lodgers."

"Lodgers! What? Hang on... who'd want to live in this dump of a building site? You've been stringing me along from the start. You're already up to something, aren't you? I'm going home now. You can make an appointment to come and see me – incognito – once I've calmed down." Laura slammed the car door and wound down the window. "And don't bother bringing your pyjamas." She put her foot down and roared off.

****

Some days later, a peculiar-looking bunch of flowers arrived – a spray of black lilies.

"Looks like you've upset the mafia," quipped the delivery driver as he handed them over.

Laura read the label, Do you still love me, hun? xx M. They were actually quite beautiful, and they smelt divine. Laura brought them in and put them in a vase.

To preserve the sense of conviviality, Laura scanned a Chalkewood complementary visitor's pass on her phone and messaged it to Monica.

****

Late Friday afternoon, Monica arrived at the house in a Jeep. She came in carrying a dainty little basket of goodies which she gave to Laura, who continued to look stern, refusing to welcome her yet. She then ushered Monica in.

"I'll take that," said Laura, relieving Monica of her pink knapsack.

"What the hell are you doing?" gasped Monica.

"Chalkewood security zone. We routinely search all bags here... and their owners, too." Laura tipped the bag out on the table, leaving Monica open-mouthed. "Right, what the hell is this? Bloody pyjamas! You're a bit damn presumptuous, aren't you? Not to mention I specifically said... Right, you now – up against the wall." Monica happily obliged, in her element now with this amusing game. Laura went through all the pockets of her black, leather biker jacket. "If I find any drugs or knives, it'll be big trouble for you, missy. And don't go looking at me like that, you're always guilty as sin."

Monica laughed.

Just then, Laura found something hard inside the lining of the jacket. She couldn't get to it at first, but then found a secret zip. She pulled out what she initially thought was a piece of jewellery, but it wasn't, of course. "This thing. What the heck is it?"

"It's a gold-plated knuckleduster from the 1920s, someone pawned it, but it was never redeemed. I just had to buy it," said Monica.

In spite of her initial reaction, Laura looked at it in wonder. It had three garnet stones set into it... but although it looked beautiful, it was still a dangerous weapon.

"Well, guilty as charged, I think. Now get your hands up." Monica raised her hands, and Laura grabbed her round the waist, giving her a tight hug. "You don't change, do you?" she said, laughing. "But remember, if you mess up here, we're done as mates. Is that clear?"

Security formalities out the way, they sat down to coffee and nibbles.

"You've changed a bit since I saw you last, physically I mean. You always used to have a skinny bottom. What have you done?"

"It's not what you think, Laura. This is all one hundred per cent natural. I just wanted to get the 'thick woman' look."

Laura Googled the expression 'thick woman'. "Oh, my word, it's a porn look, some kind of filth about having a big bum."

Monica really laughed. "Get a grip. It's nothing of the sort."

"How do you get a thick woman look? Do you go into a bun shop and say, Hey, make me thick?"

"No, don't be silly. It's all done by targeted exercise. I used the Get Thick Quick programme, so I do curtsy lunges, Bulgarian split squats, sumo walks, and clam shells. It's nothing weird. I just don't want a boy's bottom. I want to look like a woman. Hey, check this out too. Check my upper body – ha-ha, max power."

"Monica, you never cease to amaze me. Before you tell me about any more of your crazy nonsense, let me get a gin. Would you like one?" Laura brought out a range of six gin bottles. "Here, take your pick. So, what's next? How about you start by telling me what you're living off?"

"Sure, yeah, well, as I said, I'm still in a business partnership with Gaston. We have a couple of great businesses. Vlad the Impala is our strongest."

"Wait, what? Vlad the what?"

"Vlad the Impala's a bit like Wolfskin Jack, but we sell jackets made from faux antelope skin." We were doing reasonably okay, but then I used a contact I know to promote it on the web. He owns a UK company called Searchmatix Digital Marketing, in Salisbury. They got stuck into our website and the sales sky-rocketed. Even crazier, they do publishing, too, and they said that they wanted me to write a book about all of my adventures. Imagine that, next year, me, a novelist. You just couldn't make this shit up if you tried."

"Monica, I'm probably going to regret what this will do for my health, but I've just developed an urgent need to put some sticky ribs and nachos in the oven right now, because I'm starving. Fancy it? We can pop a few beers, and then do the jammies on for cocoa and snuggles after?"

****

Monica had made things very complex for herself – which was quite a natural state of affairs for her. Her mind was always active, and like Laura, she was still searching for a meaning to her life. When she had been at college, someone suggested that she take an IQ test to see if she was eligible to join Mensa, the high IQ society. In short, she had cruised it and secured herself a membership of the elite club.

She recalled her first meeting since moving to Hampden.

Walking through the door of the Duke of York pub, Monica looked around for the Mensa group she was supposed to be meeting. There were several groups seated in the pub, but only one group – made up of about fifteen people – had a Mensa magazine placed on the table, the traditional sign of recognition to members. Monica made probably one of her least flamboyant entrances ever. It was even borderline polite. She sat next to a rather sage-looking chap in his fifties. He had turned to her, saying, "Congratulations on getting in. You now have a secret that you can't share with anyone." She wasn't sure about that. Why not? Why shouldn't she tell people she was a member?

To the left of her was a young chap who was introduced to her as Ender, apparently that was short for Andrew. He wore studious looking glasses and had rather unkempt hair.

"How did you get here?" he asked.

The question made Monica wary, as it was sometimes used by men as a pretext to offer women a lift home, but that vibe just didn't fit this bloke, so she decided to answer the weedy-looking librarian type honestly.

"Well, I pretty much just jumped on a bus at Hampden."

"What bus was it?"

"Pfft. No idea. A red one."

"Well, if you'd come from Hampden directly, it would have to have been the 64. Unless you came before 18.28 in which case it could have been either the 64 or the R7. The 64s are always double-deckers, usually Scania double-deckers, but fitted with Alexander Dennis Enviro400 bodies, but they can't be used on the R7 route because of the low bridge at Calvert Lane."

Monica looked at him quizzically and wondered what he would look like hanging from a coat peg by the hood of his anorak, with her panties stuffed in his mouth. He looked like such a kind, lovely little wimp, though, so she decided to respond sincerely, "Do you think we are ever likely to be getting the electric or hydrogen-powered buses here anytime soon, rather than the ones converted to biofuel?"

Ender adored this response and keenly replied, going into massive detail.

Meanwhile, Monica looked around the room, asking herself the question, Who in this room would I genuinely be interested in shagging? There was only one guy, sitting opposite, he had been staring at her a lot. Very attractive, tall, athletic and well turned-out. He looked like the type who might just go to meetings to pull new female members, though, but at least that showed initiative.

There was a natural break in the conversation, so Monica decided to conduct a test. She went and stood at the bar with her back and her new bottom to the group. Within seconds, she sensed a presence.

"Hello, I'm Ben. Can I buy you a drink? New member's privilege. Seems nobody has remembered, though," he said jovially.

Monica turned to face him, but her intuition immediately flashed up the image of a 'serpent' in her mind. They chatted briefly, but she just couldn't shake off the image. The more she looked at him, the more she felt she was in the presence of some kind of evil. Monica squeezed her jacket to check her knuckle duster was still where it should be.

This had been Monica's most recent visit to a Mensa meeting. She wasn't yet sure if it would be her last. The organisation did have a special interest group for kinksters which sounded very appealing, but it was held up North, miles away.

****

There are those, like Monica, who follow a passion within their own vision, and there are those who follow the visions and passions of others. Is one route ever better than the other? By contrast, the culture within Laura's family, especially that of her late grandfather, the modern-era founder of Chalkewood, was to seize both and see what stuck. It was the all-encompassing imperialist view that one should aim to become master of all one surveys. Having reached the top, one would then dispense grace, wisdom and benevolence to the less well off.

Laura did not subscribe to this model, choosing, instead, to compete on equal terms in today's meritocratic society by going on a journey of self-discovery. It was therefore no surprise that she would take great exception to forces within that society that sought to destroy the equality of opportunity she so craved.

The main problem with the meritocratic journey is that it is, by nature, intensely competitive, and it requires intense periods of energy and single-minded focus. This is how the child athlete from the deprived housing estate ends up beating the privately educated kid with the soft comfortable life. Laura could see this, and she knew she could never become that driven. Chalkewood had destroyed her in that regard, but she did still possess enough resolve to focus on pet projects – one such project being helping Anna Le Pley-Dougall with the workplace culture program.

Niall Frazer was taking the heat now, but it was being applied to him in a non-confrontational and subtle way. Anna had not only videoed the play at the Young Vic theatre, she had also filmed the reactions of the individuals towards what they were seeing. A slick edited version of all the footage, complete with narration by Anna, was then sent to the CEO at HV.

Frazer was subsequently delighted to hear that he had been promoted, but not in a good way. He was to head up the launch of a new product. It was a well-paid position, but only came with a temporary contract. Many non-written verbal assurances of work thereafter were given, but HR had clearly stamped his file with no further employment. HV wasn't the kind of company to throw away successful people, though, so he would get some very nice work-from-home consultancy gigs, but he would forever be held in an external quarantine. HV was beginning to learn that the workplace was a temple and that its culture was its soul.

Anna hadn't really needed Laura's assistance. She had, with devastating efficiency, dealt with the job for which she had been hired. She did, however, send Laura a connection request on LinkedIn.

Laura was now left in a bit of a quandary. She no longer had a career focus. No doubt something would land in her in-tray soon, but until then, she planned to just be reactive rather than proactive.

Chapter Nine

— · —

Under Offer!

Selling Chalkewood was a complex process. It wasn't just the house that was being sold; it was the entire estate, with all its dwellings, tenants and hundreds of acres of land. And there was the transfer of staff to consider as well. Miranda Chilvers, from Slater Scotton & Emery, the selling agents, had been on the phone with an update about a buyer they had been nurturing. He had already had sight of the accounts and had been given a conducted tour of the estate by Gordon Peasley, so now it was time to meet the Lady of the Manor and view the main house.

The gentleman's name was James Gildagraaff. Miranda planned to arrive with him, make the introductions, show him around the house and then leave him to chat to Laura in private, whilst she sat on the drive in her car working on her laptop and making calls.

Laura was keen to meet him. She had heard rumours that a developer had been looking at the estate with a view to exploiting it unscrupulously, and needed to be very sure that this gentleman wasn't of the same mindset.

Wearing clothing carefully chosen to send out subtle signals of gravitas, Laura was ready to meet the viewer. He was a handsome chap, mid-forties, with a bit of grey hair creeping in. Undeniably metrosexual in appearance, he wore an expensive-looking, dark purple, linen jacket and looked like he may have benefitted from a regular manicure. There wasn't a hair out of place, and he carried the subtle, soft fragrance of a sophisticated cologne. He spoke with a very manly voice that had an interesting tone to it and which would not be out of place in a broadcast setting.

Laura sat down with him and conducted an interview. She couldn't find anything untoward. It seemed that he was the European Director of a company called Monrenti Biotech and he had all kinds of share options and personal assets, so everything seemed to stack up. There was also no hint of any link with a development company, so that was it – he had passed the test, and so it was just a matter of making some polite chit-chat. He was certainly very entertaining and did most of the talking.

As the meeting drew to a close, James asked if he might take the opportunity to have a wander around the estate sometime, in a more casual capacity.

"Do you play tennis?" asked Laura. "Why not pop round for a game?"

He said he did, and that he would very much enjoy that.

****

Oh. My. Word.

Laura had the hots for James, big time. She had been due to meet a Chalkewood tenant farmer at 1 p.m., but she simply postponed it. All she wanted to do now was lounge back, in peace and quiet, and run through all the possible fantasies.

First off. Laura Gildagraaff. How might that sound? Such is the luxury of personal, private thought – one can be as outrageous as one wishes. Interesting name though, most likely Dutch. Hmm... sounds quite nice, she thought, especially if there was a bit of a backstory to go with it.

Then, suddenly, Laura's mind exploded, rather like those internet memes you see. What if they got married? Her family would still get the money for the estate, and she would still get to live at Chalkewood. No, she mustn't let that colour her judgement. The quality of any relationship with James would have to be her first consideration.

What about the cons? It wouldn't be an appropriate situation to be in whilst the sale of the estate was going through. Conflict of interest, etcetera.

Laura decided, however, that in this instance, her interests came first. This guy wouldn't be a casual fling. He was massively suitable as a potential partner. This could be it! It wasn't as if her parents needed to sell the estate this instant, anyway. Her mind was set. She would throw the dice and see how it landed.

****

All the preparations were in place. Laura had just put on some casual sportswear and her steel-blue cashmere sweater. She had considered wearing her new sports bra but changed her mind at the last minute.

Her timing was perfect, getting down the stairs just as James pulled onto the drive in his dark blue Bentley Continental. Stepping out, he went to the trunk and took out his tennis bag.

Good grief, thought Laura, that looks a bit pro. It was a welcome sight, though. He looked very serious, a bit like a tennis pro. Laura wasn't looking for a lesson, though. For her, the tennis was just a backdrop to facilitate some flirting and a bit of banter.

After a pleasant greeting and some chat, they went out onto the court and started to have a knock about. It was going great. Laura hadn't played for a while, but it was all coming back to her. Then James said, "Okay, shall we get started?"

He put three balls in his pocket. Taking the first one, he squeezed it, then discarded it. Taking the second one, he bounced it on the ground with his racket a few times before reaching up to full height and smashing it in Laura's direction.

"Net," he called. Taking the final ball, he smashed it with even greater force. Same again. "Net, your service."

Laura picked up a ball, went to serve, and then thought, No, this isn't Wimbledon – we're going to do things my way. Walking towards the net, she asked, "How do you do that super-powered serve thingy? I do all that routine, but when I hit it, there's like zero power."

It was clear James had perceived the change in tempo when his body language relaxed. Laura was even more encouraged when he went with the whole mood change, turning it to their mutual advantage.

"Yeah, well, like so many things, it's not about sheer force. Technique is king, whether it's serving a ball or simply removing a tight lid off a jam jar. Technique is everything. Okay, well let's look at your serve, shall we?"

Laura served a couple of balls, with James standing by her.

"Okay, Laura, it's mainly about stance and body position, but let's start off first with the grip. Use the Continental grip, like this."

Laura got that straightaway. James then went on to describe the stance and how to line up correctly. Laura had difficulty interpreting what he was saying. Maybe he was deliberately explaining it badly? She was beginning to suspect that he might be...

"Yes, it's a little difficult to explain. I mean, I'm not a qualified coach or anything. Look, if it's okay, may I just turn your shoulders for you?" James then put Laura in the correct position. "Yes, perfect, there you go. Okay, give that a try."

Laura served and, to her delight, saw an immediate and measurable improvement. She took back everything she'd thought about not wanting a lesson!

James then went on to make the most of cutting even more coaching corners. Every 'lesson' would be prefixed by a confusing description. Laura would then fail to understand, and he'd move in with another of his short cuts. Laura loved being totally useless for his benefit. She loved his strong arms, his athletic prowess, but she especially loved having his hands go everywhere, but all very legitimately. One minute, he'd have her by the wrist, then he'd be pushing her tummy in with the palm of his hand, then his arm would be reaching across under her breasts. It was a total work of art. The fact that he was being naughty, but in such a proper way, made it even better. Laura was getting quite light-headed. Inside, she was like a chocolate fondant – all hot and gooey and ready to burst.

Being a mature woman with a degree of self-control, though, she eventually said, "Okay, let's take a break for a bit, if you don't mind." They sat down on the court chairs, and Laura took the linen cover off the water jug and the bottles of Robinson's Barley Water. "Orange or lemon?"

Later, they walked through the house to the more comfortable seats out front. The warm breeze wafted up across the lawn and this, combined with the endorphins from the earlier exercise, suffused them with a peaceful sense of well-being.

Clearly wary of outstaying his welcome, James said he ought to be leaving, as he had one or two things he still had to do before the end of the day.

Laura shook his hand at the door. "Thank you, Mr Gildagraaff, for this morning and for your expertise. If you are a true sportsman, perhaps you would allow me to challenge you to a round or two of croquet in return?"

"Ooh, ahh, you've got me there. I have to confess I've never played."

"Don't worry Mr Gildagraaff, I will allow you some free bisques to help balance your handicap and I might even help you a bit if your stance isn't quite up to it. Let's chat in the week, shall we? Cheerio, for now." Laura closed the door.

****

"Oh, my word, Monica, he's really filthy. He's like a dirty tennis coach."

"That's brilliant, Laura, but he sounds like a bit of a posh twat. I thought you'd cleansed yourself of all that pretence and fake values?"

"Well, yes, I know what you mean. I don't really notice all that when I'm with him, though. The man is very eligible, so I fully intend to let him take further advantage of me. I love how he tries to trick me. If he's like that at tennis, what's he like at everything else?"

"Why don't you turn the heat up a bit next time? Wear your riding jodhpurs, the thin white mock ones. But work on getting a bit thick first. Then what you do is stand with your feet apart and bend right over when you take a shot. Let him see the insides of your thighs, your whole thick, child-bearing zone."

"Finished? Monica, why do you have to be such a filthy whore? Have you ever seen a crinoline lady? That's how I want to be. I don't want him to even see my ankles. Just my porcelain skin protected from the sun under a wide-brimmed hat."

"It's only nature, Laura. Nothing to get all shocked about. After all, we're all just animals, anyway. Men sometimes need to be encouraged to make babies.

They are very visual creatures. It's how nature made us."

Laura slid back on the sofa, laughing to herself. Monica always brought such a refreshing slant to everything. So, status check. How was it all going with her Mr Gildagraaff? Not too bad. Forced to find a negative, she felt that there was a bit of a wall between them still; she didn't feel that they had made a deep connection yet.

****

Mr Gildagraaff was duly invited over for croquet the following week. This time, Laura wasn't interested in any kind of nonsense or game-playing. No flirting. She just wanted to see if he had the potential to become her soulmate. Laura wore an old rugby shirt and a long skirt with elasticated waist. She made a bit of an effort with her hair and put a modicum of slap on her face. Thankfully, he turned up in jeans. It turned out to be a great evening and play drew to a close framed by a beautiful sunset.

They were both hungry after the croquet, and Laura had made jambalaya, which she served with a nice bottle of Chablis. After coffee, James went in for a bit of a dirty move, but Laura needed some reassurance that he had taken the trouble to think things through, so she pushed his hand back from her thigh.

"James, I like you a lot, but do you think this is all that wise, what with all that's going on?"

James told her he had been giving the matter some thought, and he couldn't see a problem. "Things just happen naturally sometimes," he said, whilst trying to haul up her long skirt – no doubt in an attempt to gauge the thickness of her hips.

"Erm, excuse me, Mr Gildagraff, are you looking for something?"

James climbed on top of her and kissed her instead.

"Mr Gildagraff, I'm still a virgin, and it remains my avowed intent to preserve my virtue until wedlock," said Laura, tongue in cheek.

He whispered in her ear, "I want to tear your pants off with my teeth, you stupid woman."

"Do you? Do you? Well, I think you need some ice tipping down the front of your pants, Mr Gildagraaff... No, seriously, James, I'm thinking London. I fancy that... I think. I'd like things to be special."

"You'd like things to be special, would you? Well, I'd hate to disappoint, so I think you'll be needing the honeymoon suite."

"The honeymoon suite? Why, whatever goes on in there? I have no idea. I'm a virgin. Hm, oh well, sounds like honeymoon suite it is then," she said, smiling and giving his trouser budgie a quick pat.

****

James was there to meet Laura when her early train drew in at Paddington. They dropped off their bags at the hotel, but he wouldn't let her see the room, saying he wanted it to be a surprise.

"Well, mister, what's on the itinerary today for this little tourist?" asked Laura.

"First, we're going to do a bit of sight-seeing around some of the lesser-known attractions. We'll start east and move west. Late afternoon I suggest, if you would like, that I take you to be fitted for some rather nice lingerie, and after that we can go back to the hotel for a rest... maybe drift out for a spot of supper after."

"James, are you going to have me walking miles?"

"Well, you're wearing sneakers and leggings like I suggested, so you have nothing to fear if I do."

For breakfast, they went to The Prospect of Whitby, an ancient pub on the banks of the River Thames at Wapping. Laura thought it odd that they were the only people in there, then she realised James must have made some kind of private arrangement with the landlord.

As they ate hot devilled kidneys on sourdough toast, James told her a little about the place. "They used to hang pirates just outside here, right there on the foreshore at low water, and Sir Hugh Willoughby sailed from here in 1553, to try to discover the north-east passage to China."

When Laura went to the loo, she noticed some stone steps leading down to the water. After breakfast, James took her down those same steps. At the bottom, she saw an interesting-looking small motor dinghy tied up to a ring on the wall.

"Oh, look," she said, pointing to it in delight.

"Why don't we take a closer look?" suggested James.

Laura couldn't hide her surprise when James helped her into the small vessel. It was being skippered by a chap called Little-John. Apparently, he was descended from generations of lightermen and watermen. Dressed in black cotton twill and wearing a Breton cap, he looked every bit the part and spoke with an authentic South-London accent. Moments later, they were entering an inlet on the South Bank and travelling away from the Thames.

"Where on earth are we?" Laura had never seen this part of London before.

"It's Surrey Quays. Beautiful in the morning sun, wouldn't you say?"

The neighbourhood was resplendent with repurposed buildings surrounded by all manner of leisure craft and sailboats. Returning to the Thames, they continued a very short distance upstream. On the left, the Mayflower Pub.

"People think the Mayflower set sail from Plymouth. It did eventually, but it started its voyage here before calling at Southampton and then Plymouth."

Next on the left, an inlet with a low bridge. "This is the river Neckinger. Hardly anybody knows about this place. Dickens based his book Oliver Twist around it. In fact, they filmed the 1968 film right here. Isn't that right, Little-John?"

Little-John turned to them and then, all too suspiciously, broke into a smile and a song. Singing 'I'd Do Anything' from the film.

After the first verse, a man standing on a balcony above, wearing a silk dressing gown responded in song with the chorus.

This time, Laura was pleased to see James was just as astonished as she was – he hadn't been in on the plan for this part, then. It was a lovely moment, though, and Little-John and the man above continued to the end of the duet. Dropping the South-London accent 'Little-John' called out, "Lovely working with you, dahling, yes, marvellous. Lionel Bart would be proud of us. Worked with him once, you know. Lovely, lovely man."

'Little-John' took James and Laura back out onto the Thames. They waited a moment for a Thames river-cruise boat to pass and then headed back across to the North Bank, this time sailing into St. Katherine Docks. Dicken's Inn was there on the right, looking all very smart with its flower baskets filled with geraniums.

They drew alongside the Mary Christine, a beautiful, old, converted Cornish trawler with a superstructure made of polished wood. Stuart, the owner, welcomed them aboard. "Hello, me hearties," he boomed.

"Is he from Disney as well?" enquired Laura.

"No, I think he's an engineering director for Network Rail or something."

Little-John was just untying, ready to leave, when Laura leant over the side of the boat. "So, what's your real name, then?"

"St. John Huxley-Jeavons at your service, ma'am," he said, cap in hand and bowing with a flourish, one foot out at an angle. His face now full of expression, replacing the earlier cameo of Little-John, seadog extraordinaire. "Toodle-pip, must go now – things to spy, fish to fry," he said, as he drifted off around the corner.

Stuart came back out on deck, with a tray full of scallops served on their shells. Freshly caught by him and cooked in butter, with some balsamic vinegar on hand to finish. Stuart poured out schooners of sherry all round to go with it. Laura couldn't remember when she'd last enjoyed herself so much.

The morning's tour of just half a mile of the River Thames was now at a close. Stepping ashore, Laura stood in front of James. She looked into his eyes, put her arms around his neck and gave him a hug. It was part 'well done that was amazing' and part 'I'm really getting to like you'. She could tell James sensed her meaning and saw the look in his eyes. "Erm, look, do you want to do the shopping thing? Maybe see what's a-cookin' in the land of... er... underwear," he said, clearly trying not to appear too direct.

Laura thought he did a good job of covering his eagerness by not making the journey to Soho too inappropriately swift. Instead, he took Laura via Grays Antique Centre in Mayfair. She was a bit non-plussed. What was he bringing her to an antiques shop for?

"I've always wanted to see this," he said. "It follows today's theme of rivers." They went down into the basement where there was a long stone water trough carrying water "It's part of the lost river Tyburn," he said. There was a little bridge going over the hidden river, and Laura took a selfie of her and James on it.

All well and good, they made their way to Soho and to Agent Provocateur, a shop renowned for its high-quality, retro-styled lingerie. "Good afternoon, Mr Gildagraaff, we've been expecting you." They were welcomed in by two uniformed retail assistants, synonymous in style with the ubiquitous fashion icon, Dita Von Teese. The shop had subdued lighting and dark surfaces. It felt very private and carried the scent of new clothes and gentle perfume.

Laura and James browsed the range of items, many of which they were allowed to handle. She could really feel the quality. They spoke to each other in hushed tones, and James confessed he wanted to see her in a basque, seamed stockings with Cuban heels and a pair of stilettos... and he wanted it all to be sheer. Laura was equally enthusiastic about his choice. Although for her, it was heightened by being her moment of total glorification. She had spent months killing herself doing Couch to 5K, Park Run and Fat Fighters, and now, finally, this was her moment: the Laura show.

There was nothing in this damn shop-for-kids that wasn't going to fit on this occasion. Of that, she was very sure. In fact, she had secretly put in one or two sessions to make herself look 'thick', as Monica would put it.

Looking at some matching sets of waspie corsets, bra and knickers, they found a set they both liked in blush red, together with some matching stockings. The assistant confirmed they had all the colours in all the sizes, and she took Laura through to a private fitting room to get undressed and hang up her sneakers in favour of something radically different.

Meanwhile, they showed James to the Gentlemen's seating area. Here, they gave him a coffee and a copy of the catalogue, which contained sumptuous photos of barely clothed models. He had a quick flick through, but the models were all what he would call, 'kids' – in their early twenties – and they didn't look at all 'thick'. Laura was the one he wanted to see, but she seemed to be taking quite a while.

Suddenly, one of the assistants arrived. "She's ready now, if you would like to come through and have a look."

He stood in front of the black velvet curtains and the assistant pulled them back... and it wasn't just his eyes bulging at what he saw.

Laura was giggling, but only because she was so elated by what she was seeing in the mirror.

"Ta-dah!" She looked him in the eye and then did a few dirty poses that Monica had taught her. James immediately went into uncomfortable overload, so much so, he had to shuffle out backwards.

The assistants barely blinked, walking back into the shop like it was all just routine. Which it was, for them, Laura realised. It was nothing new, something they saw day in, day out.

Laura removed all the items, and the assistant returned to the counter where she wrapped them in pink tissue paper. The second assistant put a box of Kleenex tissues back on the stool in the cubicle and closed the curtains. James asked Laura what the tissues were for. "To protect the knickers," she replied. James had to think that one through.

The shoes she had tried on were a bit ordinary, so they decided to go elsewhere for them, but before leaving, James asked them to throw in a nice whip with a diamante-studded handle plus, of course, the obligatory set of handcuffs. The staff wished the happy shoppers a pleasant afternoon and opened the door for them.

Next, it was back over to Mayfair, to Christian Louboutin, where Laura chose some nice four-inch heels, in dusky pink with red soles. It nudged the day's shopping bill just over the four-figure mark.

By the time they came out of Laboutin's, they were hand in hand. "Phew, I'm tired. It's been such fun, James. A top bit of teamwork."

As they walked through the arch into Shepherd Market, they were pleased to see a few empty tables outside the Italian cafes. It was time for another snackette. They wanted to eat lightly, as in all likeliness they might be 'exercising' back at the hotel.

The drinks arrived, and James received a text message. "Seems like they've got into a bit of a pickle at work, but all's good."

They both had the chicken and avocado salad and chatted about the morning's fun. Laura was sure that the man on the balcony had been hired in, and that Stuart on the Marie Christine was really a chef.

James received another message. "Sorry, Laura, I just need to call them." He took a stroll across the street and had a brief conversation before coming back to their table. Laura wasn't sure if she really wanted another drink, so she stuck with the water, sipping it down to the lemon slice.

James's phone was busy again. "Laura, this really has turned into a crisis, and they're going round in circles. I wonder... and I know this is really rude, but if I were to just pop in to the office for an hour, I could give them a steer, and we wouldn't be disturbed again after that."

Laura was delighted. Best of all worlds: she had been up since 5 a.m. and was so desperate for sleep the evening could be seriously compromised if she didn't get some and soon. She gave him a hug and kiss and sent him on his way.

****

Wowser!

The hotel room was a-ma-zing. What a wonderful backdrop it was going to be for the fashion show she was planning on giving him later, but right now, all she wanted to do was sleep. First, though, she booked a nail technician. She didn't fancy all the work of putting on those long red nails that would top off her outfit. Someone else could do that.

Drifting off into a wonderful deep sleep, Laura dreamt she was back at the restaurant. She dreamt she couldn't find her knife and fork. Later, she dreamt James had got another message, and then she dreamt it was her phone ringing this time, but she couldn't switch it off. She woke up feeling confused. Her phone really was ringing, though. It was James.

"Look, I am so truly sorry. Nobody was looking forward to tonight more than I, but things have turned nasty, and someone is trying to implicate me in something. It's totally insane. I'm going to have to fly to Brussels right now. Could you possibly put my travel bag down at reception, and I'll have a bike collect it and bring it to Heathrow?"

Disappointed by this development, Laura called reception and had them take the bag down for her. She drifted back to sleep.

Waking shortly after, with a jolt, it took her a moment to reconnect with reality. Then it all fell into place. Wow, what a shame, but nothing could ever take away from such an amazing morning. Probably the best thing for her to do now would be to visit the spa and then have room service bring up a meal and a drink whilst she watched something on Netflix.

Light bulb moment! She decided she would phone Monica and ask her to come and stay with her instead, but Monica's phone just went to voicemail when she called it. Then Monica called back, but only to say she wouldn't be able to come.

Laura was just browsing through the menu when the phone went again. Monica had now rearranged a few things and would be on the next train to London.

****

The bedside phone rang. "Hello, reception here. I have a Monica McStrachan here for you."

Monica walked in and looked round the room. "Woah, this is some kind of place. So, this is the honeymoon suite, is it?" Monica suddenly went into predatory mode. Laura shrieked and ran whilst Monica chased her, shouting, "You're my wife now."

She chased Laura into the adjoining room and back again. Now, they were on either side of a sofa, each anticipating the other's move. Monica leapt onto the sofa and jumped over the back. Grabbing Laura's hair, she pinned her down on the bed. Laura was giggling but crying at the same time, trying to wipe her eyes in amongst the chaos.

Monica put her arm round her. "Bubsie, bubsie, bubsie, let's not have any of that. Bastards, men, aren't they? Well, never you mind, because we're going to have a great time and get wankered on champagne."

"No, Monica, I'd rather take it easy. I can't compromise the new me. You won't believe what I just managed to fit into." Laura tipped the afternoon's purchases on the bed for Monica to peruse.

"No way! Well, you sure are looking trim. It works, doesn't it? You believe me now, don't you!" Monica found the till receipts and stood there wide-eyed and open-mouthed. "No... way..." She laughed. Next, she threw off all her clothes and started rummaging in her case, whilst muttering, "Now, where's my swimsuit?"

Laura couldn't resist taking another look at Monica's bottom. Thank heavens it hadn't grown any 'thicker'.

Monica had the party started in no time. They were in their spa robes and headed down to the hot tub with a bottle of Baileys and two glasses in no time. Sweet sticky alcohol, just what the doctor ordered. The tub was super-hot, and Laura groaned with relief as her limbs sunk beneath the surface. She hadn't realised until she checked that she had done something like nineteen thousand steps that day. Every time James had tried to call a taxi, she had refused as she relished the exercise.

The tub bubbled away until their hands were going wrinkly. "Laura, you know I have this woman's intuition thing."

"No, Monica, you don't. Call it intuition if you like, but I know what you are going to say next, and if you say it, I'm going to pull your hair, hard. Got it?"

"Sure, shut me down then. The guy's a fekin arse," Monica whispered in a broad Irish accent.

"I beg your pardon? I beg your pardon?" shouted Laura, keen to shut down any discussion on that particular subject.

Monica held her hand. "Don't do that. I only want the best for you. Ooh, no, wait. I forgot something." Monica reached over and took an aerosol of Chantilly cream out of her spa bag. "We forgot this, so we did." She put a squirt in each of the drinks then filled her hand with it. "Well, this is another fine mess youse gotten yerself into," she said, slapping it right in Laura's face before laughing. All hell then broke loose, cream everywhere, fighting and splashing until...

"You stupid tit! Look what you've done." Laura stared in dismay at the yellow buttery film that now floated on the surface of the spa water. "You idiot."

"No, you're the idiot." It ended with them making a quick exit and rushing back to the room to shower and get all the thick grease off their skin.

****

"What a weird day it's been. Right now, I should be face-down in the pillows getting it from James, but instead I'm stuck with you, you great soppy circus piece."

Monica was wearing a pair of round gold-rimmed reading glasses which Laura hadn't seen before. She thought they made her look very erudite. Laura read the menu again whilst Monica was sat up in bed, her face illuminated by her laptop. "Let's have a look at who this Gildagraaff is then..."

"He's my boyfriend, that's who he is, so butt out and mind your own spooky business, please—"

"You unimaginable bastard. You utter maggot. I'll gouge your eyes out, one by one, then piss on them."

"Whaaat?"

"No, hunsie, don't look."

Monica tried to fold Laura up in a big hug, but Laura wriggled free and picked up the laptop. There was a picture of James on an African safari, standing over a giraffe that he had just shot, grinning. "Yeah, not him. Photoshopped anyway. The Net is full of stuff like this. Look, this was 2002. He was two decades younger, then."

"Stop it right there, Laura. You're scaring me now."

It was an uncomfortable night. Laura didn't enjoy the incongruity of being in utter luxury whilst James had such a damning indictment hanging over his head. Monica couldn't leave it alone, and in the small hours, she found more.

"This Monrenti company he's a director of. Have you seen what they're up to? They're a global menace, hated the world over."

Laura was too tired and heartsore to engage, so she sobbed herself to sleep.

****

When Laura awoke at 7 a.m., Monica told her she'd been talking in her sleep, whilst she hugged Laura and stroked her hair.

Laura suddenly leapt up. "Right, ding-dong. I'm taking charge of this situation now. I'm gonna deal with this. I wasn't put on this planet to be made a mug of. First, he's innocent until proven guilty, so let's find the evidence, if there is any. Second, I want out of here. Now. We'll have breakfast on the train. Third, I want you at my house tonight."

Monica peered over her glasses and gave a positive thumbs up. "Sounds like a plan, boss."

Laura took out her phone and called one of the researchers at HV. "Emma, I need a really big favour. Can you check out a contact for me? Strictly between you and me – it's the person who's making an offer on our estate. A Mr James Sebastian Beeching Gildagraaff, 24/11/77. Town of birth, Antwerp."

****

You can't quite beat having breakfast on a train. Laura had always found rail travel very evocative, even since childhood, reminding her of the lines from the Robert Louis Stevenson poem 'From a Railway Carriage'.

Faster than fairies, faster than witches,
Bridges and houses, hedges and ditches;
And charging along like troops in a battle,
All through the meadows the horses and cattle...

The train thundered along on the Down Fast line, over Brunel's magnificent brick-built Gatehampton Railway Bridge. Through Goring & Streatley, then out along the banks of the River Thames, now in its rural upstream setting. She watched the verdant landscape slide by on this grey, rainy morning, the raindrops tracking sideways across the window of the fast-moving train. Like tears being wiped away.

"Top grub." Monica gave her seal of approval. A full English breakfast and an endless supply of supplementary toast and coffee. All delivered to their linen-covered table by a liveried steward.

The carriage wasn't full. They were homeward bound, and many a crowded commuter train passed them going in the opposite direction.

Finally, the train drew slowly into Hampden under Chalkewood station, and they alighted and made their way to the taxi rank.

****

Back at the estate, they went over their discoveries, again and again, trying to make sense of it all. Then Laura took a call from Emma at HV. She mainly listened, interjecting occasionally with words like, Yep, Okay and Really? When the call ended, she sat there fiddling with her phone, barely able to meet Monica's eye.

"Well, that adds a new dimension. Remember me telling you that there was a company out there who were looking to buy Chalkewood to asset strip it, sack all the staff, turn the farm into a life-science research unit, and develop and build on large parts of the land? Well, seems that company is called Dorling B.V. and it's owned by my Mr Gildagraaff." Laura suddenly couldn't breathe properly, her respiration laboured, her throat tear-choked. Monica stood behind her and massaged her shoulders.

"I want to get that Mr Killed-A-Giraffe and take him for a long, not-for-pleasure trip to the dungeon. I want to make that dull, corporate libertine scream for mercy so loud that I have to wear ear defenders. I want to punch him in the guts so hard that Chuck Norris would be impressed."

Laura laughed, wiping away her tears. She could just imagine her naughty friend actually doing that whilst dressed as a scorpion or something equally as crazy.

They just sat there for a while, regaining their composure. Laura's phone buzzed yet again. Emma had previously been sending all the evidence over in a series of PDFs, so Laura just glanced at the screen, but this next message was from someone else. She let out a scream. "It's Killed-A-Giraffe!" She was hyperventilating too much to read the text, so she handed the phone to Monica.

Good morning, Laura, hope you're not too cross with me and again my deepest apologies. Just to say everything went well in Brussels and the storm has now passed. Are you free for a chat?

"I can't, I can't! What do I do, what do I do?" Laura was not normally given to panic, but this whole thing had really cut her to the marrow. It didn't take her long to regain her confidence, though, and compose a reply. Good morning, Mr Gildagraaff, I am just a little busy at the moment. Going through some reports and noting that you are the owner of Dorling B. V.

He replied, It's a complicated business. I wanted to speak to you about that. I wanted to suggest that if the sale went ahead that we might perhaps divide the profits of Dorling B.V? Does that appeal?

No, Mr Killed-A-Giraffe, it does not, especially as you were planning to tell me all this only after you had carnal knowledge of me.

Ahh, yes. Guilty on all charges, but please believe me when I say that I am not guilty re the giraffe. That was a Photoshop job done by someone who had a vendetta against me.

A vendetta against you, James? Surely not! And that dash to Brussels? Busy boy, aren't you?

There was no reply.

Well Mr Gildagraaff, just to confirm: We are now concluded on all matters, but I should like to thank you for a nice morning on the Thames and also for the lovely lingerie which I enjoyed wearing, and I should also like to thank you for your interest in Chalkewood.

****

Miranda Chilvers from the selling agents texted.

Laura, I'm in the area today. May I drop by for an urgent chat?

Laura doubted very much if she actually was 'in the area'. With a sale commission of half a million pounds due to Slater Scotton & Emery on completion of Chalkewood's sale, the stakes had probably never been higher for the agents, and Laura had just lost them that fee for which they had worked very hard. Thankfully, Teddy had built some caveats in about 'buyer eligibility', but it still wasn't going to be an easy conversation.

Miranda arrived, very poker-faced. She declined the offer of a coffee and went straight to the detail. Although Laura was the customer and the agent had to show due deference at all times, Miranda was spitting blood, implying that Laura had sabotaged a viable sale. But worse was to come.

"Furthermore, am I to understand it that your relationship with the potential purchaser had taken on a personal aspect?"

Laura gave no response.

"I don't wish to be impertinent in any way, and I am only passing on what I have been told, but there has been some talk that you two were even on the verge of marriage. You were testing honeymoon suites or something. Even to the point of trying out bridal lingerie. All see-through and high heels with whips and handcuffs thrown in for good measure, so I am told. Until that is, Mr Gildagraaff became distressed by an allegation you made regarding fake photos of him on a routine hunting trip in Africa."

Laura knew that Miranda's personal share of any sale commission was probably in the region of fifty grand. In fact, she had probably been lying in bed at night, already planning on how to spend it all on new kitchens or luxury holidays, so Laura was quite sympathetic, but she was the customer, and the customer was always right.

"Our family lawyers will be sending you some PDFs this week detailing our reasons for not wishing to proceed with Mr Gildagraaff. Thereafter, may I suggest you speak to my father to ensure that he still has faith in your ability to find properly screened and filtered prospective purchasers?" Laura then showed Mrs Chilvers the door, but not before they both indulged themselves in one last moment of staring each other in the eye and glaring, sharp nails twitching.

Laura sat back with a lemon tea and momentarily fantasised about having a glorious catfight with Miranda. She really wanted to pull that woman's hair so hard for all that nonsense about the 'bridal lingerie', but then she wondered if perhaps she had been spending too much time in the company of Monica McStrachan.

****

The words Daddy calling ominously appeared on Laura's phone display, as it began vibrating its way across the table.

"Darling, both your mother and I were so, so terribly saddened to hear the news of how your hopes for Mr Gildagraaff had been so cruelly dashed. It all sounded too good to be true, and so it was, unfortunately. We just want you to know how much we love you, and we want to reassure you that everything will be just fine. Thank you so much for being so professional and diligent in your preparation of all those evidential PDFs. They tell us all we needed to know."

Isn't that just what dads are for? thought Laura, as she felt her stress level drop to zero.

There was a scrabbling sound as Tice snatched the phone away. "Piggy! Poor, poor Piggy got roasted by some damn bore."

"Yes Mummy, Piggy got her trotters burnt, I'm afraid," said Laura, playing along with their piggy routine.

"Ooowh, poor old Pigster. Mummy make it all better and cook you some lovely apple sauce to fatten you up, yum, yum, yum." More glurgerific pork talk ensued. Tice would always aim to out pork Laura, until she accepted defeat and ended the call. Laura felt comforted by her mother's baby talk. Who else in the world would give you that kind of service! It reminded her of the comfort she used to get as a child.

CHAPTER TEN

—·—

SECRET GARDEN

After a restless night's sleep, Laura woke feeling uneasy about her life. Worst of all, she still had feelings for James. Over and over in her head, she kept asking herself if there had perhaps been a way it could have all worked out, but there most definitely wasn't.

What was making it all so difficult was that he was never anything other than totally wonderful when they had been together. He had always been lovely and sexy, right to the end. All the problems with him were abstract which did nothing to diminish her strong feelings for him. She felt she needed to see him again so she could challenge everything properly, have a blazing row, and end it properly. But that wouldn't be possible now, and it had robbed her of closure.

The evidence was unequivocal, though. The giraffe thing might be fake, but the deceitful property company wasn't, and what kind of a person has people out there who hate him so much to do a thing like that, anyway? She remembered how her intuition had always made her feel that there had been a wall between them.

Laura just couldn't pinpoint what had attracted her to his slick, metrosexual style in the first place. Amongst other things, he was a member of The Tarot Club in Pall Mall, a gentlemen's club which didn't allow women members or visitors. It was hardly the world Laura aspired to, especially considering her recent experiences at HV.

James Gildagraaff typified everything that Laura despised in the corporate world: lack of accountability, lack of social justice, obsession with greed and excessive materialism, lack of vision for human harmony, that baffling toxic treatment of women so at odds with what they would want for their own sisters, daughters or indeed their very own mothers to experience.

****

It was a beautiful July day, warm and dry. There were little puffy white clouds tugging one another across the blue sky, and nature was bursting forth in all its abundance. Outside, the world was getting on with its business. People out enjoying themselves and making the most of the holidays, a day for couples and families to make the most of their free time together. Laura felt forgotten. She felt trapped

on the outside, trying to get in. Today was a day for
a self-indulgent cry; it was a secret garden day.

Chalkewood had some stunning features. One
was its secret garden; a garden surrounded by
a high stone-and-flint wall. Within the walls was
a lawn with borders laid to flowers, shrubs
and an alpine rockery. At the far end was a
small single-room medieval chapel that all the
Chalkewood generations had played in as children.
The wooden entrance door to the garden had a
horseshoe loosely fixed to it, and family members
would turn the shoe sideways as a sign that the
garden was occupied, and nobody was to enter. It
was where Laura had brought her boyfriends as a
teenager.

Draining her cup of the last of its black coffee and
taking her faithful ally, Roary the teddy bear, by the
paw, she headed to the garden.

Turning the horseshoe sideways, she pressed the
latch and entered the garden, closing the door
behind her. The place was immaculate. She hadn't
quite expected that, but of course Teddy would
have laid down instructions to keep it that way to
entice potential buyers.

The light in the garden was beautiful as always.
Tice mainly used the place to paint watercolours.
There was an officious-looking, green, cast-iron sign
with white lettering wedged into the turf. Keep
of the Grass, it read. Teddy had put it there. He

thought it was hilarious, as except for the borders, it was all grass in there and you had to walk on it.

Laura crawled onto the grass with Roary and tried to cry, but it felt so self-indulgent that she couldn't quite muster the tears, so even this simple-seeming catharsis was something she was going to have to fight to get... like everything else recently. Pulling herself together, she lay on the grass, looking up at the sky, sniffing back the imaginary tears. Chalkewood was like a luxury prison; how could she be so unhappy in such a beautiful place? Maybe she ought to just grow up and pull herself together?

She placed Roary on a wrought-iron bench and they sat together. The words from the song, 'We're All Runners', came into her head.

Its whole theme of being runners in the 'game of life' and losing and getting stung, yet still running on. It always reminded her of Park Run, and so it reminded her now of Patz. At least Laura still had a life to be miserable about. And that's the way it is, isn't it? You can never complain because there is always someone else worse off and more deserving of sympathy and favour than you.

Laura sat on the grass beside some marguerites. A hover fly moved from flower to flower. A lavender bush to the other side of her had several bees on it collecting pollen. They were working away industriously, apparently without a care in the world. Happily getting on with things and reproducing with no need for Tinder. Rather like Monica. If she wanted to mate with some man, she'd just do some brief courtship routine around him, probably involving waggling her new thick bottom and then just get on with it.

Laura got up and went into the chapel. Its origins were somewhat unclear. The Stanhopes had always used it to practice their own version of the Christian faith. There were no religious icons, except for a small wooden cross on the altar. There was a picture of St. Anthony on the wall, sitting in his cave weaving mats. When Laura was young, the family had used the place for nativity plays. Family members would go there to contemplate and think about... well, anything really.

There were some books, an eclectic mix of wisdom. Nothing denominational, no books or pamphlets of turgid liturgy. There was a book about the Iona community. A copy of 'Dark Night of the Soul', a poem by St. John of the Cross. Laura picked up another, a dark red, dust-covered book: The Sayings of Sister Syncletika. Laura thought she would just open the book and see what page she landed on to see if it could possibly have any wisdom for her.

In the beginning, there is struggle and a lot of work for those who come near to God. But after that, there is indescribable joy.

In its own way, this seemed to fit. Pushing her chances, Laura read on.

It is like those who wish to light a fire; at first they are choked by the smoke and cry... we also must kindle the divine fire in ourselves through tears and hard work.

Maybe this meant all her tears and hard work were just about to pay off. What if that were true?

Laura left the garden, turned the horseshoe and went indoors. She wondered how Monica was getting on in her quest to find harmony with the male race. Maybe they could meet up and have a nice girly chat and talk about boys. Sending a text, she received a reply saying, Yeah, you might just as well come down now. Let yourself in. I'm warning you the place is in a bit of a mess, though. But the warning about the place being 'in a bit of a mess' did not prepare Laura for what she was about to see at Monica's.

****

She pulled onto the drive and made her way past all the building materials to reach the side door. Much to her surprise, it all seemed really nice and tidy inside. "Yoo-hoo," she called as she walked in through the door that had been left ajar. Laura called again, "Yoo-hoo, anybody home?"

Just then Monica walked into the hall. She was wearing black thigh-high PVC boots with four-inch heels, a leather basque and seamed stockings, but at least she was wearing knickers. Laura put her hands to her face. "Oh my word, Monica, what's going on?"

"Oh yeah, sorry, I forgot I was wearing this."

Monica's response numbed Laura. It was what you might expect from someone suffering from the onset of a progressive mental illness, something the Mad Hatter would say in Alice's Adventures in Wonderland.

"Have you got a man in here or something?"

"Two. The lodgers. They're a bit wrapped up at the moment."

Laura's head was now pulsating with anxiety.

Monica took Laura through to what was presumably a reception room. Its walls were painted red and the ceiling black... This was Monica's secret garden. Laura looked down and recoiled in shock and horror. There, lying on the floor, were two naked men, gagged and wrapped in cling film.

"I thought it would be rude not to introduce you." Monica had now lapsed into an Irish accent, which was a sign that she knew she was misbehaving.

Both men had something attached to their willies by wires. It looked like a small black box. A red LED on each indicated that whatever they were, they were switched on. "Here, grab a handset. It's a bit like Scalextric. You drive them round the bend, but in a different kind of way. When you press a button, it will shock them, right in their difference. Level one will just get their attention. Level two hurts. It's a punishment. Level three is excruciating. The guy on the right squeals like a pig," she said. "Watch this. Level three." The man on the right suddenly started squealing, just like a pig. "The one on the left is ex-marines. Al Qaeda nearly killed him once. He loves this sort of stuff, as he knows that at least I'll never kill him. Well, at least not on purpose. These guys are real players, you know? Not just some drips off the street.

"Go on, Laura, press a damn button. Pick a number."

Laura tentatively pressed button two on her handset. Her pig convulsed a little and gave a stifled moan. Laura, now had a naughty schoolgirl look on her face, but put the remote to one side. "I'll just watch if that's okay."

Standing back, she couldn't help but reflect on what she was seeing. When men do bondage, they use ropes and chains and stuff. Maybe it's more intuitive for a woman to use something perhaps more familiar to her, like cling film?

Behind the men was a large, black gothic throne, and Monica was now sitting on it using the handsets with increasing frequency and severity. "Okay guys, that's a wrap for now. My friend Laura and I are going to take a tea break," announced Monica, leaving them wrapped and gagged, and nice and fresh.

Through in the kitchen, Laura asked, "Who even are those guys?"

"They live here. They're my Pain Pigs."

"Why have you wrapped them in cling film?"

"It's what you do to keep meat fresh, isn't it? I don't know what makes me do it. I just know that I want to."

"So, you're a sadist?"

"Well, that would make me a follower of the Marquis de Sade, and he was a man. So no, I'd be more like the Countess Elizabeth Báthory from the fifteen hundreds."

"Oh, what's she famous for?"

"Killing 650 virgins and drinking their blood. I bet she never had an iron deficiency like I do."

"Why do they let you do it to them?"

"Well, they know that I'm a black belt for starters, but really, they are here under contract. They get free accommodation in exchange for working on the house extension. Bob is a chippy, and Squealer's a brickie. I'm just a kind of strict landlady, really, and that appears to suit them."

This all caused Laura's state of disquiet to deepen even further.

Monica didn't indulge in this kind of activity through any sense of revenge or misandry. She just used atonement to justify her preference. Maybe its roots lay in her past? As a middle child with four brothers, she had always been excluded and had always had to prove herself to get any kind of access to their world.

Her parents once bought her a Wendy House to try to give her a world of her own, but she had converted it into a jail for her younger brothers. For a laugh, she would lock them in there for hours on end and feed them through the windows. Her favourite game had been to place the food or drink bowls just slightly out of reach, and when they strained to get at them, she would sting their hands with nettles. Monica had simply extended these harmless games into adult life, using them as the inspirational source for much of her colourful sex life.

Monica's father was in construction and so were her brothers, and they had kept Monica at arm's length most of the time. Having her own building site now and staffing it with male slaves was an absolute delight for her – a really powerful catharsis.

Suddenly Monica's mood changed. "Laura, it's time for you to get going. I'm not sure you'll have a strong enough stomach for what comes next. I'm going to really hurt the guys now," she said, with an expressionless face, dark sunken eyes and all the conviviality of a Great White Shark.

"Is all this legal?" Laura asked.

"Sure, it's all safe, sane, and consensual. We'll probably do a bit of vanilla stuff, like making them clean the house, afterwards," said Monica, picking up a box of surgical needles.

"Are you having sex with these guys?" Laura felt it necessary to ask.

"Good grief, no. That would spoil it. Can you imagine if I did? Afterwards, they would simply start going What's for dinner? or Let's watch the football."

"Do you cook for them?"

Monica looked like she might fall over laughing. She opened a cupboard. "No, they get this. I take a couple of dog bowls, fill them up and put them on the floor." The cupboard was filled with dozens of red and blue cans of Chappie.

"Why Chappie?"

"It's the only brand of dog food that's reckoned to be safe for human consumption."

"And they eat it every day?"

"Yep, they agree to let me watch them eat like dogs once a day. It comes in different flavours, you know. Tonight, they've got chicken and rice."

Laura was numb with shock by now. Walking to the door, she asked her final question. "Is this some kind of feminist statement or expression?"

"No, not at all. I don't really like all that stuff. This isn't a reaction. It's purer than that. It's not trying to be like men. Instead, it's a pure extension of womanhood – we own it. I wrote about all this in Cosmo. Did you not know that?"

Laura didn't know anything about her article in Cosmo.

****

After Laura had left, Monica flicked the kettle on. Her Pain Pets could wait a bit longer – they'd probably like that anyway.

She didn't know why Laura thought she was so weird. Making a coffee, she pondered the subject whilst opening the mail. It included a parcel containing an Uzi air pistol. Picking it up, she went outside and sat on the patio with her coffee, some biscuits and the Uzi.

Am I really that weird? she thought, as she used the weapon to destroy some empty damp-proofing cans lying on the rubble.

****

Laura's journey home was nowhere near long enough to even begin to get her head round what she had just seen. Monica made it all look so... normal.

As Laura pulled up outside the house, she saw Guy, usual coil of steel wire over his shoulder. What the heck does he do with that stuff? She decided she go and ask him, hoping a chat with Guy would help clear her mind a bit. When she asked about the coils of wire, Guy took her through to a corner of the garden at August. She was amazed. He had created a breathtakingly beautiful steel-wire sculpture of two roe deer. "A friend of mine at horticultural college married a man who makes this stuff for a living, so I thought that I would have a go."

Is there no limit to human creativity? Laura wondered if she was becoming boring, though perhaps it was unfair to self-flagellate like that. She did, after all, have Park Run, and her health and fitness had been a total triumph recently. Maybe she needed to go clothes shopping, or something.

There was no denying it, though – she wasn't going to be able to let the subject of Monica's activities drop, so she invited Monica for a girls' sleepover.

****

Monica turned up with some goodies, and the girls changed into their jammies and got straight into Laura's sumptuous bed. "I just need to check on the Pigs," said Monica, taking out her tablet. "I sentenced Squealer to a day's solitary for stealing my chocolate. It's not like they don't get a sweetie allowance." Logging in to the app, Laura saw the tablet screen was divided into eight grainy zones. Squealer was languishing in what could only be described as a prison cell, and Bob was cleaning the kitchen. "Looks like they're all settled. That's good."

"Look, Laura, I've known you long enough to know how you work. Me being here after introducing you to the Pain Pigs is no coincidence, right? I know you want to interrogate me, and yeah, really, that's fine. Any questions – I'll be happy to answer."

"Okay, well, you're right and thank you for being open. So, the Pigs. They work for free, and you give them free accommodation and food. Is that right?"

"Correct. Chappie is always on discount down at the cash and carry."

"So, if you didn't offer all the kinky extras, would they still be up for that arrangement?"

"Probably not, but loads of people take jobs just because they like the ambience of the place."

"Ambience, indeed. Well, I calculate that, given the going rate for their skills versus the local property rental costs, you are charging them at least double the value of what they're getting in return. So, not to put too fine a point on it, does that amount to prostitution?"

"A dominatrix isn't a prostitute, not if there's no sex act. Just like strippers and lap dancers aren't. What exactly is prostitution, anyway? If you were to live with some rich guy and do nothing all day, wouldn't that constitute prostitution, by your reckoning?"

"Well, quite apart from that, you're receiving a benefit in kind, so are you paying tax on that?"

"Am I, bollocks," muttered Monica in her faint Irish accent. "Anyways, I've got bigger things to worry about. The roof is going to need to go on soon. The Pigs will do the roof trusses, but they won't tile the damn thing. Between you and me, I've got my eye on Micky the roofer down at the pub. He's a right lippy git, just the sort I'd love to beat, jail and put him to work on the roof. He's such a gobby little bastard, and I'd love to reform him."

"Exactly how long have you 'jailed' Bob and Squealer for?"

"Well, Squealer's in for a twelve stretch, months, that is. I jailed him last September, and he had to give me a ten grand bail-bond to stop him from absconding. Bob got two years, but I'll give him time off if the works are finished ahead of schedule."

Laura just sat there, incredulous, completely bewildered – yet she had to admit that it was a stroke of genius. She didn't approve of the arrangement from an ethical standpoint, but who was she to judge?

"Don't look at me like that, Laura. You know me well enough to know I'd do right by them boys. I found Bob on the streets, literally. He's an ex-serviceman – they just let him go. His wife left him because he gets disturbed and screams in his sleep, but I just gag him if he won't shut up. He ended up on the street after she turfed him out, and one day I put some money in his tin and started chatting. I found out he was a chippy, and then he made a few dirty comments about how I looked, so I took him for a coffee and suggested that jail would be the best place for him. He thought I was joking, so I took him home, so he could have a chat with Squealer, and they both got on really well, so I served him with his papers and then led him off for a beating and an introductory bowl of Chappie."

The conversation moved on to love and marriage. It turned out it wasn't just Laura who wanted a husband and a family.

"Do you really think you're increasing your chances or eligibility, what with all your dungeon shenanigans?"

"Well, I do date men. I just can't take them home at the moment."

They chatted for a while with the lights off and then started to drift off.

Then. "Did you just drop something on the floor, hunzie?"

"No."

"I think I can hear voices – listen."

"Shit! Intruders."

They both got out of bed and put dressing gowns on. Laura grabbed her mother's shotgun and filled both her dressing gown pockets with shotgun cartridges. "Just to warn you, Monica, if they try to take us on, I will kill them."

"Let's go."

Both women crept towards the interconnecting double doors.

"We'll go on the count of three," said Laura. They flicked the lights on and, bursting in like Butch

Cassidy and the Sundance Kid, took up advance positions behind the chaise-longue. Two men were huddled in the opposite corner. "Hands up. Get against the wall." The men complied, and it was all under control. But Monica waded in, turned the younger one around and punched him in the stomach for good measure.

The older guy spoke up. "Look, we're real sorry, right, we thought the place was abandoned." Those words had a familiar ring to them. By now, the young guy was sobbing quietly.

"Okay, turn round and face me. Why are you here?" said Laura.

"We're YouTubers; we film abandoned places."

"How do you know about this place?"

"We saw it on YouTube, the place with the ghost."

"Yes, but on that they keep the location a secret."

"Go on, Haz, tell 'em how you did it."

In between sobs, Haz explained he had spent two months on the net comparing the Ninjas' images of Chalkewood to pictures of the castles and stately homes of England, until he found a picture where the eves of the roof and the windows matched the Ninja footage.

"Wow, that's impressive." Laura was amazed. She broke her gun open and rested it over her forearm.

"Aye, well, that's what Haz is like. You see, he's on the autistic spectrum."

Laura glared at Monica. "You'd better make yourself scarce. We'll talk later," she whispered. Once Monica had slipped sheepishly out the door, Laura turned her attention back to the two men. "How did you get in? There had better not be any damage."

"Oh no, we lifted the coal chute grate and got in through there."

"But that's tiny!" Then Laura looked at them more closely and realised so were they. They were stick-thin.

"Let's go down to the kitchen."

Laura led the way, the two of them whispering to each other all along, saying how fantastic they thought the house was inside. In the kitchen, Laura gave them both a seat and handed some tissues to the lad, who was still doing stutter-breaths between his words as he wiped away the tears. "Okay, so from your accents, you're from the north-east?"

"Yes, ma'am. Sunderland."

"And are you a bona fide YouTube channel?"

"Well, we like to think so. We're called 'Father, Son and Holy Moly'."

Laura laughed. She then checked them out on her laptop. They weren't in the same league as the Ninjas, but they had started out impressively. Laura felt a bit awkward. These were decent people who had just made a mistake.

"Well, look, clearly you didn't mean to break into anyone's home, so let's get this wrapped up. May I just ask you to write your names and addresses down for me, just for my record, and do you have any form of ID so that I can verify you?" Whilst they wrote down their details, Laura asked what they planned to do next, and they said they were going back to Sunderland. "Wow, that's a long hike. Look, can I make you some sandwiches or something?"

The father was happy to have anything on his sandwiches, but the kid shook his head at everything. Laura went through all the common choices until the lad's father spoke up.

"Haz only really eats one type of sandwich. He'll eat a corn chip and mayo sandwich, if it has plenty of ketchup on it." Laura set about the task, but she also made some hot chocolate and gave it to them in a complimentary Chalkewood thermos flask. This still didn't fully ease her guilt though, so she went for a rummage through the merchandise cupboard to see what other goodies she could give them. In went a couple of Chalkewood Estate mugs bearing the old slogan 'Fun Day Out'. Some Chalkewood pens, a couple of Chalkewood fridge magnets and a couple of Chalkewood carry bags to put it all in.

Having bid the father-and-son duo farewell, Laura returned to bed to update Monica, concluding by saying, "And fancy punching that poor autistic kid. You're such a heartless witch."

"Instead of all that Chalkewood crap, why don't you just stock some handcuffs? Then we could have busted them properly and called in the fuzz. Plus, that fussy kid – you should have just put Chappie in his sandwiches."

When Laura woke, Monica was up and checking in on the Pigs. It seemed Bob was already up and working on site, his work being slightly hampered by the fact his workmate was still in jail.

Monica looked up from her screen. "I need to get back and let Squealer out."

"Yes, I should think so. Poor Pig. I bet he'll be delighted to go free range again."

"Well, yes, he will. But he'll have to go on the cross first for a thrashing. He ate an entire bag of chocolate raisins, and you know how sacred chocolate is to me. Greedy little bastard."

****

Once Monica had left and normality had resumed, Laura made some breakfast. She had wanted to have breakfast with Monica, so this played a bit on Laura's sense of loneliness. Wandering around outside, she spotted Guy. Somewhat bizarrely, he was holding what looked like an inflatable flower head with about eight petals on it, about six feet wide. A woman appeared, and they put it in the back of her truck.

When the woman had left, Laura went over to Guy, and he told her all about it. "It's an inflatable yoga docking station for paddleboards. Emma's a paddleboard yoga instructor and she's bought the docking station so that all the paddleboarders in her class can float their boards in and dock whilst she leads the session. I've just changed all the fixings so that now any brand of board can dock on it.

"Emma has a spot, down on Green Velvet Lake. You wouldn't know it was there. She paddles out with her clients to a place that's inaccessible by foot or by road. There's a short streamway, and it leads to a pool surrounded by rushes. It's like her secret garden. Have you ever paddleboarded?"

****

Meanwhile, back at Hampden Lodge, Monica's secret garden/penitentiary for wayward men, everything was going well. As scorpion-in-charge, she watched over her subjects whilst they hauled another bucket of mortar up to the first-floor scaffolding. Things were ahead of schedule. She was delighted. They might even get an Indian takeaway tonight as a reward, and as it was a Saturday, they might be allowed to finish early. On Sundays, she always let them out so they could go to church, and afterwards, they were allowed to roam the village until sunset.

Monica decided to walk around a bit with her bullwhip in her hand, just to create the right ambience. After that, she planned to go down to the gym and do some shopping. Monica quite enjoyed the contrast in lifestyles between her and Laura. She had, however, had a slight panic that morning whilst leaving Laura's, when she caught sight of Guy Pengersick, with whom she'd once almost had an encounter...

***

It was when she had just moved to Hampden. One evening, after she had eaten her fill of chocolate, she thought that the next thing on the menu should be a man. She didn't plan on doing anything about it, but whilst she was down at the pub drinking her usual pint of milk stout, she saw Guy. The pub was superbly set up with smoked mirrors behind the glasses shelf. This gave excellent visibility of everything and everyone, even with her back to them, allowing her to watch without being obvious about it.

Monica picked her moment. She and Guy were the only two in the bar, so she made a show of fixing her make-up a bit. He glanced up. With her back towards him, she stood up and bent over to get something from her bag. As she got up again, she momentarily glanced in the mirror. He was looking. His hand was now in the cookie jar, and there would be no escape.

She walked across the empty room and kicked the leg of his chair. "Someone's sitting there, mate, you better shift yourself, you're in their way."

A momentary exchange of facial expressions made the necessary communication, and they were soon chatting and laughing. "I'm not trying to pull you, by the way, you're too ugly for that. I'm just desperate to chat to someone in this damned doom room for the dying." Her unusual line of chat enthralled Guy, and Monica loved the look of him – his bushy hair, his unusually beautiful eyes with their far-off gaze. She noticed his manly hands, his chunky diver's watch and some ancient-looking Chelsea boots. He oozed character.

"My pint is still full, but I'll have a Tia Maria chaser if you're buying."

Guy was coping well with all of Monica's strange ways, and he bought her the drink she had asked for and watched intently as she enjoyed her milk stout interlaced with sips of Tia Maria.

They chatted, but Monica very much kept a wall up and gave nothing away. Later, as she went to leave, saying she had to get back home, he attempted to ask her out on a date.

"Whoa, hang on, now you're taking things in a whole new direction, aren't you? I just wanted someone to talk to. What are you proposing exactly? I ought to warn you I don't do lovey-dovey, and I don't do vanilla. You'd better be willing to bring along some interesting ideas, and I think you know what I'm talking about. Plus, I don't think we'd be coming here either. Let's make it the King's Arms at Westerleigh?"

****

Monica had set herself a strict set of rules for the date. She wanted no poncy time-wasting courtship rituals. At the end of the day, if they weren't sexually compatible, they were headed straight down a pointless cul-de-sac. Her tastes were varied. She'd be happy with just a basic interest in kink, but there would be no wham-bam thank you ma'am. He would have to prove his credentials.

She slipped into a generic, slinky, black, long-sleeved, polyester-Lycra-mix mini-dress and some heels and waited outside the pub in her car. Guy pulled in and flashed his lights. His eyes lit up as she got out of the car, and she gave him a warm smile to break the ice. Once settled inside the pub with their drinks, she started on him. "Do you ever have sex in the toilets? Sometimes I just can't wait." She then let the smile drift from her face. "You do have some interesting ideas to tell me about, don't you?"

"Well, I do like to give a woman a good time. I regard myself as something of a long-stayer."

"A long-stayer, well, okay, but there's an ocean of difference between something sustained and something protracted. Let me make things easier for you, because right now you're scoring around ten per cent in an arena where the pass mark is about seventy-five. Think of food. If I said name the sort of food you like, you'd be able to do that, wouldn't you?" Monica was getting a bit irritated at how reticent he was being. She wanted to keep things light and happy, though, so she slid down a bit on the leather sofa to let her dress ride up a bit – let the dog see the rabbit and all that. Guy's attention was suddenly caught by the group of men opposite who had noticed what was going on. They were grinning and whispering and their eyes were out on stalks.

"Monica, for crying out loud, pull your dress down. Those guys are watching you."

But Monica just kept smiling. Guy looked quite buoyed up by this evolving situation, and Monica continued her conversation. "Look, Guy, we're not kids and I'm not a prick tease. But I'm not subjecting myself to any mind-numbing tedium. I want sex in colour. Otherwise, it'll just be a bonk fest. You'll cough your filthy yoghurt, then roll off me, fart, and before we know it, you'll be trying to get me to make bacon sandwiches whilst you watch the football. Right, look, I'm going for a piss. You've got four minutes to come up with a proposal, okay?"

When Monica returned, Guy looked pretty flustered. It didn't bode well. "Right then. Start talking. If I came home with you, what would you do to me?"

Guy took a sip of his drink. "Right, well, I'd get you home... put some romantic music on." At these words, Monica started to get a migraine. "I'd turn the lights down real low. Pour you a drink and maybe we'd have an intimate chat about how nice you look, and who knows... maybe go upstairs."

By now Monica was glaring at him, putting all of her anger and frustration into her stare. She saw it hit home, and Guy slumped. "Well, obviously I've failed the test, so what were the right answers?"

"Erm, well, let's see. You could have had: pull my hair, use nipple clamps, thumb clamps, gags, high heels, role-play, costumes, furry play, spanking, E-Stim, latex, abduction, bimbofication, CBT, figging, Shibari, Zentai. That might have at least been a start," she growled.

Guy took a long glug of beer, the sort you take when you're either really nervous, or you want to drink up and leave. In Guy's case, she suspected it was a bit of both. "Okay, all of what you've just said, all of that then – I'll do that. Yeah, I'm game for a laugh."

That last comment made Monica snap. She leant forwards. "You useless git, you dick-splash." Realising that she had over-reacted a bit, she added a little laugh, once she had managed to stop gritting her teeth. "Nice try, but no good. You wouldn't let someone drive a forklift truck if they didn't have a certificate of competence, would you? Well, same applies to my body."

"You, madam, are impossible. I don't doubt your sincerity, but I'm in over my head here."

Monica calmed down, just wanting to finish the evening by staying friends and keeping things cordial. She pulled her dress down again properly. There was a faint booing and some laughter from the lads opposite, which she ignored.

"It's a right shame, because you, mister, are a total dish." She wasn't sure Guy had ever been complimented in that way before

Sadly, he wasn't even aware he'd received a compliment.

****

Laura told Guy that she hadn't ever tried paddling before, but she'd be up for giving it a go. They went through to the garage at August, and Guy showed her that he had built a paddleboard out of recycled two-litre, green, plastic Sprite bottles. Laura was so impressed.

"They were left over from the Chalkewood Festival."

That embarrassed Laura a little, and she vowed to look into it. Guy pulled out a more professional-looking inflatable model and told Laura that this would be hers.

They loaded everything into the truck. Laura dashed inside to change into more suitable clothes, and they were on their way.

She was both excited and nervous as they drew up to the shoreline. It didn't take long to get everything into the water. Kneeling down on their boards, they set off, paddling clear of the shallow water.

"Okay, shall we try standing up?" said Guy. "So, just give it a bit of forwards momentum, then with your paddle across the board, look ahead, bring one foot forwards and stand up with your feet either side of the handle."

Laura couldn't believe it. She was up; she was doing it; it was easy!

"It's a bit of a faff having to change sides with the paddle every two strokes. Isn't it?"

"I know. It's down to using the paddle correctly. If you do that, then, with a bit of experience, you'll soon be doing ten strokes per side. It will help if you turn your paddle round the right way, so the blade is facing the other way. That's it."

It was magical. Like walking on water. Laura had a good stable board and she already saw it as a friend. Steering was easy, and she was doing less zigzagging now. In a short space of time, they had travelled a long way down the small lake. Guy tried to do a step-back turn and fell in. Then Laura's board hit Guy's, and she overbalanced and went in with him. The water wasn't cold, and they were soon back on the boards. They sat on the edge of their boards for a moment and had a swig out of their water bottles.

Laura saw Emma paddling back with her clients, and she nudged Guy. He looked in the direction Laura had nodded, and he waved at Emma. Her clients headed on back to deflate their boards, get changed and go home, and Emma came over. Guy was keen to get her to give Laura a quick intro to yoga, and Emma was happy to oblige, suggesting they follow her. Reaching an opening in the reeds, they went a short way in along a passage to a secluded pool. It had water lilies growing all around the edges and the water was dark and clear with fish swimming just below the surface. A ray of sunlight illuminated one end, and a heron stood on the branch of a fallen tree.

In a quiet, calming tone, Emma gave them a little taster. "Just lie on your board. Let all the tension drain out of you into the water. You're at one with the water. It is you, and you are it. Go on, put your fingers in the water and feel its coolness.

"Your board is going to help to challenge your balance, whilst building both strength and flexibility throughout your whole body at the same time. Staying centred and balanced on your board, make sure you're steady, and then let's start with the Downward-Facing Dog position."

Laura felt happy and confident. She had an overwhelming feeling of beauty and positivity. Everything just felt perfect. She didn't ever want to leave the pool, but eventually the session came to an end.

Making their way out, Guy tried for a headstand. Emma was giving feedback, and for a few moments, he held it before falling in. The sun was now setting behind the treeline, and they made their way slowly back. Laura had never noticed Guy's looks before – the orange sun on his face, his beautiful eyes and his athletic body steering the board through the water. The entire situation was a picture, but also an experience. It felt right; it felt honest and uncontrived. The way they and nature were existing together so naturally. Laura was hooked. She wanted to get all the gear and go deeper. All of this sense of well-being had been achieved without any complexity, simply by choosing to stop seeing Guy as 'just an estate worker'.

That evening, Guy again invited her round to Garth and Gren's house, and this time she accepted.

Laura slipped into some comfortable clothes and headed down to Foresters Cottage on her gravel bike. Forester's was probably the most picturesque house on the estate. It was what someone would typically call an English 'chocolate box' cottage, with its thatched roof, cosy rooms, rustic beams, and quaint features such as its inglenook fireplace. But on this warm evening, the socialising had spilled outside to under the vine-covered veranda, looking out on the west-facing garden.

Guy had cycled down too, and they walked in together like a couple, through the rose-covered gated-arbour. Laura wanted to hold Guy's hand, but that would be an insane move. They could hear 1920s jazz music quietly coming from the open windows, and then there was the heart-stoppingly delicious smell of food. Laura could hear her mother's voice. "Now then, Piggy, hold back. Don't forget, humans find piggies very intimidating when it's scrummaging time. So, plenty of pig dignity, please." Laura took onboard those imaginary words of wisdom, but she was utterly starving, having had nothing since breakfast and then having spent an afternoon on the lake.

She was totally unsure of how to greet Garth and Gren. Being informal with tenants would be crossing the Rubicon for sure, but she wanted a change of dynamic. Somehow, the other three had anticipated this, and they were up for being bold. Guy held Laura back. "Gentleman and gentleman, your attention please, Her Ladyship, the Honourable Miss Laura Stanhope."

Laura was on! She stepped forwards and held out her hand for them both to kiss.

Garth said, "I shall bow first."

Gren said in an exaggerated voice, "And I shall curtsey."

Everyone fell about the place, and they had a group hug and a communal 'm'wah' kiss.

Wow, that went well, thought Laura. Even better, the canapes were immediately forthcoming. They brought out a jug of Dubonnet and lemonade, and there were lots of small strawberries in it. It went down a treat. Next, out came the Marquandy board with its banana-yellow and ebony diamonds on it. Gren started patting the table and quietly chanting, "Mar-quan-dy, Mar-quan-dy," as a sign of approval. The alcohol having made him wonderfully mellow.

Garth won the toss and puffed first. The metal ball went straight into the hole. They all put a ball in the box. When it was opened, there was no black ball, so it was oblique, but it was Gren's go now. He puffed, but the ball ran out and was bracketed. He took the buff-coloured pack of cards, shuffled them and took one. It read Disparion – the look of shock on his face.

He ran out of the room up the stairs and came back down with a pair of socks and a steam iron. "Dis - pair - I – Iron." Out came the box, in went the balls. Lid opened, two red and two blue. Oooh, difficult. That was most certainly a Gantry.

Guy had a real talent for the game, and by the time the compasses had swung on Lauds, he was well ahead. He had also taken on the job of whispering all the rules to Laura and helping her. It was, in essence, a simple game.

When the evening drew to a close, Guy and Laura left together and cycled back together. Chalkewood was first. Laura parked her bike and Guy got off his to say goodnight. They did a polite hug and then just stood there, looking at each other awkwardly. Eventually, underpinned by the potential excuse of alcohol, Laura said, "I need you to do something. I need you to kiss me. Don't argue, just get on and do as you've been instructed."

Guy approached her in his usual practical kind of way and carried out the demand. For Laura, it was a sumptuous experience, and it scored ten out of ten. He was even wearing a gorgeous cologne.

"Hmm, you're lovely," he said, before shaking her hand firmly and ironically, then saying, "Goodnight, my lady." That scored ten out of ten, as well.

Walking in, Laura felt she had somehow hideously short-changed herself. On the one hand, she had to be certain that she was doing the right thing and not walking headlong into social catastrophe. Yet, on the other hand, her hormones were driving her crazy. She pushed the door of the laundry open and wheeled her bike in. Her hip flask was lying on the side and there was a damp towel lying on the floor, getting in the way.

Flipping the top on the hip flask, it turned out to contain sloe gin. Yep, very nice. Laura threw the damp towel into the washing machine. She selected a 1600 rpm spin, reversed her bottom onto the corner of the machine, picked up the hip flask with her right hand, and then hit the start button with her left. Her legs were soon starting to twitch, and complete discombobulation followed shortly thereafter.

CHAPTER ELEVEN

— · —

FRIENDS TO LOVERS

Monday morning. With weather to match. Laura was woken by the rain beating on the sash windows as they rattled with every gust of wind. She pulled back the curtains and looked out. A lone seagull, far inland to escape the rough sea, was being carried effortlessly across the sky sideways by the strong wind. It was 9 a.m., but cars in the far distance still had their headlights on. It was very dreich out, as Scottish Uncle Cuddy would say.

Wait! What? I kissed Pengersick last night! The thought entered Laura's head like a thunderclap. She seriously needed to spend some time rationalising that, but she couldn't, as she had an important group Teams meeting booked for 10 a.m. with her boss's boss, Mark Sieniewicz. It was pronounced 'Senayvich', but they all called him 'son-of-a-bitch'. Perhaps a little unjustified, but he hadn't got where he was today through being a doormat, that was for sure.

Laura was flustered and ran about the house, trying to prepare herself and at least look decent from the waist up. A shower could wait. She threw on an old blouse from last week, fixed her hair and pulled on a random pair of old stripy leggings. Sitting at the kitchen table now, toast and jam in hand, cup of tea on the go. Ten minutes to run, laptop initialising.

It was a useful meeting. Niall Frazer was long gone, and Mark Sieniewicz was now implementing the recommendations made by Anna Le Pley-Dougall. It was a big task, and they agreed Laura would drop down to just ten hours a month, to be on hand for people to consult with until the company was in a position to complete all the new appointments and move forwards. This suited Laura perfectly, although she didn't say that, as she didn't want to appear uncommitted.

The meeting ended with the announcement that Dolly Deloitte had just been appointed to Niall's old job. A tumultuous cheer went up. It was a huge career jump for her, and Laura joined in the shouting with, "Way to go Dolly." Dolly gave a double victory salute with both hands in the air. "Brannigan's Thursday night," she yelled, to be heard over the cheering. Mark then concluded with a formal eulogy to Dolly's previous achievements, including a discreet and humbling reference to her wetting her knickers. The meeting finished with a polite ripple of applause and people making the heart sign to Dolly. The subtlety here was that Dolly was not in any way celebrating a simple personal victory; it was a victory for all the women of HV.

Coffee in hand, Laura went back upstairs, swapped her blouse for a T-shirt and got back into bed. The meeting had filled her with a rather nice sense of peace, and she was relishing the thought of having virtually no work over the summer. She had never needed the money, but was still reluctant to let go of what she had achieved in the corporate world.

Now she could luxuriate and think about the whole deal with Guy. At first, she tried to pass it on to him, thinking of him as a naughty boy. Except... she then had to admit he wasn't. She'd instructed him to kiss her. Then she thought, Maybe he didn't want to; maybe he just did it because he had been instructed to? But she knew that wasn't true, because he'd said, "Hmm, you're lovely," which was something to be thankful for.

What to do, though. Laura still carried some prejudice about him being staff, but she wanted to purge herself of that. Her day with him had been superb. It had been organic and unplugged, and had made her feel peaceful and happy. Plus, she was totally bitten by the whole stand-up paddleboard thing. Then there were Garth and Gren... Oops, that reminded her. She took out her laptop and sent them a quick message thanking them for last night and giving the usual blurb about the delicious food and the wonderful company – which it so truly had been, on both counts.

Guy, hmm, what to do? One thing was for sure, she couldn't afford to waste biological-clock time on him. In fact, the stark choice was: Either he was marriage material, or she had to completely forget he existed romantically.

It wasn't until lunchtime that Laura finally got dressed. It was hot outside, and this drew her out into the front garden, if for no other reason than to just soak up the heat like a lizard kick-starting its metabolism. She walked onto the drive. Shock, horror. It was Guy, and he was coming towards her, and she was totally unprepared. She had no idea what to say.

She went over and shook hands, which her parents had told you should never do with staff. So this, at least, was a step in the right direction. "Morning, Pengersick, everything alright?"

"Yes, miss. I think we're up to date with everything. I've had those signs made up saying that the house is 'occupied and not abandoned'."

"And the lower field, have we addressed the risk of flooding?"

"Yes, Abbotts start next week on that."

They stood there looking at each other. "Miss, I was just wondering. May I invite you out for supper one evening this week?"

Laura looked around. She put her hand up to shield her eyes from the sun as she turned and looked out at the horizon. "Yes, that would be in order," she said quietly, without making eye contact. "Right, well, I must dash, carry on as you were." She shook his hand again and walked off.

Laura went indoors and let out a moan. She would have so loved to drag him in by the hair and take him upstairs for a good morning-long workout. Looking around, she wondered if she ought to put a wash on, but she thought better of that and went for a 5k run instead.

****

Pierre Fontaine Bloechap at Le Saison Blanc Visage – well, Laura hadn't been expecting that for a dinner venue. She always welcomed a spot of two-star Michelin nose-baggage, always a delight, but unfortunately you sometimes had to go for a McDonald's afterwards because the portions were too poncey, even for a lady. She had, however, taken the precaution of doing what she called 'preeting', pre-eating by having a banana before leaving the house. Piggies know all the best hacks.

The meal was a real piece of theatre. Totally brilliant. They were served at their table with a telephone with smoke coming out of it, and they had to dial up their meal like a takeaway and everything came on a bed of quinoa. The intermezzo, rather than being a palate-cleansing sorbet, was a palate 'dirtier' – to prepare for dessert, they were asked to eat a spoonful of homemade Nutella. The chateau de chocolat menthe was then served. It was a rich, crumbly chocolate confusion, dusted with mint-green icing. Just as they cut into it, Johnny Depp's voice rang out, "Everything in this room is eatable, even I'm eatable!" When Laura did it, the voice had a slight echo, as the person behind her had gone for it at just the same moment.

****

Guy insisted on paying the bill. It was, in essence, a demonstration of his commitment, and Laura was delighted. Technically, she was his employer and landlord, and that meant it would have been completely in order for her to have paid, so it was a strong gesture from him. Laura was facing the battle of a lifetime, though – with the way that she had been brought up. She was afraid that all the values and etiquette she had grown up with had made her too judgemental of others. For instance, she had trained herself to no longer judge everyone she met by their table manners, but she still held those close to her to the high standards she expected of herself. So, it was a relief for her to see that Guy had impeccable table manners and he knew how to use a knife and fork correctly. And he had broad tastes and interests in food and drink. His line of conversation interested her as well. However, they both inhabited different worlds, and she knew that once back home, she would have a difficult decision to make.

They drew up outside the house, and he walked her to the door, where she made the decisive move: kissing him politely on both cheeks, thanking him for a wonderful evening and letting him go.

Sitting up in bed with a black coffee, she knew the stakes couldn't be higher. This exact moment in time, right now, she was teetering on a knife edge. This thing with Guy seemed so implausible; it went against everything her mother had taught her. Life was always a balancing act, though, and lucky indeed are those for whom everything just falls into place.

Laura's basic assumption had always been that she would cut out a career in the city and, in that process, she would meet a marriage prospect. The subtle difference to many other women with this same plan, however, was that she didn't need this prospect to be a breadwinner. That aside, most men she knew well at work horrified her. They were all driven people, but in all the wrong ways. She, personally, had had a whole group of them dismissed for corruption that time she called the police in. Others suffered from such toxic masculinity that a specialist management company

had had to be hired in to provide the evidence
to remove them from the management structure.
Who'd want one of those prospects as a husband,
or the father of their children?

Then there was James. Oh yeah, that bastard had
all the right table manners – he'd probably taken
classes in it, just to fool even more people and
further his Machiavellian endeavours.

Throughout the evening with Guy, Laura had
employed a very subtle line of conversation
designed to elicit his opinions on issues that were
important to her. Yes, he did want a wife and
children. However, he also had a real lust for
adventure and a fascination for global horticultural
projects, which was all very laudable, but a bit
distracting. Laura had wanted to remind him that he
too had a bio-clock, and that if he left it too late, all
the good women would be gone, and he'd end up
with some barking-mad swamp donkey. Thankfully,
she hadn't voiced that last sentence.

It was now one minute to midnight, and the only
conclusion she'd come to was there were no perfect
prospects in life. She asked herself, if there was
anything to suggest that Guy would not be suitable
as a marriage prospect. And the emphatic answer
was no, there wasn't.

Laura slid down under the covers and let out a big
sigh. No doubt about it, the man was eligible. She

hated being faced with decisions this important, but that was how it was.

Glancing at her laptop, she noticed Monica was online, so she messaged her and then they ended up face-timing. Laura put her laptop on the side so she could chat comfortably.

"Laura, you've got it all arse about face. You should bang him first to check that you are sexually compatible. If he's gonna be sniffing round your Charlie for the next seventy years, you don't want him making a bad job of it. If he turns out to be sexually mindless, which he may well be, then fek him off out of it once you've drained him, but get him to teach you how to paddleboard first."

"Well, Monica, I'll have you know we had a scintillating evening, and I'm pleased to report that he has excellent table manners. Unlike you, because I had to train you to eat with a knife and fork, didn't I? You were a really messy eater when I first met you. As for the correct way to eat mussels – you: no idea. You also didn't even hold your fork the right way up. You held it like an overloaded shovel, and you'd ram it in your face like you were stuffing a turkey's arse. If I'm going to have him sniffing around my dining table for the next seventy years, I'd be much more concerned about him making a bad job of that."

"Piss off, you stuck-up, fat snob. I still remember the time you told me off for 'cutting the nose off' on a wedge of cheese. I'd never even heard of that one."

"Don't call me a snob, you common bogtrotter."

"You're full of the mouth when I'm not there, aren't you? Aren't you? You stuck-up fat piggy. Remember, I have a key to your back door. I can come round, and we'll see how brave you are, then... Seriously though, are you planning on getting his pants off?"

"Only once I've made him beg."

This notion met with enthusiastic approval. Monica hadn't a clue what Laura was so concerned about, so they did their virtual hugs and kisses, said goodnight and ended the call.

****

Sunday

Monica decided she would accompany the Pigs to church that morning. They had been fairly agnostic when she met them, but she had told them that if they didn't become Catholics, the deal was off. It had all sounded like a brilliant wheeze, but in the cold light of day and under the gaze of The Almighty as they prepared for church that day, it all felt somewhat awkward and uncomfortable and lacking sincerity.

After a cup of tea and a slice of toast, they headed off. Monica was wearing a fitted black jacket, a matching below-the-knee skirt, some 50-denier black tights and flat shoes which made her calves ache a little, as she was so used to wearing high heels. Monica quite liked wearing black on a Sunday – to be fair though, she wore black most other days, although that stuff was usually a heck of a lot more shiny.

The Pigs were wearing tweeds and also their uniform flat leather caps, which Monica had made compulsory for them to wear outside of Hampden Lodge, just for her own amusement. She was fussing over them and doing up any loose buttons, hurrying them along, even though they were all still on time. They walked along the country lane to the sound now of the single church bell ringing out the last call, and Bob got out a paper bag of pear drops and offered them to Monica and Squealer.

"Ok, but we're not going into the church still sucking them. Is that understood?" Monica warned them.

They were just about to go down the final bridle path leading to the church when Monica said, "Right, let's get the sweets gone." She flobbed the last of hers into the hedge, and Bob kicked his down a drain grating. Squealer wasn't cooperating though, and Monica was getting very cross with him. He cheekily crunched his up and swallowed it, so Monica smacked his face 1950's style for that.

Walking into the church, Bob and Squealer both took off their caps, and a sidesman handed them hymn books, a psalter and an order of service each. Monica loved the church interior; it was nice and spooky: austere stone walls, dark everywhere, candles, chunky gothic furniture, silver chalices full of red wine, occasional bright red tapestry, eerie icons, awesome costumes – very little difference really from her dungeon back home, only this place was equipped with different paraphernalia.

They walked to their regular pew at the back. The minute Bob took his seat, he realised he had a massive fart brewing, but with tight trousers, a hard wooden pew and a silent but echoey building, the outcome would have been catastrophic, so he sucked it back in. He started sniggering and whispering to Squealer. Monica gave him a stern look and reached across and smacked him.

Monica took her spiritual duty to the Pigs very seriously. She felt it was up to her to help them find absolution for their sinful lifestyles. However, Monica's version of evangelism was somewhat alternative. She didn't believe in poncy Alpha courses, confirmation classes or seeker-friendly services. The Pigs had a choice: either go to church and repent before the cross, or stay at home and end up on the cross, complete with a pre-crucifixion whipping, for added biblical authenticity.

After a moment of quiet contemplation, the service began, and they all stood for the entrance of the priest, Father Fitzalan-Tightly. He welcomed everyone in the name of the Trinity and the congregation responded, "And with thy spirit."

Monica loved the hymns. She had a proven singing voice, but she hadn't been invited to join the choir, probably because she added a rock-and-pop lilt to everything she sang. It just didn't sound pious enough. Meatloaf singing 'Silent Night' was how she'd overheard someone in the congregation describing her vocal ability.

At the end of the service, Monica didn't want to stay for the coffee and biscuits fellowship session. "The nosey bastards ask way too many questions." Instead, she told the Pigs to wait outside whilst she saw Father Michael about a problem she was having with the Wednesday Confessions.

As soon as she was done, they headed back. When they rounded the corner and Monica was sure nobody was watching, she stood between Bob and Squealer and held their hands. Then she started swinging their hands backwards and forwards whilst singing 'Immaculate Mary'. It was such a wonderfully happy moment that she suggested, "How about we go down the pub for Sunday lunch?"

****

At Chalkewood, Laura had invited Guy, Garth and Gren round for Sunday lunch. It smelt divine. The radio was on quietly, playing 'Summertime' by Ella Fitzgerald. A warm breeze was blowing in through the open kitchen door. Laura took the beef out of the oven and added the potatoes to the pan. She basted them and put them back in.

"Guy, open this for me, will you, and leave it to breathe?" She handed him a nice bottle of oaky Malbec.

Garth and Gren were in the drawing room laughing hysterically at some anecdote. It probably wasn't that funny. More likely it was the effects of the homemade rhubarb wine Guy had brought round as an aperitif. Everyone thought it tasted bloody fantastic, but it must have been about seventeen per cent proof, or something ridiculous.

Guy stood watching Laura at the range. He was leaning against the wall, a sexy smile curving his lips. Laura looked over. "Why don't you come and give me a hug whilst I stir the gravy?" He slipped both his arms around her and gave her a hug, kissing her neck whilst gently swaying her. The moment seemed to last an eternity. They heard the footsteps of the boys on their way in, so Guy slipped away quickly.

"Golly gosh, that just smells better every time I come in here. Dahling, it smells a-may-zing," said Gren. He surreptitiously looked through the oven glass and saw it was rib of beef. Not wanting to spoil any surprise Laura might be planning, he whispered in Garth's ear, "She's only gone and bought rib."

"Rib!" shouted Garth, who was well under the influence of the rhubarb by now.

"I heard that," said Laura. "Don't get your hopes up. The beef's for the cats. You lot are having baked beans."

Garth went over to her. "Put that spoon down and dance with me, right this minute,"

****

Maybe Garth and Gren could sense the romantic tension building between Laura and Guy, because they didn't stay late into the afternoon. After they left, Laura put on the Bridge Over Troubled Water album, a nostalgic nod to those Sunday afternoons when her parents used to play it. Today, its lyrics spoke to her of uncompleted journeys.

Laura and Guy sat on the sofa, and Laura lay back against him, his arms around her whilst they chatted.

"So, do you have many job applications in the pipeline?"

It was a loaded question and Guy sensed that, but he wanted to be honest and straight. "Things here are by no means certain, Laura. I don't have a vital role at Chalkewood, and it's safe to say, any new owner will make me redundant without question."

Laura detested that answer. It was a threat to her dreams and aspirations. What irritated her most was that she could easily afford to pay his salary, but without Chalkewood, what would there be for him to do? There was no easy answer. Perhaps the way to make progress would be to throw herself at him to see whether she 'stuck'. There was no need for her to put in too much effort on that front, though, as in between kisses, Guy had finally reached second base. With both hands up inside her bra and a concentrated expression on his face, he was now twiddling her nipples as though he were trying to tune into some far-off radio station.

It was time for Laura to make a decision. She pondered allowing him to go for a home run. But for that, she wanted to be prepared and for things to be perfect. Her private garden was also in dire need of some topiary. Pulling her knickers on that morning, she'd noticed how everything was spilling out around the sides, like there was an epic spider-crab migration taking place. And it wasn't just her topiary either – her knickers were a right old pair of applecatchers. Originally white, they were now blue-tinged, having cross-dyed in the wash with her jeans. Then there was her bra. It didn't even match, and the underwiring was starting to poke through. No, that was her mind made up. On this occasion, Guy was going to have to strike out. But not before she had established a couple of things. First, she wanted him to pledge to at least some kind of commitment, and then, there was the delicate subject of endowment. In the tragic event he had been under-blessed with a spindle-dick, she was going to need to know about that in advance, so that she could manage her expectations.

Time for action! Laura took hold of his wrists and yanked both of his hands out from under her top hamper. "Well, you've turned out to be a rather dirty little house guest, haven't you? How very bad-mannered you are. How would you like it, eh? How would you like it if someone did that to you?" Hauling him to his feet, she rammed her hand down the front of his jeans for a girth check. "See, how did you like it? Not very pleasant, is it?" she said, trying not to laugh, whilst Guy's eyes were almost rolling right back in his head.

Just then, she noticed her bra was undone. "Bloody hell, what kind of black magic have you been practicing? I didn't even feel that happen. Damn well refasten it, will you?" That done, she sat him down again and sat astride his legs, facing him. "Well, thank goodness that's been dealt with, because this could so easily have ended up in the bedroom," she said, bouncing on his lap for good measure. "Yes, that would have been a real disaster, wouldn't it, Pengersick?" she said, grabbing his fleece as though it had two lapels. "A complete disaster, because there would have been me, falling for your charms, and then afterwards, you would have been telling me all about your new job a million miles away from here. Bad, very bad indeed, Pengersick.

"Right, on your feet, mister. Home time for you. You need a cold shower, and then you need to get your thinking cap on. After that, you can make an appointment with me so you can give me a presentation on why I should consider you as a partner. In the event that you get the promotion, a suitable appointment will then be made for you to come round here so that I can assess your athletic ability. If you pass that test, I might consider giving you a permanent position."

Guy left feeling a bit confused. He felt like he was playing a game for which he didn't know all the rules. But he thought that it was rather delicious and intriguing, so being a passenger was fine, for now.

Laura sat back, feeling very self-satisfied. He had been baited, tormented, girth-checked and sent off for a cold shower followed by homework. The whole thing with Guy was a massive gamble, but she just had to take the plunge.

****

Monday

Down at Hampden Lodge. Monica had just zipped up her boots ready for another day's site supervision. The Pigs were downstairs sitting at the kitchen table. They'd made themselves some toast and cereal and were eating and drinking tea. The portable TV was on quietly in the background. Monica walked in. The Pigs stood to attention and nodded their heads in respect. Monica was in a great mood. She signalled for them to sit down again. Pinching her nose, she addressed them.

"Now, hear this. Now hear this. Attention, all Pigs. You will report at twenty hundred hours, Friday seventeen, ready to go for a night out in Mapelwick. Thaaaat is all."

"Miss, miss," they called out as she went to leave, "What's the deal?"

Monica came back in, sat down and enthusiastically told them she had discovered a banging new munch in Mapelwick, the nearest large town. They'd heard the term 'munch' before but had never been to one. "It's a place for kinksters to meet up and network, in a vanilla setting, so something like a pub or café. I think it would be healthy for us all to get out and meet people. We all know that things here won't go on forever and you guys need to build some contacts."

Bob slapped his hand down on the table. "That is a banging idea. Miss, you are the best. Squealer and I had begun to talk about life hereafter."

Monica grabbed them both by the scruff of the neck. "Good, that's that sorted, then. And now, you worms can damn well get to work before I take you down and string you up."

****

Guy was down at Ten Mile Patch. He'd been called in to see why the replacement hedging saplings weren't taking. It had meant a long walk along its length and having to do some soil testing. The high winds on that grey day hadn't helped either.

Returning to his equally grey estate Land Rover, he cleaned his hands on a wet-wipe and sat in the cab, lunch box in hand. Before he started eating, he thought he might liven up his break a bit. So, he texted Laura, My Dear Lady, I should like to apply for the position of companion, please advise.

Laura was delighted to get the message. She wanted to continue the fun and make it an excruciatingly formal experience for him, so she intended wearing a business suit for the occasion. But she couldn't be arsed going through all that rigmarole specially for one interview, so she chose a time when she would already be suitably dressed, just before she was due to go up to London next. She went through a few official letter templates and sent him a formal response, offering him an interview.

Guy had just pulled the lid off his yoghurt when his phone buzzed. With heart beating fast, he put the yoghurt on the dashboard and fumbled for his phone. It was such a gratifying read, and he adored her attention to detail. She was being such a bitch, and it was delicious. Then he noticed he had a meeting with Peasley that same day. He messaged her back with the bad news.

Laura's reply was equally prompt. Dear Mr Pengersick. Get it changed, BY ORDER, Stanhope, L. He called Gordon Peasley, but he was out, and Margaret answered. She was adamant that

Gordon's plans were set, so Guy asked for Gordon to call him as, he said, he had no intention of going against Miss Stanhope. There then ensued an acrimonious three-way conversation that ended with Laura and Guy getting their way, but not before Gordon got his own little victory over Guy by rescheduling their meeting for 6 p.m. on Friday. What an arse! thought Guy

****

Guy had smartened himself up for his interview with Laura. He knocked on the kitchen door, but there was no reply. He tried again, still no answer. He opened the door a crack, his heart beating fast. He could hear Laura talking, and tentatively followed her voice, calling out, "Hellooo, hellooo." There was still no answer, so he continued to follow the voice.

He knocked on the open door of her office before peering round. She beckoned him to come in. Guy couldn't help admiring how amazing and very business-like she looked sitting behind her father's old desk. She then made him stand and wait for something like ten minutes whilst she finished a business call. When she came off the phone, she didn't look him in the eye. She just said, "Morning, Pengersick, don't take a seat, just begin your presentation."

She continued writing some notes and typing something on her laptop, whilst he began. She didn't even appear to be listening. He lumbered on with his jaunty but serious presentation. Laura looked up and smiled encouragingly. She was now making notes, and he noticed she had written his name down on a sheet of paper in front of her.

Occasionally, she asked some awkward questions, wanting to humiliate him just for the fun of it. Peering over her gold-rimmed reading spectacles, she said, "How can you assure me that you aren't a selfish lover?"

He had to really think about that one, only managing to reply with, "Well, I always take the time to consider my partner's needs."

Laura kept pressing him for more and more detail, until he was red in the face from having to go into so much anatomical detail. She then took another short business call. After that, she looked at him again, saying, "Okay, Pengersick, thank you for coming in today. I'm a very busy person, but I will try to make a decision regarding your position sometime this week. You may leave now." And then she gesticulated for him to get out.

He was just crossing the driveway on his way to August when she was leaving for London. Laura beeped at him to get out of the way as she didn't see why she should slow down to let him cross. The second her car went out of sight, he punched the air.

CHAPTER TWELVE

CONDUCTED TOUR

Monica walked up the steps of the Rectory for her meeting with Father Michael. It was a nice enough day for early July: dry but not too hot. Pulling the brass plunger on the stone pillar, she heard the tinkling of a bell in the distance. Mrs Boyle, the housekeeper, opened the door and greeted her. She showed Monica in and through to the study. Father Michael was pleased to see her and offered her a seat. He spoke with a soft southern Irish accent, and Monica couldn't help slipping back into her native accent.

"So, Monica, how can I help you today?"

"Well, Father, and this isn't a complaint, but I'm finding confession to be difficult. You see, outside the confession box you posted a sign that says, 'Make your confession direct and to the point, and confess only your sins and offences. No need to explain why you did it. Thanks very much.' And that's me whole point. I want to explain, and I want to talk about it."

This interested Father Michael – parishioners engaged him in all manner of nonsense conversations, but he felt this one had legs. In any case, the fact that she had once confessed to him that she gained sexual gratification from hurting men pretty much guaranteed her his attention at any time. "Monica, would you like a sherry?" Her eyes lit up. "I take it, that's a yes? Sweet or dry."

"Dry, please."

Having received the correct answer, he indulged her further. "Or perhaps you'd prefer a Madeira?"

"Sure, why not?"

She took a sip and clearly liked it. He could tell she had never tried it before and was happy to have been the one to initiate her.

"Ours is an omniscient God, Monica. He already knows 'why you did it'. He just needs to be reassured that you know what you did was wrong and that you genuinely want to repent and change. Even if that takes several attempts." He nodded reassuringly.

At that moment, Mrs Boyle knocked and popped her head round the door. Father Michael vaguely waved his hand from side to side in a signal to her that this one wouldn't be having any tea or coffee.

Monica had now slipped further into her Irish accent. "Oi knows dat, Father. It's jost dat I doos wanna talk about it."

"Well, Monica, that would be kind of drifting over into a more specialist kind of ministry. One beyond simple prayer. One perhaps involving deliverance or even exorcism."

This really spooked Monica up, conjuring up images of blokes canoeing through the swamps of Louisiana or that girl, Regan, doing her backwards spider walk down the stairs.

"But Father, people do talk about these things. Down at the evangelical church, I hear that they really focus on spiritual development."

Father Michael looked pensive. "Ah well, you see Monica, that would be an ecumenical matter."

Monica was beginning to feel a bit bewildered, so she moved on to her next complaint. "Okay, Father, I get that. Can I ask you about services? Would it be possible for me to do just confession and no services? It's just that I find the repetitious liturgy a bit pointless. It's a bit like coming into work each day and reciting the entire employee handbook before starting work."

"Monica, do you find Hail Marys and Our Fathers to be repetitious and pointless?"

"No, because they're penitential,"

Her reply was like putting another coin in the slot. It was a trick question, and her answer was spot on.

"Monica, do you own a rosary? You might find it helpful in penitence."

"Oi! 'ave a look on Amazon, so I will," vowed Monica, before moving on to her final question. "Father, is it possible to say confession on behalf of another." She was specifically thinking of Bob and Squealer.

"Oh, who did you have in mind?"

With a somewhat startling slip of the tongue, she said, "My Pigs," and there was no real way back after that – correcting it would just make matters gravely worse.

Father Michael relaxed back in his chair. "Oh, bless you, my dear. St. Francis would be proud of you. He used to preach to animals. So yes, by all means, give it a go," he said, laughing. "I hope you don't think I'm ribbing you, but if there's any penance required, I'm sure we can chop it short. I hope you don't think I'm hamming it up, but I'd be loin if I said I wasn't."

"Yes, Father, plenty of belly laughs here, eh?" Monica was about done with it all now. She could be quite a serious person, and she felt like she had made no progress. All she really wanted him to do was to scoop her up in his priestly robes, sit her on his lap and tell her that she was a good girl really and she wouldn't be going to hell.

****

Guy looked at his phone. Still no WhatsApp message from Laura. He didn't know what to make of it. Maybe she had changed her mind on the whole thing? Maybe she just thought it would all be too complicated? Maybe her parents had talked her out of it? That was a real possibility.

Guy had been looking at his phone constantly these last few days and was beginning to give up hope. He really liked Laura, but he was also ready for a woman in his life. He wanted the excitement of meeting up on Friday night, dressed-up and walking hand in hand, seeing neon lights coming on in a distant town as a setting sun cast its orange glow. Knowing that the weekend was theirs.

Today shouldn't be too bad, he thought. A couple of meetings, a bit of lab work and an afternoon doing research on the net. The toast was in, but he had nowhere to put it, as the kitchen table was full of junk mail – mainly stuff addressed to the previous tenant, which he had been putting in a box to sort through later.

He picked up the complete sheaf of mail and stood between the box and the rubbish bin, sorting the items. That done, he was left with three items. One was a credit card statement, one was his payslip from the estate office, and the other had his name written on it in what looked like fountain pen ink. It also had no stamp, just the words by hand written on the right-hand side. Opening the envelope, he pulled out a note written on a thermographically printed Chalkewood correspondence card. It's raised dark blue letters adding to the imposing effect of Laura's fountain pen script.

Dear Guy,

You are invited to supper, for two. Please message to arrange.

L. 2/7

It had been lying there since the second of July, four days ago. He'd better reply quickly, but first, he took a moment to just stand there looking at it, soaking up the delicious implications.

Blue smoke was now drifting across the kitchen ceiling. Guy quickly whipped the toast out from the toaster. It had been his last two slices of bread, and they were quite black. Taking a table knife, he scraped the charcoal off, and thankfully, they were still edible.

****

The big day had arrived. Laura started to prepare early – like, 4 p.m. early. Guy wasn't due to arrive for another four hours, but there was much to do. Carmen Roland, the housekeeper, had been in earlier, and the kitchen, drawing room, bedroom and en-suite had all been cleaned and new sheets put on the bed.

A week ago, Guy had put the new signs up in a couple of the windows: This building is occupied and NOT abandoned. The signs also had a picture of a policeman on them and a CCTV symbol. Hopefully, they would prevent any more unwanted guests.

Her clothes were all laid out now, and she had her nail technician booked for 7 p.m. The plan was to serve drinks and then a starter course, nothing too heavy. After which, she would take him to bed, and following that, it would be club sandwiches, a half-bottle of Louis Cristal and some Belgian chocolates.

****

Oksana, the nail technician, had packed up all of her bits and was just leaving. She had talked Laura into having French tips. Laura thought they looked a bit slutty, but that would be fine for tonight. She also liked how men found that sort of thing esoteric and baffling, and the way it exploited the joyous physical difference between man and woman, in much the same way as all her ironic retro-lingerie. She wasn't planning on wearing any of that on this occasion, though. Instead, she had just poured herself into a pair of soft, beige, lightweight jodhpurs. They were for dress only and wouldn't last more than a few moments if she ever went riding in them. She checked herself in the mirror and knew for sure that all those Park Runs and the careful eating had been well worth the effort.

Twelve minutes to go. Laura scrolled through the music app on her phone and selected 'Hotel Cheese'. It was a four-hour loop of ambient hotel-lobby piano music, but it also had the hubbub of people talking in the background, designed to make any place sound less empty. She thought it was hilarious. Ideal for Chalkewood with its dozens of empty rooms. It was almost time. She just hoped that he wouldn't turn up wearing his usual baggy trousers. She hadn't even got around to having a proper look at his bottom yet.

'Fashionably late' is a subjective term at the best of times, but by ten-past, Laura was getting a bit twitchy. She went to check her phone again for any messages but was pierced by a shot of adrenaline when the doorbell went.

A nice informal cuddly greeting confirmed that he was wearing that wonderful cologne of his again. He handed her a bottle of wine, in a bag, of course. Guy wasn't just house-trained; he did actually care about things like that. She went to put the bag on the side, so she could then turn and have a good look at her. Cheekily, he was wearing some army surplus trousers. She wasn't sure if they were faux, but they were superbly tight. Oh, my word. Delicious. His buns were like two basketballs, firm and muscular. The trousers also had the slight overtones of a military uniform. All quite a contrast to his usual sagging blue jeans, always with junk in the back pockets. Guy's camo pants were held up with a wide leather belt and his T-shirt was tucked in. Laura sensed it might be a tight-fitting -shirt, so she helped him off with his jacket, which she took through to hang up.

Well, clearly there was no need for him to work out, what with all the outdoor work he did. His upper body was a well-toned inverted triangle shape and with his dark blue, finely ribbed, muscle T-shirt... He'd obviously dressed like this on purpose – that was quite obvious, but very much appreciated.

The atmosphere was charged, and Laura was doing her usual routine of being all very matter-of-fact about things, not smiling much and just asking him about Emma and the paddleboarding. Guy was having a bit more difficulty keeping it together. He knew exactly why he had been summoned to her house and exactly what he would be expected to do to her later, and the pressure was making him a bit light-headed.

Laura had been standing, warming her bum on the Aga. Now she decided it was time to turn up the heat in a different way. Bending down in a way that her mother had specifically told her never to do, with locked straight legs, she reached for a random lid for a Le Creuset casserole dish out of the bottom drawer of the unit. She had an extended rummage in the drawer to be certain she had the correct, random, un-needed lid... and then stood up. Guy looked a bit pained. Quite frankly, she thought it served him right. Two can play at dress-up tease.

Guy suddenly looked confused. "Is there someone else here?" He must have just noticed the voices on the 'Hotel Cheese' selection.

"Yes, indeed there are. I've invited the Peasleys. Let's take our drinks and go through and greet them, shall we? They must be wondering where on earth we are," she said, picking up her phone and taking Guy through to the drawing room. It was empty, of course. He looked confused. She scrolled on her phone. "Here, listen – the voices are on here."

The look of relief on his face once he realised she was joking about the Peasleys, was no less than you'd expect to see on an earthquake survivor. Laura spat her drink out, laughing. She laughed so much her drink started running out of her nose. Guy was more than happy to offer his clean hanky so she could wipe her face.

This had lowered the temperature a bit, and Laura took him back through to the kitchen so they could start eating. One or two light canapes, a measured top-up of their drinks, and it was time for the starter – scallops on black pudding. Laura had once overheard him say how much he adored them. She served them with a pea puree and some pancetta and a drizzle of truffle oil.

Guy took just one bite and gave a kind of shivery moan, thinking, Well that's the 'Angel in the Kitchen' box ticked, and we'll see about the rest later.

"Guy, what I thought I would do now is take you on a tour of the house. Would you like that?"

Guy was very interested. He had worked on the estate all these years and had only ever seen as far as the kitchen and drawing room.

Laura started in the ball room and then moved on to the chart room in the newer part of the building, where on the entire face of one wall was a modern map of the world. In the centre of the room was a large bench, originally used for housing her grandfather's maps and drawings in its drawers. You could easily sit twenty people around it. It was where Laura and Daisy used to come as children to do their homework, and in the holidays, they would use it for crafts. Guy was seriously impressed and said that he would have loved this when he was growing up. It was such an inspiring room.

Next, it was back into the old part of the building and into the beautiful and imposing library with its wood panelling on the walls and fifteenth-century, carved-oak, ceiling panels. At one end stood a grand bookshelf. The centrepiece had a carved-oak pediment on top. The wall that had no windows had more bookshelves and was broken in the centre by a grand marble fireplace. Huge Corinthian pillars supported the ceiling. On the floor: wide, polished oak floorboards and two huge Persian rugs. It truly was a special place, and Guy felt very privileged to be there. Normally, he'd have to buy a ticket to visit this kind of place. In there, Laura subjected Guy to a long and boring talk on the history of the room and the furniture and paintings in it. She was doing this with a twinkle in her eye, and he began to wonder if she might be boring him on purpose, to tease him.

"So, let's now look at the bedrooms." Walking round a series of stairs and corridors, they looked at the various bedrooms. Not surprisingly, many had a tedious story for Laura to tell. "And now, if you'd like to step this way, we will take a look at the master bedroom." Laura had now perfected the formal style of the average country-house tour guide. "And this is the bed where the Lady of the Manor would sleep. As you can see, it's very sumptuous and comfortable." Laura then stood at the side of the bed, facing it. She placed her feet about a foot apart and bent right over, arching her back downwards, placing the palms of her hands on the mattress. "One feature of this bed is its very springy mattress. Look how it bounces; do you see that? Can you see everything okay there? Look, let me show you again," she said, vigorously pushing down on the bed. Momentarily, she felt just like a firefly, wiggling her illuminated bottom in order to attract a mate. Humans aren't really that different, she thought.

She continued to push on the mattress and wiggle, to see if she could attract her mate. Suddenly, out of the corner of her eye, she saw his boots standing right behind her. Then his strong hands gripped her hips. It just felt so natural. She wriggled out from the tight space between him and the bed and stood beside him. His eyes had darkened, and he was breathing heavily. He looked drunk. His nostrils were even flaring. She had successfully ruined him, and now he looked just like a stag – proud and ready to mate. An imposing tower of lean meat, he reminded her of the painting Monarch of the Glen, a huge red stag, his bushy hair like antlers.

"You look a little overcome, sir. May I offer you a glass of water... or something else, perhaps?" Guy reached out and grabbed hold of one of Laura's bum cheeks. "Ooh, no, sir, we can't have that. I'm afraid I'm going to have to report you to the chief guide and have security remove you."

Guy stood there, his face expressionless. "Whatever is the matter, sir. What do you want from me?" Guy whispered softly in her ear. She pulled back from him. "Ooh, no, sir, that's absolutely disgusting. Utterly disgusting. You should be ashamed of yourself speaking to a lady in such a disgusting manner. Look, sir, I have a better idea. Why don't you go downstairs to the kitchen and wait there? I'll slip into a nightie and get into bed then message you, so you can come up and see the Lady of the Manor in her natural setting, in bed."

Guy now looked like he was recovering badly from a lobotomy. He turned towards the door, and Laura

skipped alongside him. She gave him a hard smack
on his pert bottom when he got to the doorway. He
attempted a confident smile, and she giggled.

Once he was gone, she set about trying to remove
her jodhpurs. They were stuck to her like paint,
and she was very glad he wasn't there to see her
wrestling her way out of them. All the time, Laura
was sniggering to herself about how Guy looked so
totally ruined with lust. It had been a joy to watch.
Sprucing herself up, she slipped into a cream satin
and lace camisole with cami-knickers and got into
bed.

Ready, she messaged

Back came a raging-bull icon on her phone.

Laura waited. She looked at the large photo
beside her bed. It was of Monica, a black-and-white
portrait of her in a silver frame, taken when they
first met. Monica had even had the gall to sign her
name across it. She had been giving them away to
her friends after one of her gigs. You couldn't quite
tell if she was smiling or frowning, and just like the
Mona Lisa, her eyes would follow you round the
room wherever you went. Laura loved it, though,
and she grinned at Monica, knowing how proud she
would be of the way she was teasing Guy.

Laura grabbed a book and pretended to read,
wearing some gold-rimmed reading glasses. Just
then, the sound of floorboards creaking announced
Guy's entrance to the room.

Whilst Laura had been wrestling with her jodhpurs, he'd been out to the car and brought his overnight bag into the kitchen, making his own transformation for the occasion.

Looking up from her book, she said, "Oooh, you're a smart boy, aren't you?" He was wearing blue-and-white striped pyjamas. They were so new she could still see the creases. He really was making a magnificent effort. Then she noticed he had his toothbrush in his hand. It was so cute. "Come and stand by my bed, please. I like your pyjamas – they're lovely, but I'm going to ask you to take them off now. Please, fold them up and put them over the back of the chair. Don't worry, you can change back into them later... That's good. Now I'd like you to walk up and down the room." Guy walked a route around the enormous suite. Laura watched intently, then suddenly became curious about something. "Hey, hang on, how come you have an all-over tan?"

"Down the far end of Green Velvet Lake, you can't be seen. I love to go down there when the morning mist is clearing, to paddleboard." She imagined him there just like the painting, Piper at the Gates of Dawn, naked, at one with nature, standing there, gliding along on his board, in all his manly glory, his lovely hair rippling with each stroke of the paddle.

"Okay, keep walking, please." It was fun to have him endlessly walk around the large bedroom suite in the nude with all his rigid glory on display, watching his powerful leg muscles contracting and relaxing. He even had a confident, artistic way of walking. It was a little bit catwalk, in style. Such a contrast to the usual impression of a scruffy git he gave when wandering around the estate in his baggy jeans. "Okay, thank you, that will do for now. Right, pyjamas on and into bed, please." Laura took a quick glance at his fingers to confirm a suspicion, as she had another interlude planned for later.

Guy was just marvelling at the paradise world he had fallen into, clambering into bed with the delectable Laura, when it all came crashing down around him. He had spotted the menacing framed picture of McStrachan glaring at him, her eyes following him. Until that moment, he'd had no idea she was friends with Laura. He should have known his luck tonight would run out at some point, and the woeful memory of their date together rushed into his thoughts. He could hear her hissing at him like a snake, "You useless git. You dick-splash."

Guy drew close to Laura and petted her a bit. She lay back, dreamy-eyed. He very gently lay on top of her, kind of crab-walked his way over her and turned diagonally. Reaching out of bed with his right leg, he found the bedside unit with his toes and kicked McStrachan in the face, knocking her down. He then carefully made the return journey, passing over Laura as though she were a speed bump.

"Guy, what's going on?" Laura had never encountered this particular move in the Karma Sutra.

"Nothing… I'm fine. Just a bit of cramp in my calf muscle."

"Cramp! We can't have that. Would you like me to massage it? Look, why don't I get you a glass of water? That ought to help." Laura dashed off to the en-suite to get one.

In the meantime, Guy grabbed McStrachan and shoved her down the side of the drawers. Laura returned, and he took a sip, but naturally didn't want more. The very last thing he needed would to be to want the loo right in the middle of anything.

Commotion over, they both settled back into bed, ready to attempt the mating ritual once again. Laura knew Monica would be proud of how she was handling things. Guy, meanwhile, was determined to shed his vacuous 'dick-splash' image. He'd make McStrachan proud as well. The couple's intentions were now on a conflicting path, as they both fought to be 'in charge'.

Guy slid his hand right down the front of Laura's top. "Hey, mister. Who do you think you are, rummaging around in there like that? Santa? I'm half expecting you to pull out a kaleidoscope or an orange or something. Hands out now!" she shouted in a harsh but feminine voice. Laura was loving it. Monica would piss herself if she could see this.

Based upon her earlier observation, Laura let out a fake scream. "What the heck? Just look at those nails. You dirty, dirty little boy." She well and truly had something on him now. Leaping out of bed, she grabbed him by the ear and led him off to the en-suite. Once in there, she found a nail file. "Right, use the end of that to get right under those nails, and you make them spotless, do you understand? And don't you ever get into my bed again with hands like that. I don't want them coming anywhere near me. Do you understand?" she shouted at him. He nodded, and got on with the job, whilst she stood staring deep into his eyes.

Out came all the soil and the automotive grease, and whilst he was working his way along all ten fingers, it finally dawned on him why a woman might not want exploring fingers to be loaded with bacteria. Her Freudian slip, however, had pleased him, when she had said, And don't you ever get into my bed again with hands like that, clearly showing that there might well be a next time. The prospect filled Guy with a sense of well-being. He picked up the bar of Pear's soap and lathered up the palms of his hands. What a complete idiot he felt. Fancy coming to bed with hands like that. "Laura, I'm really sorry."

"It's okay," she said softly as she stroked his hair, "get your hands dried now, and we'll say no more about it".

They settled back into bed again. She had spent the evening teasing him and playing games, but he had loved all of her attention to detail, her creativity and her play-acting. The mood was uplifting and fun, and they ascended together to a place of heavenly bliss.

****

Laura woke from her short snooze. She lay there, feeling the profound nature of the situation. They had just become one. Guy was proving to be an interesting contrast to her usual bed-mate: Monica. Although she and Monica were both very hetero, they loved each other, and the absence of sex in their relationship made for a great simplicity.

Reaching out, Laura could feel Guy's hairy, muscular arm. He was different, though. He was a powerful baby-making machine, and they had now just become one flesh. But to make a marriage work, they would need to become 'one' emotionally, spiritually, financially and aspirationally. In her haste to solve the problem of a two-year stint of loneliness, since things had fallen apart with Mike, Laura had taken on a fresh set of problems which would require some careful contemplation.

Guy lay next to her. He couldn't quite believe that he had just shagged the Lady of the Manor. Laura was a truly fantastic experience. He'd been through a bit of a dry patch recently. He'd had a good sniff around Emma last month, but he didn't really see her as sexual. Kaz was good, though on the Dana McLendon scale, she was a seven hot, but an eight crazy. Then there was Tish. She was only a five hot, but a four crazy. Monica would have been a ten hot and a ten crazy – clearly in the danger zone, which, according to McLendon, is for redheads, strippers and anyone called Tiffany. On this matrix, anything below a five crazy is classed as being in the unicorn zone. They don't exist. Below a four crazy and it's probably a dude you're talking to. Laura would be a ten hot and a seven crazy, but that was only because of the delightful crazy games that she loved to play, like the embarrassing presentation interviews, the frustrating tour guide tease and the catwalk experience. In reality, Laura was only a five crazy, and that placed her firmly in the wife zone. Guy understood that. Unfortunately, though, Guy was currently betrothed to the person whose company he loved most: himself.

Laura was sassy, and last night and the journey leading up to it was probably the most fantastic sexual experience he had ever had. It seemed weird that he was now in bed with her, having known her all these years. Guy had no idea if they were compatible. He tended to stay away from all the poncey stuff, like hunt balls and dressing-up, but he truly admired Laura's efforts to ditch all those aristocratic trappings. He just lay there dreaming.

Fully awake now, Laura thought that she really ought to try to become friends with Guy. He must be starving by now, so she should probably get her knickers back on and fetch him some food.

Laura sat up. She reached for her antique crystal atomiser with gold puffer and used it to gently freshen herself. Some of the wonderful light, fruity, ginger smelling spray landed on Guy, this esoteric feminine routine fascinating him.

In every way, Laura felt re-humanised. She felt vital again. She felt wanted, and she felt her life button had just been switched back on.

Guy sneezed. "Sorry, that might have been me," she said, climbing on top of him to kiss him. "You've been a very good hard-working boy, haven't you? I expect you need to be fed and watered now." Laura handed him the glass of water which he gulped down appreciatively. Was there no end to her thoughtfulness? thought Guy.

Down in the kitchen, Laura assembled the pre-prepared club sandwiches and brought them upstairs.

Guy was starving, so he really hoped that she would leave some of hers. She was posh, so he guessed she would never eat the last one. All he had to do was offer to take the plate back downstairs afterwards, and then scoff her leftover sandwich in the corridor, just leaving the plate on a windowsill somewhere because in reality he had no intention of going all the way to the kitchen.

Laura placed the tray on the bed. The sandwiches were already divided onto two side plates, because piggies were no idiots when it came to food. Guy picked up a sandwich and politely broke a piece off. He fed it to Laura as a romantic gesture. But she was on to him. She thought to herself, You double-crossing bastard. I bet you're planning to feed me one of yours and then take two back in return. He looked just that sort of a cad – exactly the type who might take more than his fair share of meat at a Viking restaurant banquet.

By the time they had eaten the sandwiches, drunk the Louis Cristal and eaten the Belgian chocolates, they were both stuffed, anyway.

****

Laura woke in the morning to the sensation of Guy stroking her arm. He was sitting up and gazing at her. It reminded her of the Aerosmith song 'I Don't Want to Miss a Thing', and the lines about not wanting to fall asleep in case of missing anything.

Guy kind of felt this way too, although he also felt a pressing need to demonstrate his fitness levels to Laura again.

After lovemaking, they lay together, divinely entwined, and he said exactly what she wanted to hear.

"I don't know what you fancy doing today? But we could get the boards out and paddle along to Compton Mill, have some lunch there, and then deflate the boards, catch a taxi back, and maybe this evening stroll into town along the canal path. I hear there's some good musicians playing there tonight. Maybe meet up with Garth and Gren?"

It was already looking like being a boiling hot day, and Laura's heart soared. She pulled back the bedroom curtains and opened the largest of the sash windows. A warm breeze swept into the room, carrying with it the scent of fennel and camomile from the garden. She glanced across and saw the shared joy on Guy's face.

Guy decided Laura was having too much fun, so he started a play fight with her. She made a strong effort at first but ended up losing badly, pinned down and with her arm up behind her back. Kneeling up on the bed now, she rubbed her face. Two cabbage white butterflies flew in through the window, dancing intensely around each other. It seemed that the whole of nature was celebrating creation today.

Chapter Thirteen

—•—

A Fete Worse than Death

Carmen was working, as usual, through her wide range of tasks. She had been with the Stanhope family at Chalkewood for nearly two decades now, and the family loved her for her friendship and loyalty. Carmen was the height of discretion, and the family knew that they could trust her with their innermost thoughts without fear of them being spread around the village. She was stylish and always cheerful, and she liked to dress fashionably rather than wear overalls. She also came with the bonus that her devoted husband Jeff was an engineer, and he could always be relied upon him to fix something in the event of a disaster whilst the family were away. He'd also water the plants and top up the swimming pool chemicals, as part of the bargain.

"Hello, Laura, how are you?"

"Fine thank you, Carmen, and you?"

"Fine thanks, it's just them others." It was her catchphrase, and they'd always have a giggle over it.

"Laura, the Chalkewood Festival. How's it going?"

Laura laughed nervously and gave a vague answer. Asking the question was Carmen's way of warning Laura that she was behind with the arrangements. The festival, in its current form, had been held every year since the end of World War II. A gift to the village from the estate. It was one of many traditions that still survived at Chalkewood, and it was part of the glue that held the communities of Hampden and Chalkewood together.

Although Teddy and Tice strived to escape their life of privilege and any appearance of it, they always felt they had a responsibility to preserve such much-loved and popular traditions. The villagers all had a part to play and could apply to have their own stall, which would then be their own responsibility. The proceeds from the event were traditionally split between the Anglican church and the village. Teddy would open the fete and the Lord-Lieutenant of the county, Lt Col Peter Cockcrow Retd. would represent Her Majesty, The Queen.

Laura's main problem with the festival, however, was that it had a tendency to bring out the worst in a very small minority of the community. These people tended to be of Teddy and Tice's generation, and although they lived in modest accommodation, some in houses on the Chalkewood estate, they had a fanatical obsession with being 'posh'. They would speak in an affected way, more so in 'polite company', and would, almost without exception, dress like Toad of Toad Hall, women included.

The Stanhopes and their estate staff referred to sufferers of this condition as 'Toads'. Gordon Peasley, as estate manager, however, avoided using the term at management meetings. It cut a little too close to home, as he was friendly with most of the Toads, mainly because he ran the estate like his own personal fiefdom from which he would go around dispensing recognition, social access and favour.

Laura continued her parents' efforts to discourage this unhealthy Toadocracy. It was a tricky gig, though, because if the family went too far and broke any rules or traditions, it would make them look like bad custodians. Laura had created a private Facebook Group called, Things You Hear at Chalkewood to which she had invited the family and trusted staff. Laura administered it under the fake profile name of 'Unfortunate Girl'. This epithet had been taken from a stallholder who once called her that as a teenager, when Laura had dared to argue with the crazy old bat for only giving her change from fifty pence when she'd paid with a one-pound note.

Posts in recent years had included:

"Don't you know who I am?"

"It's such a shame that Oxbridge doesn't focus on the classics anymore." From someone who had dropped out of high school.

"I think you've come to the wrong place. The town's that way." From a volunteering Toad to a member of the public who turned up at the gates not wearing waxed cotton clothing.

Carmen was the only sane voice amongst the volunteers on the Festival Committee that Gordon had created. She was there because Laura insisted, and she was Laura's eyes and ears. It was highly unusual for an estate manager to run such a committee, but Teddy and Tice had allowed it, as it enabled them to stay impartial.

Reaching in her handbag, Carmen brought out a list of things for Laura's attention, and they both sat down over a coffee and discussed the outstanding arrangements. At that moment, Miranda Chilvers from Slater Scotton & Emery called. She had two new prospects interested in buying the estate, and she wondered if she might bring them to the festival, as it could be an ideal opportunity to showcase the estate at its best. Laura had the phone on speaker so Carmen could hear.

Miranda went on to explain that one was a nice chap who had won the EuroMillions Lottery and the other was a Russian oligarch. "It's okay, he hasn't been sanctioned," Miranda added, before saying, "and you don't have to worry, Laura, both of them are married."

Laura was furious.

Carmen knew exactly what that was about, and when Laura came off the phone, she said, "Oooh, I bet you wish you could climb down the phone and smack her face. Stuck-up bitch."

The Stanhopes had made the festival as autonomous for the participants as they could, and now their role was mostly symbolic. Tice, however, had loathed the thought she would ever have to stand up and say over the PA, "I now declare this festival open."

****

Laura had now had quite enough of sitting around for one day, so she decided it was time for something active. She had an overwhelming desire to take her horse out so she could hunt Pengersick down and generally annoy and tease him. In her excitement, she got a bit carried away, though, putting on jodhpurs, her dark blue riding jacket, silk scarf and a lady's top-hat riding hat, with a tulle veil covering her whole face. It was the type of costume normally associated with side-saddle riding . Guy knew nothing about equestrianism, though, and she knew he'd be intimidated by the overall look.

She took a quick trot down the drive: no sign. Then she went through the woods behind August, so she could look into his garden as he sometimes went home for lunch. Again, nothing and no sign of his Land Rover either. Just as she was running out of ideas, she spotted her quarry. There he was, making his way along the perimeter roadway, driving towards the estate's exit. She had to stop him escaping, so she cantered diagonally across the open field to cut him off, only just beating him to the gate.

She managed to have her horse standing stationary, blocking the open lane, when Guy pulled up in front of her. Managing to keep a dead-straight face, she said, "I'll have you know, it's ten miles per hour in here."

"Hi Laura, how are you?"

"It's not 'Laura', it's 'miss' to you when I'm on duty. Now turn off your engine, get out of your vehicle and stand beside it. As I've just told you, Pengersick, the speed limit in here is ten miles per hour. Don't let me catch you speeding again. Don't you smirk at me either, mister. Under the manorial rights of this estate, bestowed upon me, I preside at the Court Baron, and I have the power to summon you, try you and, if necessary, punish you, and I wouldn't hesitate to do it for one moment."

Laura was now getting Honey to do the occasional dressage manoeuvre. She also subtly directed the horse to push Guy around a bit. "Calm down, Honey," pretending the horse was being skittish, though she was following Laura's commands perfectly.

Guy was desperate to get hold of Laura for a quick cuddle and a kiss, but she was miles above him, up on the horse. He was desperately trying to think of a way of getting her to come down, but then he realised it would be pretty pointless as she had that veil over her whole face, and he could see it was fastened around her neck.

"Erm, miss, I was just wondering if perhaps I might be permitted to come round and see you later this evening?"

Laura took out her riding crop, she held it under his chin and tipped his head back so that she could look him in the eye. "You, mister, are just a little too presumptuous."

"Yes, I know I'm being rude, but I'd really like to come and see you, please."

"Well, you can't, because I have Miss McStrachan coming over."

"Oh, okay. Is there any chance I could possibly come over, perhaps after she has gone?"

"How downright impertinent you are. I don't take kindly to the implications of that, and no – it's a sleepover, so Miss McStrachan will be sleeping with me tonight." This was doubly torturous, as Guy already had his issues with McStrachan, and now she'd be taking the place in Laura's bed that he wanted to occupy.

"No, of course, I'm very sorry. I didn't mean to be so impertinent. When might be a good day?"

"Tomorrow, I'm washing my hair; the day after, I'm washing my hair, and after that, I've no idea. Maybe I'm too busy to see you at all? People who ask don't get, so maybe you should wait to be asked. Maybe that would be the gentlemanly thing to do. Meanwhile, get on with your work and make sure you obey the speed limit on my estate."

With that, she rode off. What an absolute bloody bitch. Guy was crippled with lust for her. He so wanted to yank her down off that horse. He watched as she disappeared into the distance and vowed to get his own back on her, when she was least expecting it.

****

Monica came bounding into the kitchen that evening, all excited like a little puppy. She ran up to Laura, throwing her arms round her with force.

"Hunzie, hunzie, hunzie, hunzie, hunzie." She shook Laura's hand with force. "Congratulations on getting laid. Well done. Now, I want to hear all about it, down to the very last, filthy, minute detail, so don't go selling me short."

Laura took her thumb and used it to wipe Monica's face, which was all grubby from her building site. She put her nose in Monica's hair, and it smelt of stale piss, sweat and Chappie. Laura became a bit tearful. "Hunzie, look at you. When did you last have your beehive down?" Monica didn't answer. "Okay, I've decided. I'm going to run you a bath, give you a good scrub and then re-do your hair for you."

They spent the next five hours in the bathroom whilst Laura told Monica everything. "Oooh, you're a bit naughty. Respect to you, sister, and that bit about you setting off on your horse to go 'bloke-hunting' – that is class and so good that you captured him and put him in his place. In a way, he's like an inmate in your open-prison, and that, madam, is very cool indeed. But I would just be careful. Still waters run deep with men. He will try to punish you back for that. A prime piece of stag meat is never going to be deterred for long, not now the rut has started."

"Yes, I expect he will. I've wound him up to breaking point," said Laura with a mischievous smile.

****

Laura decided working from home was great.

Up with the lark as ever, Monica had left early to go back and feed the Pigs. What a lovely night they had had. Finally, it was Monica who was in awe of Laura, and that felt great. It had also been lovely to hear that Monica had had a great night out recently with her Pigs at this munch thing in Mapelwick, and that they had made lots of new friends of their sort and been encouraged to come to a local club called the Torture Garden, where they were told the 'really interesting' stuff goes on.

Apparently, Monica had also met a new contact. She referred to him as 'Roofer Pig', and it seemed that following recent committal proceedings, he would be getting sentenced to two weeks' jail with hard labour down at Hampden Lodge.

It was a quarter to twelve, and Laura had just checked her shopping list and was thinking about going for a 5k run. She had already put her trackies on and was looking for her socks and shoes.

Suddenly she looked up to see Guy walking in through the kitchen door. "Hello, miss, I've got a rather pressing matter that needs attention. Don't worry, I won't keep you long." He walked over and kissed her hard on the mouth, tongue exploring as she responded, his hand sliding down the front of her trackies and into her knickers.

Brushing everything off the large, heavy, wooden kitchen table. He lifted her up and sat her on it. In a very matter-of-fact way, he pulled her trackies off and gently pushed her back onto the table. She looked up at him. "You disgusting bastard. You untamed filthy animal."

Later, in between breaths, she said, "I hope you're keeping a note of the time, because I'm going to have this deducted from your pay."

Getting up, she cleaned up and put her trackies back on. "My legs are all wobbly now. They're completely shot. I hope you're happy with what you've gone and done. That's my run ruined because of you. Selfish isn't the word."

Guy stood at the door, wiping his sweaty maw with the back of his hand. "I think that makes us equal now, miss," he said as he opened the door and walked off.

****

Tuesday

Laura had completed all of her Teams meetings for the day. She then remembered that she needed to make the house secure. So, she locked the kitchen door. Guy often snooped about around this time. In fact, there he was now. She went over and waved at him through the French windows, before going to put the dishwasher on.

She saw him walking towards the kitchen door. He tried the handle.

"I'm sorry, I've locked it." She smiled and walked away. Suddenly, she noticed him walking round the house. The side door! She raced through to it and just managed to turn the key in the lock before he started rattling the handle.

Safe and secure, she walked back into the kitchen, where she saw him standing at the large French windows. She walked over and put her hand on the glass, and he did the same. They kissed each other through the glass. Reaching down, she pulled up her bra and her top, and pushed herself against the glass. That'll teach him. She took out her phone: 2–1 to me. Now why don't you go and get on with some work?

****

It was mid-week now. Mainly a clear up day. Laura also managed to get a 5k run in without getting captured by Guy, and she was now safely indoors with the all the doors and windows locked. She was having to wait for a document to arrive before she could get on with any more work. Just then, she saw the orange jacket of the postal worker as he walked past the windows in the hall. She opened the door, just as he was looking down, sifting through the letters. It looked like it was all junk mail.

He took a step forwards and put his foot in the doorway. Lifting his cap, he said, "Congratulations, miss, looks like you just got male."

Guy? He walked in, closed the door behind him and stood there with his arms folded, staring her straight in the eye. She took a breath. "Okay, fine. Fair cop. I've been careless, haven't I? Where do you want me?"

"Kitchen table again," he said, taking her by the arm.

Later, and with all postal formalities now completed, he tugged on his postal worker's hat. "Well, ma'am, you have yourself a good day." He went to walk away, before turning back. "That'll be two-all, now."

Laura was so angry. She was very competitive and hated losing any type of game to a man. But fair do's – he'd thought it all through really well.

****

Thursday

Laura had been very security-minded right from the start. All locks and windows were checked. She knew he'd try again, but no matter how much she racked her brains, she couldn't second-guess what he might try. By three in the afternoon, it seemed obvious that he wasn't going to make a fresh attempt. She gave up expecting anything and sat down to watch the news – the usual manmade disasters of war and famine. The village had even done its bit recently by taking in a displaced Muslim family. What crazy times.

Laura went for a top-up of tea. Good grief. There on the drive was one of the refugee family members, all clothed in black and wearing the full niqab. She was carrying a basket and seemed a bit lost. Probably couldn't find the entrance. Laura hurried to the door and put her hand on the lock.

No, no, no, silly girl. Stop! she thought.

She opened the letter box. "Hello, can I help you? What do you want?"

"Aw, yes, I'm a very poor person," came the feeble reply, as the veiled person came right up to the door.

"You tasteless, fraudulent git." Laura shouted through the letterbox.

Just then something came through the letterbox that she was quite sure had never been mailed to Chalkewood before. She looked at it. Hmm, it would be a shame to let that go to waste, she thought.

Some time later, as Guy was regathering his composure, Laura looked through the letterbox. "I think that kind of still makes us even, doesn't it?"

Guy then noticed that someone was standing right behind him. It was Connie Nugent, the churchwarden from St. Georges, the local Anglican church, in the process of delivering the church newsletter.

Always delighted to walk the long drive – one never knows, one might get the chance to hobnob with someone important – Connie had seen the 'Muslim woman' from a while back and had approached her with curiosity. "Hello," she said, loudly so that woman would understand. "Do you speak English?"

Guy shook his head, kind of contradicting 'herself', and started making all kinds of strange hand gestures.

"You speaky English?" She put the newsletter through the letterbox. "Bloody foreign bastards. Put them on the next boat back, I say," she said under her breath as she walked off.

Laura opened the door. Guy came in and slipped out of his devout clothing. They hugged, and he swayed her from side to side. "Guy, I'm fed up with games. Take me away for the weekend, will you?"

"Ah, sorry, I can't. I'm going to a horticultural symposium in Harrogate at the weekend."

"Tell them to shove it?"

"Well, nice idea, except that I'm doing one of the talks."

"Take me with you!"

"Erm, well, no, there'd be a lot of waiting about and hanging around. Total waste of your time." Guy wasn't going to be persuaded.

****

Saturday

Laura was somewhat pacified that Guy's symposium was going to be broadcast live online. She would perhaps have it on in the kitchen. His lecture was due to start at 11 a.m.

It was a grey day which suited her mood. Had it been a beautiful day, his absence would have been an even more painful sacrifice. The morning came and went. Guy's presentation was incredible. Laura felt it was equally as good as anything she could do. She was almost jealous, but in a good way.

The whole event was being headed up by a Professor Mariette Kreutzmann. She introduced Guy and could be seen chatting to him afterwards. Laura Googled her. She had an impressive resume for someone of the same age as her. Guy must be impressed. The delegates got up to leave, and Guy left the auditorium with the professor.

Laura called Guy. He didn't answer. Texting instead, she asked how things were going. Still no answer. Just then, she had an unexpected pang of jealousy. This woman would have a lot to offer Guy, not least in terms of profession, but possibly romantically, too. The afternoon session started. Laura casually looked in. Guy was now sitting next to her. This went on throughout the day, and Laura went to bed not having heard from Guy. She lay there feeling unhappy, but surely, her concerns were all in her head? She had sown this seed of pain all by herself; her jealous agony was of her own making.

****

Professor Kreutzmann fascinated Guy. She knew so much about his favourite subject and was involved with some truly fascinating and ground-breaking projects. Over lunch, she told him to call her Mariette, and she showed him the details of a project she was about to start, out in the Cloud Mountains of Irian Jaya. She even went so far as to offer him a job, one that would partly involve teaching. Guy was totally blown away by it all. Professor Mariette was South African, and during their discussions, she alluded to the fact that she'd had a tough upbringing that had been borderline abusive, and it had given her a slightly hard edge.

It had been a long day and the concluding lecture was mainly about politics, so Guy went for an hour's snooze. Coming back down, he bumped into Mariette again. She said to him, "Oh, hello. Long day, eh? I'm quite parched. Come and let me buy you a drink."

The professor was the same age as Guy. She had big red hair, wore nice clothes and had a lot of gravitas about her. She had an entourage that had followed her around during the day. They were all women, and to Guy, they just appeared like verbose underlings, all short-haired and trying to look like men. They were the total opposite to the professor who was very feminine.

One of the entourage, who was quite an activist, came up to her. "Professor, would you be willing to come over to our group and do a Q and A with us?"

She got a quick answer. "Look, this is my time now. Do you understand? Now just piss off." Guy was completely shocked. Mariette didn't even flinch, then took a sip of her drink. "I get this all the time in my job. Those silly tits just don't get it. They're young, I guess. Look, how would you like to join me for supper? I'd really love to have a bit of mature, adult company". Sensing Guy's slight reticence, she added, "Come on, I'll pay. This is all on expenses, you know."

Guy agreed to have supper, and Mariette went upstairs to change. He only had one set of clothes, but he decided to have a shower. He had meant to call Laura, but time was running short now.

Mariette was turned up for dinner looking even smarter, fabulous even, and Guy simply had to compliment her. "You're looking beautiful, Mariette."

They took their seats, and Guy noticed she was now wearing some rather intimidating, long, sharp-looking false nails. They were bright red and matched with her hair. Guy remembered the hot vs crazy matrix. She would be right there in the danger zone, up there with the strippers and people called Tiffany.

Mariette talked effusively about her subject, and Guy was mesmerised. He couldn't really contribute and just sat there making uncomfortable comparisons between her and Laura in his mind. After all, it wasn't like he was married, or anything like that. He was free to do what he wanted. Both she and Laura looked great, same age, but Mariette was an expert in his main interest, plus the whole Irian Jaya thing was irresistible. It's all so strange. This time last year, I was so lonely, and now there's all this top-end totty to choose from.

"Guy, just think, we could end up on the other side of the world together, working on the same project.

You'd be working strictly under my supervision, and everything would be just dandy."

It was a complete no-brainer, surely? Guy couldn't understand, though, what force was making him bend to this crushing temptation. It would take enormous strength to fight it. But he couldn't shake the thought that he had never banged a redhead before.

"You're quite a pretty man, aren't you? And you have such beautiful eyes. Look, it's getting late. May I ask you to walk me safely to my room, and we can chat tomorrow?"

Guy happily agreed.

They stepped into the lift and pressed the button for the sixth floor. As the doors closed, Mariette leant forwards, held Guy softly by the face and whispered in his ear. What she said was disgusting. Guy panicked. The doors opened on the sixth floor, and they had to get out.

Guy said, "Look, I'm flattered in so many ways, but there's no easy way to say this – next year I'm getting married to my boyfriend Pete."

"Pah, well, ain't that a thing? Life can just be so disappointing at times. What a shame. What a shame." Mariette shook her head. "Look, you gay people are pretty broad-minded, right? You don't get to be gay without seeing a bit of the world, do you? Well, Guy, I'd like you to come with me to my room. I want you to get undressed and walk around with no clothes on, whilst I lie on the bed and masturbate. Is that clear?"

"Ha, that's a coincidence! That's exactly what my girlfr—" Guy stopped, realising what he'd said.

"You lying little bastard." She led him along the corridor and opened the bedroom door. "Get in!" She bundled him in and closed the door.

"Right, pants off now. Do it." Guy sat on the bed and shrugged his shoulders. Mariette stood by the bed, blocking the route to the door.

"Pants off now, or I am going to scream and scream and scream." His blood ran cold. This must be what it feels like to be a victim of sexual assault. It was not good. Things had turned really nasty now. He looked at her with all her bright red hair. Maybe God paints them that colour, he wondered, as a warning! In nature, red signals danger. And the McLendon's matrix never lies.

"I will count to ten." She started counting. Guy picked up the bedside lamp and broke the bulb in it so the room went dark. He dived out past her, got the door open, and ran. Just as he left the room, he felt her claws scratch down his back.

Jogging down the corridor and looking over his shoulder to make sure she wasn't pursuing him, Guy arrived at the lift. Thankfully, it was still at that floor, so he hopped in quick. The doors opened at his floor, and he looked out with trepidation, half expecting to see her standing there. Once in his room, he checked the en-suite, then checked the room door was locked.

He sat on the bed and rubbed his face with his hands. Obviously, there had been no job offer. She had just been amusing herself with that nonsense to seduce him. The whole thing had simply been a boredom cure for her. He checked to see if she had had any way of knowing what he looked like before she chose him as a speaker, and he realised that there was a fair chance he had been selected just for his appearance.

Clearly, he couldn't risk meeting her the following morning. So, throwing his few items back in his day bag, he vowed to get up and leave early at 6 a.m.

He didn't sleep very well that night and let out an audible sigh of relief the moment he was in his car ready to leave. He jumped with shock when he noticed a shadow just behind his driver's door, but it turned out to only be a lamp post.

Very pleased to be seeing the hotel shrinking in his rear-view mirror, he made his way out onto the service road. He briefly used the rear-view mirror to confirm that his rear seats were empty and then pressed the door-lock button. He wasn't sure what he was feeling, but it felt an awful lot like he imagined mild PTSD would feel.

Service station breakfasts can be hit-or-miss, but this one was great, the best. Guy sat there with a coffee refill and checked the time: it was 9 a.m.

Hopefully not too early to call Laura on a Sunday. He started with a message, but she face-timed him straight back. He found he couldn't wait to see her in a couple of hours' time. He looked at her honest and well-meaning face, as it froze on his phone at the end of the call. It was a really expressive and appealing image. He screenshotted it and saved it as his screensaver.

Chapter Fourteen

— • —

Chalkewood Festival

The day of the Chalkewood Festival had arrived. Sliding open the sash window in her bedroom, Laura could feel, even at 7 a.m., it was already warm outside. She poured herself a black coffee and climbed back into bed. Sitting up, amongst a sea of soft pillows, she opened the festival document on her phone and ran down her list of responsibilities and the timetable for the day. In Teddy and Tice's absence, this was the first time she would be the senior authority figure present.

Everything had been precisely organised. Peasley had made a professional job of things, but in a way that suited his own agenda. Carmen, however, had ensured Laura hadn't been side-lined. She had also just arrived at the house to prepare Laura for the day ahead. One of Carmen's many talents was hairdressing, and she had come to give Laura a shampoo and set and to help her get dressed in all her finery.

Carmen knew everything that went on at Chalkewood, and as she was leaving, she gave Guy a disapproving look when she found him loitering about round the kitchen door. Using her official house key, she locked the door behind her as she left. "The Lady of the Manor is busy. She won't want to see you."

Ironically, though, what Laura genuinely needed for the event was an official partner, and she didn't have one. It was a real shame that she wasn't in a position to use Guy.

She unlocked and opened the side door. "What do you want?"

"Oh, hi, Laura. Wow, you look absolutely stunning."

"Stop right there, Pengersick. Do not speak, do not touch and do not cross this line," she said, drawing an imaginary line backwards and forwards with the side of her hand. "I don't want anything smudged or creased."

Guy reached towards her. "What underwear are you wearing? Can I have a quick look?"

"Aaawh! Oh, my word, you did all three. You spoke, you touched, you stepped... Look, here, today, you will not address me as 'Laura', in public, and if you have to address me on the PA, you will do so formally. Is that clear? Now get out."

Laura's first job was to inspect the stalls. To do this, she would be escorted by Lt. Col. Peter

Cockcrow Retd., Lord-Lieutenant of the County, standing resplendent in full-dress military uniform. He knew her father well and was a friend of the Peasleys, and he was infamous for having once told someone off at work for wearing brown shoes in the City of London, when brown should only be worn West of Knightsbridge. He was busy now greeting important women guests and going mwah, mwah to them, as one doesn't directly kiss a lady who is wearing a hat. He saw Laura and, removing his white glove, he came forwards to shake her hand, as someone in her position would consider kissing to be over-familiar.

They made some small talk and then went on to make the inspection. The first stall was St. George's. They, traditionally, were the joint beneficiaries of the festival proceeds. The Rector, the Reverend Giles Pottinger, easily recognisable from a distance by his white clerical collar, saw them coming and stepped out smartly from behind the stall to walk towards them. He would be opening the festival soon with Laura, so naturally, he didn't wish to be seen getting inspected like some ordinary stallholder. Gordon Peasley was one of the churchwardens, but as estate manager, he didn't want to get 'inspected' either, so he'd made himself scarce at that same moment. Connie Nugent, the other churchwarden, was there and was more than keen to hobnob with the inspection team.

She didn't know how to address Laura, so she skipped any introductions. "Ooh hello, I was over your way recently. One of the Muslim ladies was on your doorstep, quite a tall lady. She seemed a tad confused. I did try to help her, but I'm afraid that Islam isn't one of the languages that I speak terribly well. The lady seemed to be pushing something through your letterbox with her hips. It must have been quite large, or long, or something."

Reverend Giles had now loosely attached himself to the inspection team, and the trio had moved on to the next stall which was called 'Digital Source' – the name emblazoned in graffiti-style lettering on a large board. It was the work of YouTubers, Tommo and Benji, who were there in their expensive-looking Blue Ninja costumes. Colonel Cockcrow didn't know what to make of them – he thought they looked a right pair of oiks and very much the type who might wear brown shoes the wrong side of Knightsbridge. Even Laura was slightly nervous, as the Ninjas had both seen her bare breasts and had rated them like they were some exhibit in the garden produce contest. She covered her cleavage with her shawl as they approached.

Tommo was keen to explain his stall, and Laura translated what he was saying for the benefit of the Colonel. He was keen to 'get down with the kids', but he couldn't understand what full fibre broadband was or what benefits the Ninja's digital vision promised for the village. Both he and the Rector had more than sufficient 'bandwidth' to read the Daily Mail online each day, anyway, so they were both a bit non-plussed by the suggested need for any change.

The Colonel then gave a monologue in his very loud and tuneful voice on what life was like before the internet. Laura looked quite shocked when, in a stellar moment of crassness, he asked the Ninjas if they were 'purveyors of graphic art' or whether they had managed to find employment locally? Not aware that they earnt three times his final salary from the army. Laura put her finger to her lips, winked at them, and the Ninjas stifled their smiles.

They moved on. "Now, this next stall is one that I think is particularly promising, and its owner is doing some splendid kind of presentation on horticulture for us this afternoon." The Colonel approached the stallholder. "Good morning, Mr Pengersick. I do hope I have pronounced your name correctly. Penger...? Ah, right, Pergerhousearthen. Oh, I do apologise, I should have known that." Laura had to bite her lip. "Ma'am, may I introduce you to Mr... erm, er... the stallholder?"

Laura introduced herself to Mr Pengersick using a particularly exaggerated upper-class accent in which 'oh hello' becomes 'air-hair-lair'. By now, the Colonel and the Rector were busy chatting.

Looking down her nose, she engaged Pengersick in some small talk. "You're a horticulturist, I hear. I do rather like receiving flowers myself. May I just say how delighted I am to see that you have managed to lose the rampant erection that I saw in your pants earlier? I do hope that you continue to engage in self-control today." Guy could see the Colonel approaching. He reached out to shake Laura's hand. "No, Pengersick, one does not shake hands and one does not ask questions. I ask the questions and you just stand there and grin like the depraved beast you are. Anyway, do carry on."

The rest of the stalls were more minor in nature, so they didn't attract the same level of inspection – things like bric-a-brac, apple bobbing and splat the rat, plus numerous others. One spectacular exception was the 'Houdini Challenge', where Paul Woodman, the pastor at the local evangelical church, would be put in a straight-jacket and hauled up into the air by a crane, the atmospheric voiceover would then explain that this was a metaphor for how we can all throw off the mental chains in our own lives and achieve true freedom. He hadn't arrived yet, so he was spared the inspection.

Laura spotted Carmen and Jeff. They were taking round a trolley and giving free tea, coffee, and Danish pastries to all the stallholders. Laura looked on hungrily at all the delicious food, but she was on show and couldn't go filling her face. Carmen knew this and put a pastry in a plastic bag. When nobody was watching, she opened Laura's handbag and slipped it in.

Thankfully, the inspection was over now. Laura vowed she would not end up doing all this again. There simply had to be a more contemporary way of meeting the stallholders, but she couldn't think of one. The trio made their way to the PA tent where Wayne Hollingdale was in residence as MC. He was wearing an extremely pro-looking set of headphones and was welcoming festival goers with a rundown of the day's events to a backing track of 'At the Sign of the Swingin' Cymbal', but nobody was sure if that choice of music was meant to be ironic or not – it sounded great though, and he had the pauses and the fading in and out just perfect.

Wayne had discovered at an early age that he had been born with a voice for broadcasting, and for years he had worked his way around hospital radio and slots like this today, all of which he did for free.

It was now one minute to ten, and everyone was in position, ready for the festival to open. Wayne called for the attention of the crowd and then handed over to the Rector, who began by thanking the Lord for this wonderful day and for the beautiful weather, before blessing the festival. It was then Laura's turn to take the stand. Public speaking was Laura's forte, and she made a short, endearing speech, starting first with welcoming friends old and new to her home, Chalkewood. She thanked the organisers and stallholders, and she presented a bouquet to Carmen. "So, ladies and gentlemen, without further ado, it now gives me great pleasure to declare this festival open."

Initial duties now complete, Laura was at a bit of a loose end. The formality of the event meant she couldn't just wander about on her own without a consort or a companion. Guy would have been ideal, but he hadn't yet been officially presented to the world as her partner. Laura was also having to exercise some control over her relationship with him. Because they were, in effect, next-door neighbours, there had been an enormous temptation just to have him move in with her. But, she knew, in the circumstances, this would be considered inappropriate... and she also took great pleasure in rationing his access to her.

Fortunately, Guy was quite relaxed about their living arrangements. One of the things she liked about him was that he was happy in his own company but still had plenty of friends to call on if he wanted to be sociable. She knew that there was many an evening, though, when he'd get quite frustrated having her only a few hundred yards away but behind locked doors. She knew because he'd text her to say so, and she'd increase his frustration by face-timing him for some saucy fun and then remind him that all her doors were locked just before she cut the call.

Just then, Peasley spotted her and started making his way over. He had his son Julian with him, both looking very earnest in their pursuit of her. Laura already knew Julian, but clearly Peasley had spotted a great opportunity here for him. "Ahh, Laura, you know Julian, don't you? Why not show him around a little?"

Julian really was an outrageously bombastic Toad. He was bloody posh and then some. However, she had to admit he was very well turned-out and dapper-looking in his regulation tweeds. Quite the country gent, and socially aspirational with it. It was painfully obvious what his agenda was, but Laura was pretty sure she had things under control.

They promenaded around the festival together for the morning whilst she held on to his arm. Julian was loving it, his proud oily face and greased-back hair soaking up the sun. Laura on his arm. Seeing and being seen. It was a glorious day, and Laura could hear Guy's faint voice on a PA system, as he enthused the gathered youngsters with his interactive session on overseas aid.

Over the other side of the festival site, the Mapelwick Town Silver Band, in their smart blue uniforms, played a medley of uplifting music. Meanwhile, Julian was making a full-on effort to impress Laura and was adroitly moving from one boastful story to another. He didn't ask Laura anything about herself, but that suited her perfectly.

"Julian, I'd very much like to see the horticultural stand. Can we go there, please?" He enthusiastically obliged and escorted her in that direction. Guy was on the stand with a couple of his helpers, Chris and Dave. He had just finished another well-attended presentation to rapturous applause, and they were tidying up in preparation for the afternoon session. Guy knew the whole deal with Julian, so he had a wry smile on his face when Julian arrived escorting Laura.

Laura positioned herself right in front of the stand and started flirting with Julian. She placed her hand on his chest and gently rubbed it as she talked to him whilst gazing into his eyes. Julian had no idea what the real story was and looked boastfully across at Guy.

She turned to chat to Guy. "Good morning, Pengersick. I hear that your talk thing went reasonably well."

Julian was now, rather boldly, holding Laura's hand. Just then, Dave and Chris appeared. "Guy, we're off for a quick bevvy."

With a cold look on her face, Laura swung round and said to Julian, "I want a drink as well. Get me one, will you? A Pimm's please and make it a large one." With a full-fat grin on his face, Julian waddled off into the distance towards the bar tent.

Laura walked up to the now empty horticultural stand. She pulled back a canvas sheet and walked into the stock room. "Well, you have about three minutes to do whatever you want, Mr Pengersick." It was like releasing a bag of ferrets. His hands were everywhere. "But don't kiss me. I don't want my face smudged. Just do the dirty stuff."

"I want you tonight," he whispered in her ear.

"Oh, I'm really not sure about that. Julian might be wanting to take me to dinner tonight. You had better stay glued to your phone all day, until we see what Julian decides."

Guy was reasonably sure Laura would contact him, but she was quite high on the crazy scale today, so nothing was certain, and the not knowing was going to drive him mad.

"Right, he's coming back, bless him. Quick, get your hands out and straighten me up."

Julian arrived, looking somewhat pained. It had been a long and wobbly journey, there and back, to buy her an expensive drink.

Miranda Chilvers arrived on the scene. Laura had almost forgotten she was coming. She had Gary Smedley with her, the recent EuroMillions winner and prospective purchaser of the Chalkewood estate. He was in his early sixties, silver-haired and wearing some nice new white trainers and a sleeveless, diamond-patterned golfing jumper in yellow and grey. You couldn't want for a nicer man. He looked like the cat that had got the cream, though, and was very interested in everyone and everything. He spoke with an endearing West Midlands accent, and he explained to Laura and Julian how he had recently become 'considerably richer'. "Would I have to get up and do a speech, like?" he enquired.

"Yes, Mr Smedley, indeed you would." Laura was getting a bit fidgety. Guy hadn't put her knickers straight after he had finished with her, and they were now chafing a bit. "But don't worry, I could coach you on all public engagement matters."

"And me next question is, do you think that electric dirt bikes might go down well at this festival? They're a bit of a passion of mine, like." This didn't bode well for someone who was considering taking on a 662-acre estate. Laura wished him well and let Miranda continue with the tour.

Julian had now gone a strange shade of sunburnt purple. "Are they serious? Some damn Brummie chav? Preposterous blighter. He looks like some touron here on holiday. Can you possibly imagine that at the Hunt Ball? Hopefully, someone on the door would tell him where to go!"

At that moment, Laura became overwhelmed by the fantasy of Gary becoming the new owner of Chalkewood. She decided he was exactly what the place needed, and she would work really hard to help him succeed if he bought the place. In her view, he had the most important quality she was looking for: he was a thoroughly decent person.

Laura looked at her watch. "You may now escort me to the dining marquee. It's midday, and I have a luncheon engagement." The dining marquee was traditionally for 'top-table' guests only. "Do you have an invitation, Julian?"

"Erm, sure. I guess so. Father was supposed to be covering all that. I'll be on the guest list." They arrived at the tent, and Laura was courteously ushered in. Julian had a bit of a discussion with the door-supervisor and was given directions for the public dining tent at the other end of the field. Laura raised her glass to him as he left, thanking him for the drink and for escorting her.

Julian went to ask her out to dinner, but she had already faded out of earshot, and he didn't dare shout.

The top table was being hosted by Peasley Snr. where he had assembled a party of all the usual Toads. Everyone greeted Laura, and she took her seat between Lt. Col. Cockcrow and Reverend Pottinger. She nudged the Rector. "Okay, we're all here now, so you can get on with it."

Giles took to his feet. He clasped his hands together and bowed his head just slightly. Everyone stopped talking. "For good food and for friends, Lord, we thank you. Amen." Everyone whispered amen and lively conversation flourished forth.

Laura knew Guy would be glued to his phone all afternoon, so she decided to message him. I've just spent the last half hour with my panties chafing. All because you simply couldn't be bothered to put them back how you found them. It wasn't a very good way to encourage me to honour you with a date tonight. It didn't quite exclude that possibility, but it would drive Guy crazy for a few more hours.

The luncheon wore on. The apprentice Toads had their eyes swivelling from side to side, watching how everyone did things, as they didn't want to be shown up for having shoddy table manners. A lot of the seniors were military types, and they brought with them all the received wisdom of how one apparently does things in the officers' mess. Does one cut the bread, or just break it open? Which way does one pass the sauce? At what point does one help oneself to more? Does one make sure that they don't finish their plate before the host? Exactly how much food does one leave on one's plate to be polite? Are many people cocking their little finger whilst raising a glass? Do you do that just with wine, or water as well? Does one leave the table to visit the restroom? Or is that banned? Like it is with some British regiments, where officers are expected to piss in a wine bottle under the table, rather than dare leave their seat. Laura didn't have to worry about any of that nonsense. The Toads would just copy her whatever she did, even if she flipped her food in the air and caught it in her mouth like a sea lion.

Everyone was waiting for Laura to rise before they could leave the table. She signalled to Cockcrow, and he eased her chair out from behind her. As she stepped away from the throne-sized chair at the head of the table, Laura caught Peasley by the arm. "You know the deal – I'm done now. Official duties all complete. You have control. Anyone drops dead with a heart attack you can message me. Other than that, I'm not to be disturbed."

"Right you are, ma'am," replied Gordon in a rare moment of due deference.

Stepping out into the sunshine, Laura took a deep breath. She climbed into her Land Rover and drove across the field to her house. She had left the kitchen door open – no naughty boyfriend to worry about today. Her shoes were hurting her, though, so she took those off and her dress, and then she straightened her knickers and sat down with a cool glass of water.

The festival always went through a distinct change of character after lunch. Much of the organisational tension had drained away by then, most of the major events were over and alcohol would now play an increasingly dominant part in the proceedings until the bad behaviour started at about the time it began to get in the way of those still burdened with clearing up and putting everything away.

It was Laura's time now, though. A chance to meet, chat and drink alcohol with her real friends. A time to be discreetly inappropriate. She swapped her cotton dress and fancy lingerie for some jeans, beach sandals and a hippy top. Next, she piled her hair up, put on a wide-brimmed leather hat and her mother's large, dark brown sunglasses from the 1960s. Most people would not recognise her now, though there would be the odd person bound to say, "I think that's her ladyship, there." Other than that, she was pretty safe.

Julian walked right past her, almost into her. He was going round the field, trying to track her down to ensnare her with a dinner date. Thankfully, her disguise was working perfectly. Queueing up to buy another Pimm's, she heard two guys in front of her talking. "So, who owns all this Chalkewood thing?"

"Don't know, some stuck-up posh twonk, probably,"

Laura intervened. "It's that bloke in the military uniform, isn't it? Some lord or something."

"Is it? Yeah. He looks like a real bell-end."

"You're right, he is," replied Laura, with some satisfaction. The guys were, however, now showing an interest in latching on to her, so she nipped off.

She stopped to chat to Eleanor Riggins at her jewellery stall. She had picked up some reconstituted rice that she had since made into matrimonial jewellery. Laura talked to her about her times at Central St. Martin's college.

Next, it was horticulture. Guy was standing with his back to her. She crept up on him and did the thing where you knee someone in the back of their knee. He turned round, looking surprised, but his face lit up when he saw her. He grabbed her for a hug.

"I hear your talks were rubbish, and that you made a complete fool of yourself," she said.

That earned her a pinch on her bottom.

"So, can I date you tonight?"

"Not sure yet. I've been searching everywhere for Julian, to find out what's happening."

"Laura, come with me. I want to show you this brilliant trick." He took her through to the empty store tent, where he placed a wooden chair up against the large central tent post. "Here, take a seat." When she sat down, he took her hands behind the post, and using some soft, natural jute rope, he expertly bound her wrists together before she even realised what he was doing.

Realising her predicament, she commented, "Hmm, quite the boy scout, aren't you? What have you done that for?"

"I don't want you chasing after Julian. So just sit there for a while and have a doze or something. Because now it's my turn to play games. Stay silent too, otherwise I'll have to gag you, as well."

Laura realised she had to hand a win to Guy on this occasion, and all because she had been careless.

"How can I drink like this?"

Guy fed her the rest of her Pimm's. Then pulled the brim of her hat down a bit and left the tent.

Standing out the front was Julian. "Hi Guy, have you seen Miss Stanhope anywhere?"

"Well, last I saw her, she was a bit tied up," he replied with a Sean Connery smirk on his face.

"Okay. Look, old chap, if you see her, tell her to call me, will you?"

After Julian had wandered off, Guy took a quick peek in the store tent. Laura had now dozed off, so he left her for a bit. Standing at the front of his stand, Guy watched the world go by. The great and the good all enjoying the last of the afternoon sun. And him, a proud stag, with the Lady of the Manor imprisoned and bound by her wrists in his store tent.

A lone kid had turned up and was poking holes in a polystyrene cup with a pen and letting the cold coffee run out. Guy looked at him, "Oi... piss off," he said quietly, out the corner of his mouth. The kid wandered off.

Guy popped in to see how Laura was getting on. She was still dozing, so he gave her breasts a little tweak. She woke up.

"Julian was looking for you earlier. He wants you to call him. Oh, wait, no, I'm forgetting – you can't."

"I'm tired of this now, Guy."

"Okay, if you want to be set free it works like this... Firstly, I call Julian for you, and I hold the phone whilst you tell him you're otherwise engaged tonight, and then you solemnly swear to have a date tonight with me instead."

"Yeah, whatever. Just do it. You win this time." They made the call, and then Guy set her free.

Laura was a bit drunk by now. What a crappy fall from grace she'd had. One minute, opening the festival in all her finery, escorted by the military and the clergy. Then ending the day tied up like a farm animal in some dingy tent. Having escaped Guy's evil horticultural prison, Laura wandered out into the festival where she was immediately spotted by Monica. They gave each other a big hug and then Laura spotted the two Pain Pigs, Squealer and Bob, not far off. Oddly, they were both wearing identical black leather flat caps and needle-striped, pale blue, summer blazers. On their feet, they wore bloody awful pairs of Mince Trotters, complete with the random tassels and no socks. There was nothing wrong with it all, but there was nothing right either. They just looked weird. "Why have you dressed them like that?"

"No reason, really. I just wanted a silly-looking uniform for them, one I could spot them in a mile off."

Laura felt excruciatingly embarrassed as they nodded to her, recalling she had recently seen them looking like chicken fillets, all shrink-wrapped whilst being electrocuted. Laura went over. "Hello, guys, I didn't recognise you without your cling film." They didn't answer.

"No, Laura, don't speak to them. They can't answer. I've fixed their mouths shut with special dental devices so they can't eat, drink or speak," Monica said, holding up a tiny Allen key. "I've given them some pocket money, so they can still get a fekkin balloon, or something." Confiding in Laura, she also hinted that she might have a date that night, but she was remaining tight-lipped about who it might be with.

Many people had now left the festival, and the clearing up was well underway, although some stands would be left for the following morning. Laura wandered over to see Guy at his stand, where he was busy putting packets into a picnic box. "Are you still here? Come on, let's get going."

Finally, he finished, and they left. They were heading towards the car when Laura saw some kind of a commotion going on with Monica at the apple bobbing stall. On closer inspection, it turned out that Monica had found the Houdini straight-jacket.

She had put one of her Pain Pigs in it, and she was now holding his head underwater for fun. Laura hurried over. "No, no, Monica, that's naughty, we mustn't do that, not here. Stop it, stop it!"

"He's got another twenty seconds."

"No, Monica, no! That's enough! Which one of them is it?"

"It's Bob. Bob by name, Bob by nature. First name Bob, second name Frapples," said Monica, laughing crudely and dragging him up out of the water, coughing and gasping for breath.

Laura was shocked. "Where's poor Squealer? Monica, I demand to know where he is."

Monica had now switched to her Irish accent. "He's round da back o' da pavilion, nursing his airse. Oi juss gave him a fokking bad toim an da splat da rat." Laura dashed round the back where she found Squealer lying on the ground with his trousers and pants down, and a bright red bottom from where Monica had used the splat-the-rat bat to spank him.

This unnerved Laura. "Right, come on, we're leaving right now." The four of them walked towards the car – Guy had had the good sense to leave at the start of the commotion. "Monica, what's the matter with you?"

As they walked, Monica tried to justify her actions, though she was slurring her words a bit. "Laura, don't you know anything? It's traditional. You do know that in the sixteenth century they used to have old maids' ducking stools at these events? Men used them as a torture method, specifically for women, just for fun. For fake crimes like 'excessive arguing', they would tie the women to the stools and hold them underwater. That's why that pub in Cheshunt is called the Old Pond. It's a hereditary sin... and Bob must atone for it. The sins of the forefathers must be assuaged," shouted Monica, staggering from side to side.

There was something admirably laudable about Monica's historical re-enactment. Only she would have the nerve to do it, although it was safe to say her motives were perhaps not entirely altruistic.

CHAPTER FIFTEEN

— · —

VALLEY OF LOVE

Laura and Guy made it home, eventually. Guy lifted the heavy picnic box he'd been packing earlier onto the kitchen table.

"Some fabulous food stalls today, I thought. And you know what? They throw a lot away at the end of the day. Except for all this lot, that is." He and some other team members had been offered leftover delicious hot snacks of all types. "This is going to be a grand, global tapas." He hugged Laura. "Let's have a lovely night, shall we?"

****

Down in Hampden, Monica had just put the Pigs to bed and was making herself look glamourous, ready for a night out. She was planning on going sharking in the warm, shallow waters of the Three Tuns pub. It had been a great day, and Monica had a craving for a romantic encounter, preferably more.

She circled the pub a few times, looking in through the windows to see who was in there first before committing herself. Bingo, Steven Jollyman was there! She had been watching him for some weeks – mainly indirectly through the pub's smoked mirrors on the shelf behind the bar.

He didn't look up from the book he was reading when she entered, and Monica took up a position on a stool at the other end of the bar. Ron Vaughn, the pub landlord, came from out the back and took her order for a milk stout, placing it on the bar in front of her. They chatted briefly.

Steven was as jolly as his name. He always looked happy and had an expressive face. He had Titian hair and chose clothing that went well with that. Looking comfortable, rather than smart, he was wearing a reddish-brown suede jacket and blue jeans.

Monica went over to make one of her trademark impactful introductions. "What you reading then? Is it 101 Reasons Why I'm so Rubbish in Bed?" she said, laughing at him.

"Yes, it's a surprisingly long read. I'm on chapter nineteen, 'Why it's Important to Shower'." Steven's subtle refusal to come back with a defensive answer reflected his rock-solid sense of confidence.

Monica loved the musky aftershave he was wearing. It invoked an inexplicably strong sense of optimism and adventure. "Have you ordered the sequel yet?" she enquired.

"Nah, it was cheaper to get the box set. Plus, that came with a free prequel on erectile dysfunction."

Monica almost spat her drink out. This idiot was turning out to be seriously cute, and she found herself liking him more than she had first expected. Just then a load of festival goers burst into the pub, and Monica moved closer to Steven, so that she stood some chance of continuing to talk to him.

"What do you do for a living?

"You guess."

"Okay, let's think… erm… gravedigger? No? Okay. How about mortuary attendant? Alright then, what about armpit sniffer?"

"What?"

"Armpit sniffer. Deodorant manufacturers use them to test their products. You don't look convinced. Okay, here's one for you. How about pet food taster?"

"Yeah, another one that doesn't exist."

"Oh… I can assure you that it does, Mr Jollyperson."

"Never mind about me. What about you?"

"No, noo. I asked first. Okay. Are you any of the following: glazier, plasterer, decorator, plumber or electrician?"

"Nope," he said, smiling.

"Right," said Monica, getting a bit frustrated. "How about useless git?"

"Well, hopefully not. Okay, look, you won't get it. I'm an actuary."

"Hmm, okay. That's cool."

"Do you know what that is?"

"Err, yeah, you write wills for people? That sort of thing?" said Monica, guessing.

"No, not quite. I deal with the measurement and management of risk and uncertainty."

"Okay, so you're like an accountant, except way worse?"

"Well, not really. Technically, I'm a scientist." Monica looked on with an increasing sense of irritation. "My correct title is an actuarial scientist,"

"So, you're an academic swot?"

"No, I skipped the first six grades of school when all the other kids were learning short words."

"Okay, enough of this, Mr Jolly-smart-arse. Anyway, I can't hear myself speak in this place, so why don't we move on to the Cricketers and get a drink in there?"

****

Back at Chalkewood, the food was heating up nicely in the warmer. Guy and Laura were enjoying an intimate moment beside the kitchen table, rather than on it. They were chatting, and Guy was gently rubbing her arm, where it was outstretched on the table. They'd both had a great day, individually. "I'd much rather have had you escorting me today than Peasley's random son."

Guy smiled. "Oh, but I was fully occupied on the stand." He perfectly understood the significance of her remark. He'd spent a lot of time recently thinking about her and thinking about how well they worked together as a couple. His initial lust and all the game-playing was also turning more and more to love with each and every encounter. The incident at the Harrogate symposium had also helped concentrate his mind considerably.

He often thought that a relationship was a bit like a plate spinning on the top of stick. First, you had to find a suitable plate and stick, during what often felt like a national stick and plate shortage. Then you had to give the plate a spin to get it going. Every time something good happened, it would wag the stick and the plate would spin faster. But every time something bad happened, the stick would stop wagging, and the plate would slow down, until eventually, it stopped spinning and crashed to the ground. Right now, the plate was spinning really fast.

Guy and Laura had gone out on the veranda with a Martini and were enjoying the wonderful view over Hampden on the delightfully warm evening. Guy had brought over his fancy portable fire-pit and the logs were glowing away. He stood behind Laura, massaging her shoulders whilst she looked at the lights of the village flickering in the heat haze, wondering what kind of evening everyone down there was having.

****

Monica's sharking was going well. She had her prey in her jaws now. The Cricketers was so much more conducive to intimate interrogation. Having pretty much decided how she wanted the evening to end, it was going to be a well overdue meal for this voracious female predator.

All she had to do now was play the polite waiting game before going in for the final kill. Steven's complimentary remarks earlier in the evening and his astute observations about her had encouraged her all the more. It was a beautiful evening, and Monica wanted to stay up all night. She had decided that all Catholic guilt and first night protocols would go out the window. Steven didn't look like the sort to judge.

Quite unexpectedly, the conversation turned a bit sexual, but not in a good way for Monica. Steven startled her when he said, "You're a bit dangerous, aren't you?" He then went on to give an exact description of what had been going on in Monica's back garden. Obviously, someone had seen everything, because his description was completely accurate. Monica's head was spinning.

Upon further interrogation, Steven explained. "Okay, so there's a chap I know. His name is... well, let's just call him Paul. I'm certain he hasn't mentioned anything to anyone else. He has an addictive personality and spends most of his time at home on benefits, gaming for sixteen hours a day.

"He's only interested in things that are extra-normal. He can't in any way focus on the mundane. So, when he needs to get out of the house, he goes poking around. He'll lie on drain gratings, peering down them with a torch, wondering what secret world is down there. It will drive him crazy. He pokes around in woods and abandoned buildings. He used to be a detectorist, but the gains were never high enough, so he gave that up. One day he was round the back of your house and he heard an unusual cry. You might think your place is private, but he got up into a big old hornbeam tree where he could get a bird's eye view."

Monica was enraged. "I'm going to get the wimp and sting him."

"No, Monica, not a good idea. That will get you into genuine trouble. He's classed as a vulnerable adult. The guy isn't malevolent. He's like you in some ways. And do you know what? There's an even stranger truth in all this. He now spends so much time in that tree that his life has massively improved because it's broken his gaming addiction. I only know this as I'm a volunteer counsellor and he told me all this in confidence. You needed to know so you didn't end up spotting him, without having had the full picture, and you'd probably end up doing him some harm."

"Okay, so what the hell now?"

"Well, my suggestion would be to catch him at it, take him in and tell him you're going to call the police... unless he's willing to accept your alternative punishment? Do that, and I reckon you'll have him going mental inside. It would be like a thousand Christmases all at once. You could get him to do all of your washing up." Monica was incredulous at the direction this ridiculous first-date conversation was taking, but then she realised that this was exactly the life she had created for herself. The call for last orders rang across the bar, and they decided to drink up and go for a walk.

"You're an amazing, intelligent, beautiful and interesting woman, Monica, but you're too wrapped up in all that stuff, and it makes you dangerous. I mean, are you screwing those guys?"

Monica explained the whole situation, and Steven became more understanding and reassured.

"I have to say, you're a genius; it's an inspired thing you've done. It's your world, and you're within your rights to live to those rules. There's just one problem from an 'us' point of view – I don't do the 'sex in colour' thing, as you put it. Yeah, I'm much more your old black-and-white kind of a guy. Stick an old movie on, cheap beer in my hand and a packet of unsalted peanuts and I'm happy. Really boring, isn't it?"

Steven pulled Monica towards him. "You've got a pretty face."

"You can hold my hand if you want." Said Monica reaching out a hand to him. "Do you remember the game we all used to play as kids... you know, 'you show me yours and I'll show you mine'? Why don't we do that?"

"Monica, you're thirty-four now!"

"You're a scaredy cat, aren't you?"

"Okay, you go first."

"No, it was my idea, so that means you have to go first."

"Tell you what, let's flip a coin for it. Have you got one?"

"No, I ain't... Don't worry. Look, I'll download a coin flip app." Monica waited whilst the app loaded. "Here you go. Okay then. Ready? You call."

"Heads."

Monica pressed the button. "Haha! Brilliant. It's tails." She thought the outcome was hilarious. "Okay, let's get out of the road then, in case some car comes. Right, here will do. Okay, go on then, do it." Steven stood there with a reluctant expression on his face, and Monica switched her phone light on, so that she could see everything. "Come on, do it. You lost fair and square." Steven reluctantly unzipped himself. "No, no, I'm sorry, that's not good enough.

Let's have your jeans and pants down, please."
Steven complied with his side of the bargain. "Okay,
good. I can see you're quite excited about this. Okay,
so me next. Right, you hold the phone. You're going
to get fifteen seconds, okay?" Monica lifted her skirt
up; she wasn't wearing any knickers.

Steven made a growling sound. "Hmm, that's a
really spot-on, well-trimmed pelt. Huh, trust you not
to be wearing any knickers. Clear what your agenda
was tonight."

"Luckily for you, you passed all my tests then, eh?"

Steven pulled Monica close to him. "You really are
a gorgeous sexpot, aren't you, babe? Shall we try
and find somewhere?"

"At least everywhere round here is dry... well,
with one exception," she said, giggling. "But look,
there's shitty brambles and nettles everywhere. I
don't want my arse stung. How about those thick
round railings over there? I could go over them for
you."

"Oh, actually, Monica, I might know somewhere.
There's a farm gate up here somewhere..."

The metal gate was stuck shut. Steven was about
to help Monica over, but she did a gate vault before
he got the chance. She had learnt how to do them
at school during cross-country running. Steven then
proceeded to make a bit of a meal out of climbing
the gate. Monica laughed at him. "Come on then,
you useless wanker. Get your leg over."

Jumping down, Steven took her by the hand. "Okee dokes. Follow me. It's looking good."

They went round a corner and there was a large area of hard standing with several bays on it. One was filled with plastic bags of peat. "Well, looky here." They took their shoes off and clambered up onto the stacked bags. "Check this out. You can move them around however you want, to support you in any position."

Monica pulled a bag out. "Blummin heck, Steve. The bags underneath are warm. Check it out. Wow, this is like some kind of alfresco heaven; it's a gigantic bed. Okay, go on, Steve, you decide how we do it."

Steven picked Monica up and nuzzled into her neck. "Monica, Monica, Monica. There's so much to commend you," he whispered.

****

Guy and Laura were in the bedroom now. Laura had dug out some brass candle cone-lanterns. She had lit the tea lights on each of the circular brass base plates and then put the large cones over them. The little star and crescent cut-outs in the cones were now projecting a flourish of celestial shapes across the ceiling and walls. The shapes flickered with each movement of the candle flame. Over on the other side were some subtly scented candles.

Laura stood in the middle of the room. Her blue crop-top shirt went well with her honey-blonde hair.

She wasn't wearing anything else except her pearls and a wide, white, plastic bangle on her wrist. She had put Lionel Richie's 'All Night Long' EP on to play, and it had looped a couple of times. With her hips gently swaying to the music, she sipped from her Veuve Clicquot champagne saucer. She had a distant look on her face, losing herself in the music, and the alcohol was making her feel nice and floaty.

The duvet had been taken off the bed, and Laura had replaced it with a pale blue fleece-lined mattress protector. On it lay a large bottle of baby oil. Guy had seen it. He had no idea what it was all about. Probably just one of those things that women do. He didn't feel the need to ask, as he knew she would explain things to him in a kind, confident, practical and mature way.

He stood leaning against the wall, small beer in hand and wearing only his grey boxer briefs. The candlelight cast small shadows across the muscles of his well-exercised body whilst he stood there waiting for the call to action. Laura glanced at him. He looked at her, trying to work out what appealed to him most. Was it the way her silver-lacquered toenails pressed into the carpet as she danced? Or was it the large globes gently bouncing around beneath her shirt? Perhaps it was her carefully trimmed mohawk landing strip? Guy looked on as the floorshow continued, taking another swig of beer. No, what he loved most was the broad, confident, happy smile on her face as she quietly sang to herself. He loved watching his girlfriend being so happy. Isn't this the way it should be for everyone on the planet?

****

The warm wind of love was drifting across the valley tonight. Streams of fairies with magic wands were spiralling up out of the pine forest and into the sky. sprinkling their shimmering pixie dust down on all those who were making love below.

Margaret Peasley was peacefully enjoying a nice mind-numbing, spirit-crushing game show on TV when Gordon first had the notion. She had been sat there wearing her camel-faced expression whilst watching a contestant almost win £250,000 before slipping back to £1,000. "Awwh," she went.

Fat, old Gordon had a slight twinge in his balls, and he wondered if perhaps they might enjoy some 'conjugals', as he used to called it. This was precarious territory though, as Margaret, in sexual terms, had, in Gordon's view, prematurely 'dried-up like a prune'. There was no direct channel of dialogue by which he would be able to successfully raise the subject. Instead, he would have to tread on eggshells and express himself through clever euphemisms, like, "Oooh, I think I might... erm... er... have an early night." But no, he'd have to wait another thirty-five minutes until the TV spirit-crushing had come to an end, as nothing could compete with that.

Margaret knew exactly what the early night codeword stood for, and she could sense it brewing from the other side of the room. She lived in dread of Gordon's sexual euphemisms, underwhelmed by the prospect of what his version of a night of passion meant she would have to endure. The thought of the fat, pasty-faced arsehole on top of her, attempting to feign an interest in 'making love', when all he was really wanted was to drain what little he had left in his balls to satisfy his bodily urges, and then at the end of it all, he'd turn over, let out a huge, eggy fart and immediately start snoring.

Oh well, thought Margaret, better get upstairs quick before the old twat follows me. So, the second the show finished, Margaret vanished upstairs. Gordon breathlessly dashed up behind her and got into bed quickly. The door of the en-suite was ajar. There was the usual sound of hissing, tinkling piss followed by a quick toot on the foghorn.

Margaret never got undressed in front of Gordon, so she took off her tent-shaped dress in the bathroom. It was something she'd bought online from the same catalogue her maiden aunt shopped from. It was green and light and airy. She'd gone past the point of getting away with an elasticated waist. Margaret combed her hair – an increasingly easier task, as she had now joined the race for a progressively shorter, man-like hairstyle. Mind you, Peasley wasn't exactly a park-run athlete himself, as he was pushing twenty stone. Margaret then did her well perfected 'door open, light off, into bed' single movement. It sounded a bit like: bang-click-schlumpf.

With the possibility of using any more euphemisms gone, Gordon was now into the subtle body-language zone. He tried to gently stroke her foot with his, but she recoiled violently. Next, he tried to stroke her hand...

"What do you want?" bellowed the old boiler.

Gordon found that amusing, he felt like replying, Ooh, now let me see... I know. How about a piano recital? He tried again. This time there was a mildly encouraging response, but he could tell this was going to be like starting a diesel engine on a bitterly cold morning.

Some degree of success was beginning to show for his efforts, but they still had to get through the usual argument about who was going on top, due to the crushing weight that they were both carrying these days. Suddenly, it all went wrong, their patience was done and the deal was off, and now proceedings had entered the 'huffing phase'. Within seconds, Margaret was asleep, beginning her twelve hours of futile beauty sleep. This was Gordon's moment – a chance to explore the corners of his own mind, grow wings and fly, and examine the contents of his 'spank-bank'.

Things started out discreetly. It was difficult though, as Margaret's off-putting, fat-induced sleep apnoea snoring sounded like a bath emptying next to him. Gordon pulled the duvet up around his ears, though, so he ploughed on. But suddenly, Margaret's self-abuse warning sensors got triggered.

"Stop that fidgeting, will you?" she bellowed, before instantly recommencing her self-indulgent snoring.

Once Gordon had finally spilled his dirty water, he just lay there, feeling empty and restless. His stomach was now starting to rumble a bit from all the fat-soaked spicy food that Margaret loved to cook. As she lay there in the silence beside the hulking whale that Gordon had become, she thought of all the things they could have had: a relationship based on mutual respect, fun and excitement – all ruined by his controlling behaviour. Margaret had her own plans for the future anyway, and they didn't necessarily include Gordon.

****

The warm peat bags had been a beyond exquisite experience. Holding hands, Steven and Monica lay there in their infinity-sized bed, gazing up at the constellations in the night sky. Steven was mature enough not to start trying to name them. Monica looked at the vastness of the cosmos above, and it brought about her usual feelings of perplexity. It did look beautiful, though.

Suddenly she sat bolt upright. "Tuscany. I want to go to Tuscany. I want to walk through a lemon grove and pick a lemon off a lemon tree. Please, Steven, take me to Tuscany."

Steven, wearing his usual jovial, affable expression, replied, "Well. Now, look. There's a thing, isn't it? You see, I think the answer is no. The problem with you, Monica, is that you have no off-button. So, what would happen is that, at 6 a.m, I'd be lying there asleep; you'd burst into the room dressed in military fatigues, blowing a whistle and yelling, "Alright, soldier, on your feet, out of bed," and you'd throw a shovel at me. Then, at gunpoint, probably, and under pain of death, you'd march me down to the shoreline, make me dig a hole in the sand in which you'd delight in burying me up to my neck, and then you'd just love to watch the waves wash over me before 'saving my life' at the last minute. In all honesty, am I right or wrong?"

"Bloody excellent idea, Steve. You're a real dark horse, aren't you? I'd love to do that to you. It would be superb fun."

"Well, there you go. Where's that off-button? Oh look, it's missing again."

Monica let out a heavy sigh and cuddled Steven instead. "Whoa!" Monica had had another revelation. "Brilliant idea. Look, I'll go to the doctors and get them to give me lithium bromide, or something. Then that will be my off-button. Please, please, Steve, say you'll give it a go?"

"Hmm. Well, I'd need to see the drugs and witness you taking them. Would you be agreeable to that?" Monica clambered around the peat bags. "Where the hell are my panties?"

"Hun, you took it upon yourself not to bother wearing any this evening, remember?"

"Oh yeah."

Chapter Sixteen

—·—

Tuscany

Walking into the terminal building at London Heathrow, Steven realised he was quite early. He checked the departures board and saw the flight to Florence was listed way down at the bottom.

Coffee in hand, he wondered what the week ahead would bring. What might a best-case scenario look like and what might a worst-case scenario look like? Within seven days, he would have an answer.

Monica messaged, I'm here, and a little frisson of excitement rippled through him. He wandered over to the entrance area to make it easier for her to find him. After about a quarter of an hour, he started to search for her, but there was no sign.

Twenty minutes later Steven messaged Monica. Where are you? You are at the right terminal, aren't you?

Yeah, I am. We must keep missing each other, I guess. After a few more minutes, she sent another, Are you avoiding me? LOL

You're up to something, aren't you?

No, honestly, I'm not.

He stood there, somewhat perplexed. Then he heard a voice behind him. "Do you want to go on holiday with me, or not?" Steven looked round, but all he saw were three strange women standing there. This was seriously weird. He looked again, and two had moved on. He looked at the remaining woman. She can't be Monica. She looks like her, though. Is it her sister or something? But she's about a foot shorter than Monica—

"Don't you like me anymore?"

He barely recognised her. Gone was the tall beehive hairdo, replaced with long, glossy hair that had been gently styled, and instead of the insane high heels, she wore flat shoes in pastel pink. Dressed in a beautiful summer dress and a woollen cardigan with pearl buttons. No make-up. Obviously, it was her, as she was smiling at him. He felt like a confused dog. He went to sniff and cuddle her.

"Is it really you?"

"You mean Monica McStrachan? Yes."

Her transformation was incredible. He gave her another hug. She whispered in his ear, "It's okay, I've taken my anti-sex drugs this morning. So, you're safe."

He looked at her. "These drugs... they aren't too powerful... are they?"

She gave him a smile. "We'll be okay. I've been experimenting with the dosage. They're amazing. Just help me remember to take them – that way you'll stay safe, and I won't 'harm' you."

Steven laughed nervously. Monica was, of course, hamming it up a little.

They made their way to the executive check-in and lounge. His Gold membership allowed him to take one guest in with him. Bags gone in an instant, and they were free to roam through the impressive lounge entrance. There was a buffet providing a variety of delicious food, and they had a delightful and relaxing breakfast with a glass of champagne.

"I still can't believe it's you. What exactly are these tablets?"

"They're used by both men and women. But mainly by men. Here, take a look." Monica handed him the packet. "Mycoxafloppin, or something."

"Amazing."

On the plane, Monica leant in and snuggled against Steven as the plane took off into the blue skies and the white clouds.

****

Walking hand in hand through the halls of Florence's Amerigo Vespucci Airport, Monica was struck by the wonderful sense of well-being that foreign travel had provided. They collected their bags, and when they reached the entrance hall, there was a man with a board which had Steven's name on it. He took them through to the hire car that was waiting for them – a vintage red Alfa Romeo Spider Duetto that already had its roof down.

Monica looked across at Steven. "I don't recall us booking this."

"Ah yes, careless mistake by me on the booking site," replied Steven with a mischievous grin.

Soon they were away from the airport and driving along the smaller country roads that took them to Villa Campagiano, an agriturismo working farm, subsidised by the Italian government to offer tourist accommodation. Two sisters, Giulia and Concetta, welcomed them in. They made coffee and brought out some flatbread and a tomato salad, which Steven and Monica ate sitting in the shade of the linen drapes that covered the wooden copertura. "Steven, was this also a slip-up on the booking form? You have indeed been quite careless, it seems."

"Yes, I mean... What can I say? Imagine how rubbish I'd be if I were a travel agent."

Their accommodation was a detached building a short walk from the main house. It was private and rustic, yet comfy and romantic. Inside, it was all stone walls and antique furniture. The colours, textures and materials acknowledged the history and aesthetics of the vernacular. The fine bed linen was also locally made. Monica ran her hand along it, enjoying its rustic quality.

Each window had a shutter to make the rooms cool and welcoming to guests. It was late afternoon now, and Monica went along, opening each one to reveal picture-postcard views. Reaching for the large shutter in the main reception room, she folded back its wooden panels. There, taking up the full view, was a mature lemon tree, illuminated now by the sun.

Steven stood behind her, watching. He loved the excited look on her face as she rushed outside and up to the tree. Taking hold of one of the fruits, she scratched the surface and put her nose to it. "Lemon!"

Monica's day was almost complete, but there was just one more thing... She led Steven through to the bedroom.

"If there's one thing I hate, it's a tidy bed," she said, as she pulled back the covers.

****

Monica awoke in that glorious haze that comes after the deep sleep to oblivion. She didn't even try to work out what time it was. Why would she need to know? A partially open shutter was letting in just enough soft, Tuscan sun to light the room a little. Steven was asleep. Peaceful, with a rested expression on his face. The second hand on his watch was the only thing moving. The fragrance of his sexy cologne completed the moment. This was how life could be. Maybe this was how it should be?

This reminded Monica that she needed to take her sex tablets.

She gazed around the room, appreciating its features. A beguiling mixture of French and Italian architectural influences had brought a charming and enchanting sophistication to the ancient, former farm dwelling. It was hard to tell if the antique wooden ceiling was original or not, but it hardly mattered.

Giulia and Concetta, the sisters who owned the place, had been really interesting and chatty. They had had some exciting ideas, and Monica was keen to chat with them over dinner in the main house.

The sun had now just about set, and Steven was still sleeping. She didn't want to wake him. He had been quite tired, as it had been a real challenge to get everything done at work the previous week before leaving for their holiday. Monica took a shower, instead.

Very nice soft towels. It's all the small things that make up the big picture. When she stepped back into the bedroom, Steven accosted her. He had her in a tight grip whilst he whispered some appreciative filth into her ear. She thought it added a nice dimension to all the other wonderful experiences. This felt like the relationship she had craved so long for. The feeling of being wanted by someone whom she wanted, too.

Sitting in front of the mirror was still a strange experience for Monica. Her new sugar-and-spice girly look was taking some getting used to, but it was pleasantly easy to maintain. Her beehive hairdo had previously taken her over fifteen minutes to put in place each time.

Dinner was what Giulia and Concetta described as a 'zero-kilometre meal' – locally sourced, providing elegant and welcoming flavours that reflected the local country life, including Sangiovese wine from a nearby village. They ate roasted garlic soup, followed by a casserole of duck and cannellini beans. Both Steven and Monica were hearty eaters. There was nothing they didn't eat, and they relished this gastronomic safari. Everything was fresh and interesting.

****

Giulia and Concetta were interested in their guests and wanted to know more about what they did for a living. Steven always dreaded having to explain what an actuary was, but was totally surprised to hear that Concetta's brother taught actuarial science in Florence. "Monica, what do you do?" asked Concetta.

"Bank clerk." Monica always felt awkward explaining about her life. She could have simply said, "Gothic fashion retailer," but the follow-up question would have been, "And how did you get into that?" Articulating the whole because my mate and I were into BDSM, and she killed a man thing just had a little too much potential for disaster.

"Wow," said Guilia. "That's how I started out. I used to work for BNP Paribas, in Paris."

Steven laughed. He was about to attempt a hilarious rescue attempt, but just then there was a loud sisssh, as a pan boiled over in the kitchen, and Concetta dashed out to deal with it.

Upon her return, the evening transitioned to cheese, wine and coffee. Everyone had eaten and drunk far too much, and a great night's sleep was now most certainly assured.

****

Vaginal dryness wasn't something Monica normally experienced. Maybe it was her new sex tablets? She'd have to read the leaflet to find out. Maybe it was something else? No bother though. It had still been a nice enough start to the day. Steven was a very ardent lover.

"You've got a fantastic body, hun. Enzo Ferrari would be proud had he designed curves as beautiful as yours." Even with his customary sophistication, Steven had just, inadvertently, done the oafish male thing and compared her to a machine he'd ride. But she knew he had simply wanted to compliment her, and she appreciated that, as well as rather liking the image of herself as an achingly beautiful machine, in all its noisy, powerful glory. She waddled off to the en-suite.

"Oh no. What the hell's this, Monica? Monica, get back in here now!"

Monica was still in her man-trapping see-through negligee with matching marabou trim. She couldn't imagine what the problem was. But then she realised she had left her suitcase open, and her Uzi was lying there on top of her knickers.

Steven was in a state of jaw-dropping disbelief. "What the heck is it?"

"It's my Uzi."

"Why?"

"It's in case my tablets wear off."

"What's it for?"

"To shoot you with, I'm afraid, sweetie," she said, picking it up and pulling back the priming lever.

"Are you insane?" She was now pointing the weapon at him. "Hey, are you supposed to be pointing a loaded machine-gun at someone?"

"Relax, soft boy. It's a mini. It runs on CO_2 cartridges. It could still kill you, though. But I only fill it with leather rounds. Don't get me wrong, they'd leave a nasty purple mark, regardless," she said, inserting a CO_2 cartridge and loading a mag of leather pellets.

Steven stood there, confronted with 5'11" of imposing womanhood, clothed only in her see-through negligee, Uzi in hand. However this was going to end, he was more than happy to overlook the incident, purely on the merit of its anecdotal value. Who else did he know who could claim to have found themself in a scene from a James Bond movie, for real?

"Okay, Steven. You have four minutes to cure my vaginal dryness, or I'm going to stand you up against the wall and shoot you," she said, releasing a few rapid-fire shots into the fireplace, to show she wasn't messing about. A small plume of dust went up. "By law, this is only supposed to be a single shot, but I went on YouTube and looked up Mini Uzi Mod, and it showed me how to file off the locking bar and make it into an automatic weapon. So it's now a repeater... Let's hope the same can be said about you, Steven."

Realising she had now cured her earlier problem without any help from Steven, she ordered the poor man onto the bed for round two.

****

Steven popped his head around the door to the outside world. As promised, the breakfast hamper was on the doorstep. They sat up in bed, going through it, as though it were a Christmas stocking, and it didn't disappoint. Monica talked excitedly about the day ahead, and the first of the activities they had booked after having it suggested by their hosts: kizomba lessons.

****

After a short drive, they arrived at another agriturismo. Owned by Tara, who taught dance classes there. It was a beautiful and private place, and Monica and Steven had booked a two-hour lesson. Tara instantly understood that Monica was looking for something with sensual overtones. Courtship and foreplay are essentially at the heart of most types of dancing, and that was what Monica and Tara were going to focus on.

Steven wasn't yet part of this agenda. For him, it was more of a skills test, like the TV series Strictly Come Dancing. He stood looking into the mirrored wall, thinking how best not to look uncool in front of the women.

Out the back, Tara was fitting Monica into a black turtleneck, backless jumpsuit, that she had just sold to her, whilst also lending her a pair of heels. Steven had heard them giggling, but his eyes nearly popped out of his head when Tara brought Monica out. The outfit looked almost pornographic. He didn't know what to say… and he really did feel like he was going to come dancing, without even moving a muscle. Much to his embarrassment, the sight before him had produced an instant standing ovation. Worse still, Tara said, "Don't worry, it's quite natural. That's a very good sign."

Nothing in all this was unusual to Monica, given her lifestyle. For her, though, it represented a deadly serious challenge: exploring a more vanilla sex life so that she could form a stronger bond with Steven.

Tara's 'New Style' sensual dance lessons had their origins in kizomba which, in turn, had its origins in the late seventies. The African dance had a slow, insistent, somewhat harsh, yet sensuous, rhythm to it, and much to Steven's relief, most of the moves were made by the female and involved a kind of pseudo twerking. He relaxed once he realised how well things were going, but Monica was upping the intensity and embellishing the routine with some moves of her own.

"Remember, very smoothly, slowly and sensuously." Their progress delighted Tara, and Steven was really enjoying the simple pleasure that came from expressing himself through dance.

At the end of the session, Tara suggested that they have their refreshments down by the lake whilst she took a naked swim. There was a huge four-poster bed by the waterside, and clearly, this was meant as a place to cool off in whatever way they preferred. Monica climbed onto the bed.

"Look, this suit even has a zip, just in case you need to visit the bathroom... or something," she said, unzipping it slowly whilst she lay back on the scatter pillows.

****

They were back indoors, and the girls were having a conversation which excluded Steven. But all he cared about was getting back to their ranch, as he was starving. On the way home, Monica revealed that Tara had talked to her about a possible franchise-style opportunity. What did he think about her teaching New Style back in Hampden, once her house was finished? Did he think it could work?

****

The Tuscan holiday had been one of the best holidays ever for both Steven and Monica. It had been superb in so many ways, but as the plane lifted off into the sky and headed into the glorious red sunset, they both wondered what the future held.

CHAPTER SEVENTEEN

—·—

THE TORTURE GARDEN

Summer was drawing to a close now at Chalkewood, and Laura felt her life had moved on significantly. Her relationship with Guy had matured, and they both had a deep affection for one another. Neither was holding back either and their days had now become gilded by a range of rewarding activities.

Laura loved Guy's organic lifestyle – what else might one expect from a horticulturist? It was uncontrived and unplugged and it came with no reliance on any ostentatious inputs of money. The trip James had organised on the Thames motor dinghy, staffed by an actor, had been a wonderful and special. Guy would be blown away by such a story, but if he had arranged something like that, they would have been on paddleboards instead, and they would have owned the trip rather than been passengers on it. It was subtle difference in approach like this that added a whole new dimension to their lives together. Guy's world was one of skill, judgement, planning, exploration and just a soupçon of risk, just enough to keep you alert. His belief was that risk was necessary to achieve a sense of accomplishment and authenticity.

Marriage was unmistakably the next relationship goal for Laura. Although they had never discussed the subject, Guy had initially expressed a firm interest in getting married and having a family one day. Laura wasn't prepared to wait for a proposal, though, so she had resolved to move the subject along.

Guy had been spending more and more time at Laura's house recently. She sometimes wondered if he liked the old building more than her. He'd spend hours just wandering around the halls and corridors of the house, looking in all the rooms. He especially loved the library and would often sit in there on one of the sofas, reading books. Laura wasn't keen on Guy moving into her bed as a permanent occupant, though, and whilst it made sense that it was too extravagant for him to occupy the six-bedroomed August alone, she was therefore happy for him to move into the main house with her, but only on the strict proviso that he had a section of it all to himself, one which she could lock off, so he couldn't just 'help himself' as though he was married to her. She still loved the fun of teasing him and denying him. Holding on to the option of texting and sexting him at night, as though they lived apart, as that was more than just a little bit appealing.

****

Monday morning dawned grey and dark, with rain lashing down. Everywhere outside was awash with water. According to the forecast, it was set in for the day, so there was no chance of going for a run. For the first time in ages, Laura had nothing to do for the day. Her work at Hauptman Vyse had finished until the big restart in September. So, what was she to do with herself on a rainy Monday?

There was, of course, the undeniable fact that Guy was at home – in his new quarters, in the west wing, on the other side of a recently installed locked door that led off from the passageway to the library.

The east and west wings opposed and looked onto one another. Laura peeked across to see if anything was happening. Guy's Land Rover was still on the drive. Surely, he wouldn't be working in this weather? Although, knowing him, anything was possible; he'd probably have found a way to turn the rain to his advantage in some clever way. "No such thing as bad weather," he'd say. "Just bad clothing." She could already hear him saying it.

Laura had recently found her mother's pair of antique French opera glasses, and she had been using them to openly spy on Guy. Not to be outdone, Guy had retaliated by taking Teddy's nautical brass telescope from the library, using it to peep on Laura.

Not much seemed to be happening in the west wing. Then suddenly, a light came on. Laura brushed her hair and took off her pyjamas. Then she walked up and down, pretending to check her phone. After a while, she became aware that she might be being watched. She walked clear of the large bedroom window and peeped round the side of the curtains. Guy was at his window, in just his manly grey boxer briefs, telescope fully extended and pointing her way.

With butterflies in her stomach, Laura stepped out, naked. She stood by the bed with her back to the window. The duvet looked a bit untidy, so with feet about a foot apart, she bent over to pat it down and smooth out the fabric. She stood on tiptoes, arched her back down and held the pose for a while.

Standing back up again, she walked over to the window, pretending she hadn't seen Guy. She opened her arms wide, clasped the curtains, and yanked them shut.

Climbing back into bed, phone in hand... 5-4-3-2-1... zuzz-zuzz. Why are men so incredibly predictable? "Rather grey old day, isn't it?"

"Yes, Pengersick, it's most inclement. Aren't you a bit late for work?"

"What? In this?"

"Yes, but that's hardly the right attitude, is it? There's no such thing as bad weather, just bad clothing. So why don't you pull yourself together and get out there and do some work before I notify Peasley and have your pay docked?" Boom! That'll teach him. "And I'm being serious," she added for good measure.

"As you wish, but my wellington boots are still in the kitchen, so I'll need to come through and collect them."

Oooh, nice move, Pengersick, thought Laura, as she slipped on her chiffon housecoat in all its sheer woeful inadequacy. Laura went downstairs and stood by the interconnecting oak door, key in hand. "Are you there? Okay, so you come in and go straight to the kitchen, get your boots and get out. Understand?" There was no answer. She turned the key in the lock and stood back, watching as the china, willow-patterned handle magically turned, all by itself.

Guy walked in.

"Okay, get your boots and go, understand? And stop staring at me like that, will you? It's not my fault that I only have this see-through robe to wear."

Guy grabbed Laura from behind in a big bear hug. Lifting her feet off the ground, he wrestled her into the library and placed her face-down over the back of the nearest Chesterfield.

****

They were sat up in bed together.

"Now then, Pengersick, I'm afraid I'm going to have to report you to Mr Peasley for time-theft," said Laura, picking up her phone. "No, wait. I might be prepared to overlook your disgusting behaviour... if you were to bring me breakfast in bed. I think croissants and freshly squeezed orange juice should do nicely. If it's up to scratch and done properly, then I might decide to drop the charges."

Breakfast was very well done. Guy really took that kind of thing seriously. Knowing Laura kept her mother's shotgun under the bed, he didn't fancy being ordered out into the rain.

"Oh, my word. Damn it." Laura was in a panic. "Monica is due here any moment, I totally forgot. Aaarrrrrrgh!"

"I can't stand that damn woman."

"Who?"

"McStrachan. She's a big-headed arsehole."

"That's my best friend you're talking about. You will retract that statement forthwith, or when she gets here, we will both get you in the bathroom and wash your damn mouth out with soap. Well?"

"Okay, okay, sorry, I take it back"

"Don't worry. I know all about you two dating that one time. I also heard how it went. It's okay, Monica's a bit mad. I think you're perfectly gorgeous. It's her loss, for sure."

"Yoo-hoo, anyone home?"

"Shit, it's her."

"What? Does she have a key?"

"Yes, Guy – she does, and you don't, so just remember that."

Monica walked in. "Oh. My. Word. How disgusting. Have you two been doing it?" She walked over to Laura and looked into her eyes. "You have, haven't you? I can tell." Monica could always tell if Laura had had sex recently – her pupils would remain dilated for quite a while. Walking round to Guy, Monica grabbed him by the ear, twisting it. "Did he make a good job of it? Did he?"

"Yes. He was most satisfactory. I threatened to report him to Peasley for time-theft, so he had to be."

Monica glared into Guy's eyes, whispering, "I should bloody well hope you did." She then went over and pulled the curtains back, before helping herself to what was left of their coffee. "Who exactly is that old codger, Peasley?"

"He's our estate manager."

"Hmm, yeah, I know him. He's the sad old wanker I've seen at The Torture Garden in Mapelwick."

It took Laura a little while to process that last comment. "You're saying that Peasley goes to one of those clubs, like the one you invited me, Martha and Beth to that time?"

"Yeah. Regular as clockwork. I didn't really know who he was at first, but he does kind of stand out.

He's one of a few who go pretty much naked, apart from a strappy leather, body slave-harness type of thing."

Guy sat there, open-mouthed whilst developing a joyous grin.

Laura was similarly shocked. "The filthy old codger."

"Well, don't you be so quick to judge. You're either being pervophobic or ageist – neither is anything to be proud of. He's just expressing himself in a way that suits him, whilst amongst friends."

"Sorry, yes, you're right, I guess. But I can't stand the man, so can I just indulge myself in that judgement?"

"Well, that just makes you as bad as him, doesn't it? It's the very heart of prejudice – using a difference to orchestrate hate. Would you be saying the same thing if he'd been seen in a gay club?"

Laura painfully faced her prejudice head-on. "Hunzie, you are totally correct. It just seems strange, though – him going there alone and wandering about like that."

"Alone? No, he never goes alone,"

"What? Not Margaret, surely?" Laura laughed.

"Who's that? His wife? No. He always goes with Mistress Zelda; she generally drags him around all night on a lead."

"How do you know all this?"

"Zelda's well-known. She's one of the top dominatrices in the area. She's just a bit younger than us, absolutely stunning, blonde bombshell of a woman"

"So, he would be paying her?"

"Yeah, damn right he would."

Guy was now crying with laughter.

"How much?"

"I'd reckon £1,000 a night, absolute minimum."

Laura's focus suddenly switched ninety degrees. "How often would you say he goes?"

"Well, I tend to go to every fortnightly gathering, and I've always seen him there"

"So that's £26k a year," Guy said, almost breathless with laughter.

"That's £26k net. But you'd have to be on a salary of £35k to get that, and you'd have to spend your money on nothing else," said Laura, doing a quick calculation.

"Well, it's his money. What's it to you?"

"Monica. His salary is just under £40k"

Guy stopped laughing. "Oh."

Laura's mind was frizzing like a slice of bacon that had just been dropped into a pan of hot fat. She had direct experience of fraud and corruption at Hauptman Vyse and, just maybe, it was rife here at Chalkewood, and worse still, there was usually more than one person involved in these situations.

"Guy, you had better be getting along now. You should be at work." Laura watched him as he got dressed and left the room. They sat in silence until they heard Guy drive off, then Laura beckoned Monica to get into bed with her. She couldn't get the image of Guy and those coils of steel wire and the expensive-looking garden sculptures out of her head. She wondered if she was just piloting some huge, gravy-train to which her careless parents had given the green signal.

"If Peasley's been nicking money, would you like me to have him executed?" said Monica with a cold, dark expression on her face. Laura was too shocked to even answer. "Us women are always in control with events. I could arrange for him to have a mis-adventurous visit to a dungeon somewhere. He would die screaming." Laura hated Mondays. Sometimes they are just like that.

****

By lunchtime, the rain had stopped, and with a few calls made and questions asked, they had not only managed to establish that Guy was innocent, but that he had done quite a bit of work that he had never even been paid for, and that he had also donated one of the wire sculptures to the estate, for free.

Guy had been her main consideration at the start of all this, and Laura was having a moment of remorse, regretting how quick she had been to think that Guy might have been on-the-fiddle. What she had now learnt from her investigations just made her love him all the more.

Now her focus switched to Monica. "Hunzie, would you seriously have a man executed? You being a Catholic and all that? No, wait, that last sentence probably doesn't add up, but hey, you know what I mean."

"Well, Laura, no. I probably wouldn't actually do that. I'd do anything for you, Hunzie, but a one-way ticket to hell might just be too high a price to pay."

Having dealt with the most important issues, Laura felt it was now time to have lunch in bed, and it was going to be a medley of toasted bacon sandwiches, croissants, coffee, Prosecco and possibly chocolate, as well.

Lunch complete, it was time to deliberate on Peasley. Standard practice in any investigation would be to gather evidence first. So, it was decided that a trip to The Torture Garden in Maplewick would be needed, to confirm it really was Peasley who had been seen there, and then Monica would speak to Zelda, whose real name was Karen. If everything added up how they suspected, then Laura would commission one of the contract auditors she knew at Hauptman Vyse to visit Chalkewood. Yes, contract auditors – rather than contract killers – was definitely the way to go.

Monica also decided that Guy would have to attend this fetish club as Laura's partner. It most certainly wouldn't be his thing, but if he loved her he would just have to endure being dressed-up in a swathe of fetish gear, to shield latex sex-spangle Laura from any tedious, single-male spectators boring her all night with requests to lick her boots.

Later that evening, the subject was broached with Guy. He was immediately emphatic that he was having absolutely no part of it. They were in the library, and Monica the enforcer got up and slowly walked over to him. She took hold of his wrist with just one hand, and merely by using her fingers, she had him yelping in pain from a rather unique type of one-handed Chinese burn that she had perfected on her Pigs. "You damn well will escort your woman to Mapelwick, boy." Once he agreed, she let him go.

Finally, it was agreed that Guy and Laura would wear masquerade masks as part of their costumes, and Guy was much calmer about the prospect of going after that.

****

Monica had assumed Steven would agree to come along. If Guy was up for it, then surely Steven would be? But he flatly refused.

"Remember, I'm an unsalted peanut kind of guy," he had said.

It was difficult for Monica to accept. This, plus the Goth scene, was her world, and if Steven wasn't willing to go just once, just out of curiosity, then it was a bit of a deal-breaker for her. Also, if she was in a committed relationship with Steven, then how could she then go to a fetish club on her own? This pretty much meant she would never be able to go again.

These nights out for Monica were about more than just sex. Even if she took her tablets for the rest of her life, she would still crave the dressing-up, the cosplay, the exhibitionism, the exuberance and the way it made her feel amazing and special. She just couldn't understand Steven's complete disinterest in something that she saw as healthy and fun, unlike most mainstream social activities that involved consuming thousands of calories in food and alcohol, or making mundane conversation all night. Steven, for now, would have to go on the back burner. Maybe she'd have to ask him to explain to her what he could offer that was so good it could fill the void left in her life were she to give all this up?

Naturally, Monica didn't need to find a costume for this night out. She would pretty much just be wearing her day clothes. Instead, she spent a lot of time with Laura, helping her to choose an outfit. Subconsciously, she probably wanted her friend to take a step into her world. Guy was simply told to go on Amazon and get himself some black PVC trousers.

****

The night had finally arrived, and the three of them were at Laura's getting ready to go out. The theme for the night was 'Fairy-tale or Mythological Characters', and Laura looked fabulous in her red, PVC, Little Red Riding Hood outfit with matching pretty, red Oxford heels. Guy was getting most excited. Seeing her in her outfit was a lightbulb moment for him. He could suddenly see the merit in it all, and he began to appreciate Monica a little more. Moreover, he felt really comfortable in his new soft, stretchy, black PU jeans. The girls thought he looked the part but pretty much ignored him... that was until he opened a carrier bag and put on his headpiece of black, Maleficent witch-queen horns. He proudly adjusted them on his head and admired himself in the mirror – complete with purple blusher and black lipstick.

"Oh – my – fekkin – word." Monica had just seen him and put her hands to her open mouth. She thought he looked hysterically funny, probably just because of the extreme contrast to his normal day-look. She just couldn't contain herself. She ended up on the floor laughing so much that she thought she was going to die, and she actually wet herself and had to go and quickly rinse and dry her panties and dry them with her hair dryer.

It was just then that Laura noticed Guy was wearing a grey cotton T-shirt. Still choking back her laughter, she told him, "They won't let you in, in that, will they, Monica?"

Monica still couldn't speak, but she joined Laura in supporting the notion that Guy would have to go topless. So, they lifted his shirt off him, and Laura got some baby oil and rubbed it into his torso to make it shine a bit. "There you are. If you've got it – flaunt it!"

They set off in the car, with Monica still having aftershocks of laughter whilst trying to dry her eyes without smudging her make-up. Guy, forever confident and sanguine, was just pleased that he had made her happy. To him, it was just fancy dress, so it was supposed to be funny... wasn't it?

****

They joined the queue outside the club, their costumes all hidden under their trench coats. The queue went down quickly, and once inside, the helpful cloakroom staff took their chrysalis-like overcoats from them. Like butterflies, they were now free to fly.

Inside, the dimly lit building was huge. It had been converted from a derelict bus station. There were galleries above and various rooms below. It was like entering a scene from a sci-fi movie. The whole aesthetic was designed to be a celebration of sexuality, fetish and fantasy, all in a safe and private environment.

Laura had been to something similar once before, so she was fairly relaxed, and Guy was just relieved to see that he was actually underdressed compared to other people attending. Monica was instantly off and chatting to friends, whilst Guy and Laura held hands as they walked around the huge main hall.

"Whoah, what the hell?" Guy stopped in his tracks. Hoisted way up towards the high ceiling was a naked man, suspended by hundreds of what looked like fishing hooks stuck through his flesh, all connected by wire to a large wooden cross. Several feet below, on a low-raised circular stage, were three topless women wearing tutus, walking in a circle playing violins. You could actually see some blood running out of some of the hooks in the man's flesh. Guy was incredulous.

"I think I want to be sick. Can we move on, please?" said Laura. She wasn't judging – it was just a bit beyond her squeam threshold.

Throughout the venue, there were various installations and stalls. One was a large, wooden St. Andrew's Cross. A woman had a man strapped to it and was thrashing him with a long-tailed whip, identical to the one Monica had at home in her dungeon.

The building benefitted from a state-of-the-art sound system which was playing club-type music, at quite a low volume whilst the violin and fish-hook thing was still going on.

There was a stall selling herbal tea, and Laura felt a lot more normal after having one. It was a kind of milky honey flavour and was curiously soothing.

"Hey, check this out." Guy was utterly fascinated by a stall offering to make plaster casts of people's genitals for them. Women as well. Laura felt slightly uncomfortable watching Guy study some lady having the treatment, as others looked on, but she could see that, true to form, it was the technical process he was interested in. Much to her embarrassment, he started asking questions, but the artisan was very enthusiastic in telling Guy all about the process, although Guy declined the offer of having himself preserved for posterity.

They walked on. Guy suddenly clutched Laura by the arm and stopped. "Well, there's a sight you don't see every day. That's just incredible." It was Peasley. Naked, but for his black harness, being towed around on a collar and lead by Mistress Zelda, who was quite the doyenne of the venue in all her majestic beauty.

"Guy, I think Peasley might be equally as surprised if he were to see you here and also looking quite the perv, I might add," said Laura.

Zelda unclipped Peasley, and he lay back on a low wall, opened his legs and inserted a cigarette in his anus.

"Now, you see, Laura – at least I don't smoke," said Guy, laughing and choking at the same time.

Monica was now chatting to Zelda whilst she took a short Peasley break. They seemed to know each other very well.

Zelda finished her coffee and re-clipped Peasley to his lead after his 'cigarette break'. She led him over and had him kneel on the floor to spend a few minutes licking Monica's boots. He really had no idea who she was. Monica looked across at the open-mouthed Guy and Laura with a grin as she pointed down at Peasley with both forefingers. She then winked and gave the thumbs up. This really was peak Monica McStrachan at work. She knew just how it would have looked to Guy and Laura.

"Well, there's an image I shall never forget as long as I live," said Laura, clasping her Red Riding Hood basket that contained nothing but an empty polystyrene teacup.

There must have been well over a thousand people there that evening, so it was easy to stay clear of Peasley and his expensive companion for the rest of the night and just enjoy the many sights and delights.

Monica had been off chatting with other people for some time, when she suddenly returned, bringing a man called Cavan with her. This tall, attractive man on her arm was utterly charming and quite deferential. Clearly experienced in the scene and well-costumed, he was very welcoming towards Guy and Laura, who were later to discover that

Monica had told Cavan all about Laura being landed gentry who owned an entire valley of farmland.

****

The journey home was the perfect opportunity to compare notes and chat about the night's experiences. The key question, though, was Peasley, and their worst fears had now been confirmed. He was spending vast sums of money on his escort. Apparently, she even did the club nights for him at mate's rates, because he was paying so much for additional mid-week sessions.

CHAPTER EIGHTEEN

FINAL RECKONINGS

Tice and Teddy were boomers, products of the swinging sixties. They prided themselves on being broad-minded and avant-garde, but nothing could have prepared them for Laura's phone call that Monday morning. If their daughter's suspicions were true, this was a serious matter, and it was something that went quite beyond what Teddy would normally accept as just a case of opportunistic 'taxation' by a petty criminal. He was in complete agreement with Laura that a financial audit of the estate was called for, but upon Laura's insistence, he also agreed that the Peasleys would be given no notice of the inspection.

****

Down at Hampden Lodge, it was the big prison discharge day. Both Pigs had now served their prison sentences, and Monica was giving them one last slap round the face each. The final can of Chappie had been eaten, and she had just been online to transfer Squealer's £10,000 bail-bond back into his bank account. Bob was a different matter, though – he had been homeless, and Monica had no intention of returning him to the streets. So over the last few months, she had managed to secure a council house for him, down on The Maltings, and also a job working for the Brookwood estate.

The three of them were now sitting outside in their jeans, in the sun, having a leisurely brunch and chatting about how their time together had gone. The house was looking amazing. The shell was complete and fully weatherproof now that Monica had had a firm of glaziers in to fit the heritage-style, wooden, double-glazed window units and doors.

In a spectacular and audacious attempt to get the interior finished, Monica had used her visits to The Torture Garden to network with a group of tradesmen, and she had arranged a one-week jail camp spanning the August bank holiday weekend. She had a team of nine, made up of plasterers, plumbers, painters and electricians, plus one handyman, coming in.

One of the electricians was called 'Bob' – short for Robyn. She was androgenous in appearance, but still a keen player. Monica had originally fobbed her off, but she was insistent that she should be included – equal opportunities, anti-discrimination and all that. Monica had once described herself as 'painfully hetero', so she had invited in a female friend to act as Bob's supervisor. Their presence would add an extra frisson of excitement to the whole weekend with everyone hoping that Bob would get into whole mass of trouble.

****

It was at 10 a.m. on a Wednesday morning in September, when the auditor, Zoë Hammerton, made her fateful visit. She had encouraged Chin-Mae Sakata to accompany her. He was a twenty- two-year-old Korean, one of the Hauptmann Vyse interns, who looked rather menacing. She had instructed him to merely sift papers around and look generally displeased and a bit grumpy.

The estate office was ticking along slowly as usual. Margaret had just put some items of correspondence in Gordon's in-tray. She was only expecting Laura for the regular monthly meeting, so she was surprised to see two other people accompanying her. Gordon was quick to pop his head out of his office and a rather indignant row quickly ensued once he realised who the visitors were.

Peasley was informed that the office computer, and everything on it, plus everything else in the office, was the property of the Chalkewood estate and Laura would do whatever she wanted with it.

More ranting then ensued. There was a sprinkling of threats and then some more pompous posturing.

Indignancy levels were maintained, and there were complaints that Zoë was 'touching things'.

Laura wandered over to a pot plant in the corner of the room. "It doesn't look like this has been watered much recently. You could at least look after it. I think it probably needs some plant feed too, wouldn't you say?" said Laura, closely examining it. She took what was left in Margaret's teacup and tipped it into the plant pot. This successfully added to the atmosphere of unsettling confusion for the Peasleys.

Next there was a faint smell of shit in the air, but it was unclear, as yet, as to its source. Gordon's Adam's apple was doing a fair bit of bobbing. Occasional words along the lines of 'irregular' and 'unwarranted' were being used, and he was getting quite animated whilst throwing in one or two super-posh words to try and claw back some much-needed gravitas.

Gordon was a regular wet-shaver, and his super-smooth face had now gone a rather slimy ash-and-puce colour as the blood drained from it and the sweat began to form. The intern opened the window just behind Margaret to freshen the atmosphere a little. Whatever her last meal had been, it seemed keen to escape.

After rather a lot of clanking about with drawers, cupboards and files, Gordon left the office saying that he had a full morning ahead. Margaret realised she had been left to face the encroaching molten lava. Suddenly, she came up with the brilliant ruse that her 'migraine had returned', and she walked out only to find that Gordon had driven off in their car.

Margaret embarked on the three-quarters-of-a-mile journey down the gravel drive, in her pencil skirt and heels. Lungs huffing away in the process. After about a quarter of a mile, she was just thinking how she seemed to be no further along the straight, featureless road, when she saw Gordon racing back to collect her. He hadn't done so for her sake, that was for sure, and he performed a rather messy three-point-turn, driving up onto the grass in the process.

"Migraine return," said Chin-Mae in his thick Korean accent, laughing as he sprawled back on a swivel chair, cracking his knuckles.

Zoë and Chin spent a couple of hours gleaning evidence from the files before going off to visit some of the estate residents, to ask questions and photograph documents, before returning on the train to London.

****

Laura pulled onto the newly gravelled drive down at Hampden Lodge. Monica was wearing very ordinary clothes and kneeling at the side of the building, planting something.

"Watcha, mate," she said, brushing her hair back with the back of her hand.

"What's that you're planting?"

"Virginia creeper. By the time it engulfs this wall, this place will look just like an old manor house."

"Wow, you're green-fingered."

"Nah, that lovely boyfriend of yours told me to plant it. I've stuck in a whole load of Aubrieta on the garden wall, as well. That was his idea, too."

Laura went and kissed her. "So lovely to see you looking normal. Is everything finished now?"

"Yep, do you fancy a quick tour?"

Laura couldn't quite believe the place. It had six bedrooms, three receptions, a vast and beautiful kitchen diner and a connecting door leading through to the dungeon and prison cell complex in the outbuildings.

"So, no Pigs then?"

"No, all gone. They were brilliant. There was never a dull moment, and sometimes I really miss them. What I really miss, though, is all the work they did: cooking meals, washing, cleaning, fetching this, fetching that. They didn't just build me a million-pound mansion, they did the lot and licked my boots in the evening, too."

Sitting outside on the wrought-iron patio furniture, in the last of the summer sun, Laura briefed Monica on the situation with Peasley.

****

It was a Friday afternoon when the parcel arrived containing ten copies of Zoë's inspection report. Laura sat down and tried to digest the details. Just that moment, she saw Guy outside. He was loading his bike onto the back of his car, ready to go off for a boy's cycling week. She hurried out and handed him a copy of the report to read. He laughed at how thick it was and put it in the car before giving Laura an affectionate goodbye.

In short, Peasley had taken her parents for tens of thousands of pounds over the years. It could even be as much as £100,000. He had mainly been pocketing sundry income from things like lucrative small-scale bird-shoots and from informally letting small parcels of land for cash. The report concluded that there had been wholesale mismanagement of the estate, including theft of revenue, and that Peasley had also falsely accrued valuable salary bonus credits and, in so doing, had obtained 'a pecuniary advantage by deception'. He had also been 'in a position of trust' and all this made him liable to a term of imprisonment upon conviction.

The report then went on to give instances of mismanagement, and it included a rather long section on Guy Pengersick, saying how an expensive horticulturist had been used for tasks unrelated to horticulture and that he appeared to have created a niche for himself in which he was freely using estate assets, and time, for his own personal use.

In the recommendations, it even went so as far as to suggest his dismissal. Laura didn't hold with any of the charges against Guy. Her family had chosen to utilise Guy in that way, and some of what was described were simply favours that they had bestowed upon him for all the extra work he did. But, printed in black-and-white, it made for ugly reading, and Laura instantly regretted giving Guy a copy. Zoë simply hadn't understood the subtlety of the situation. In retrospect, the simple solution would have been to ask her to remove the entire section, but now it was too late.

Although Laura knew Guy could be sensitive, she hoped he would understand the oversight, but just to make sure, she texted him a quick, jaunty message.

Have a lovely weekend. Do be careful. Enjoy the report. It makes for some brilliant reading. PS Obvs ignore that bit about you. I forgot to explain to Zoë about your unique position here. Looking forward to having you back Sunday week xxxx Laura.

****

On the Wednesday, Laura had Monica round for a sleepover, and they sat up in bed talking until the small hours. Laura explained that calling the police would be a simple matter, and her parents were completely in agreement with that course of action. The legal matters surrounding Peasley's terms of employment were more complicated, though. She had spoken with their HR advisers and been told to serve Peasley with a letter informing him that, due to gross misconduct, he was going to be suspended immediately and indefinitely, without pay, pending a police investigation. The same applied to Margaret, and that he should pass on to her a similar letter, which they had prepared.

By this point, the Prosecco had taken effect and was running amok. Laura and Monica decided that they were going to have a bit of fun with Peasley when it came to serving the formalities. Since the auditor's visit, Peasley had been told to stay at home on full pay and Laura now wrote to him on official Chalkewood Estate notepaper saying that he had been summoned to appear before a court baron that coming Friday at 6.30 p.m. – summoning subordinates to meetings at that time was one of Peasley's favourite tricks, so it seemed only fair she returned the gesture. She also wanted to make it sound ultra-formal and scary. Interestingly, this would be the first court baron to take place at Chalkewood for nearly a hundred and fifty years, the last one having been in 1876.

****

Friday afternoon arrived, and Laura and Monica spent a couple of hours preparing for Peasley's demise. First, they set out a large shiny court-room bench in the library. Then Laura dressed in her usual business clothes, and Monica changed into the dark jacket and skirt that she wore for church.

Carmen had also been called in for an hour to act as court usher, and not to be left out, she had turned up in a dark suit, too. She was delighted to hear about what was happening and was only sorry that she wasn't permitted to be there during the actual proceedings.

Peasley crunched his way up the gravel path to the tradesman's entrance, as instructed. Carmen had been watching out of the window and opened the door as he approached. With a face like stone, she said, "Come in, Mr Peasley. I hear there have been some unpleasant goings on."

He knew straightaway that she knew everything, as usual.

After being left to wait for a pre-planned fifteen minutes in silence, Carmen came back into the reception hall. "Well, Mr Peasley, you had better come with me. The court is ready for you now." She led him through the passages and corridors to the splendid library, which he had never seen before in all his years at Chalkewood.

Carmen ushered him in, before withdrawing and going to wait in the kitchen with her mobile phone so she'd know when to collect him.

Peasley noticed that there was no chair there for him to sit on, so he stood silent in front of the bench, at ease, head bowed, hands clasped behind his back.

Laura then spent half an hour laboriously going through every detail of the charges against him, whilst Monica pretended to sift through official documents, glowering at him, all the time hoping there would be an opportunity for some violence later on.

At the end of the formalities, Laura called the police. "Hello, I'd like to report a crime, please." She then spent a moment or so explaining the crime and was given a reference number and told that a detective would contact her early the following week. Finally, Monica asked him to approach the bench, and she served him with his papers. "Here you are. Now resume your position before the bench, Peasley."

This was the final straw. They had spent their powder, plus he had nothing left to lose, so Peasley decided it was his turn to cause a bit of mischief, or so he intended. "Erm, exactly who the hell is she?" he asked, pointing to Monica.

"She's my steward." Laura leant over and whispered to Monica. "Okay, he's all yours."

Monica stood up. "I'll tell you who I am, Mr Peasley," she said.

As she walked out from behind the bench, Peasley noticed, with complete shock, that she was wearing thigh-length black boots with four-inch heels.

Walking slowly towards him and pointing to her boots, she said, "And these still have your saliva staining them, don't they, Mr Pee-Hole?"

There was utter silence.

Laura spoke. "What's up, Peasley? Feeling tired? Stressed? Why not have a cigarette break? You can stuff one right up your arse whilst you take five, if you like? No Mistress Zelda to take care of you now, eh?"

Suddenly, the penny dropped, and Peasley understood what they were talking about, and how much they knew. Monica went up close to him. "You, chum, are going to jail for real. Oooh yeah. And the inmates in there are going to bugger your arsehole relentlessly for years and years and years to come. They don't like posh twonks inside, and you can bother which way you pass the marmalade all you like. Just be sure to hope they don't pass it right up your arsehole."

Laura was smirking and filming the whole thing on her phone to show Guy. Monica led Peasley across the room to test him a bit. "Face the wall, you frickin dollop. Hands on your head." He complied without a word. "I think we ought to teach you a lesson. What do you think?" He nodded. "Do we have your permission?" He nodded. "Well, say yes, then."

"Yes," stated Peasley, loud enough for his consent to be recorded on Laura's phone. Monica winked at Laura.

"Get undressed." Peasley took off all his clothes, much to their amusement, and Monica retrieved her black doctor's bag from behind the bench and took out a really nasty-looking whip, without Peasley seeing it. "Look at you, you bloated, pasty dollop. You're built like a bag of milk, aren't you? Right, up against the wall."

Monica then took a step back, raised the whip high in the air and brought the thongs down on him, full force, in one single blow. He let out a blood-curdling scream and swung round.

"What the bloody hell did you do that for? Are you mad?"

"Ha, careful what you wish for, eh, Mr Pee-Hole," said Monica, half laughing. "Alright, ya frickin dollop, get ya stuff back on, ya bloat-ball."

Whilst Peasley struggled to get dressed, Laura called Carmen. "Hello, Mrs Roland, would you come and escort Mr Peasley from the building, please? His business with Chalkewood is concluded now."

On hearing this, Peasley rushed to finish getting dressed, so that Carmen wouldn't see him naked. He wasn't up for any further embarrassment.

"Oh, and Peasley. Proceeds of crime? I'm going to take your house as well," concluded Laura.

Peasley pulled everything into place just in time for Carmen to walk in.

"Right, Mr Peasley, let's be having you, shall we?"

And that was Peasley's last moment at Chalkewood, after twenty-six years. He left the building, blood running down his back.

****

The following week saw the first of the fallout from the Peasley debacle. Laura's first mistake had been sharing her phone's video footage with her mother. It elicited a quite unexpected response.

Tice was utterly horrified. "Poor, poor man. What a wicked thing to do. A hundred grand? What's a hundred grand in the big scheme of things? We employed that man on a low salary for decades. Good luck to him if he taxed us a bit. And no, we most certainly won't be taking his house. How horrible. And what Monica did. Why did she do that?"

"Well, Mummy, she hoped to brand him with a mark that he'd have for the rest of his life."

Tice started crying, and it was then that Laura realised her mother had perhaps fancied Gordon a bit, back in the day, when he had been fit and didn't look like he was 'built like bag of milk'.

Parents. Parents are crazy people. I'll never understand how they think, thought Laura as she tried to back out and end the call as quickly as practicable. The next thing to happen that week was the arrival of the police, in all their cold reality. Also, the estate office was now unattended, and chaos was sure to ensue if the situation wasn't rectified fast. Luckily, Laura had a good network of contacts, and she had been able to quickly appoint a Mr Chris Willington as Peasley's temporary replacement, with a view to him being appointed permanently, subject to a probationary period of one year.

By far the worst fallout, however, came from Guy. Laura had eagerly showed him the phone footage and quickly got the impression he didn't approve.

"Yeah, funny at first, but then... Okay, so Gordon's a complete tosser, but you lot let him get away with it all that time. And McStrachan, what the heck? What she did was actually GBH. Even with his recorded consent, she'd be the one getting the jail sentence, if the police got hold of that footage. Nah, count me out of all this."

Laura went to her room to reflect, and later that evening it got even worse when she discovered Guy was still feeling very upset about the remarks in the report. He totally understood all the explanations, but he just couldn't get past having seen the accusations against him in black-and-white – not just once, but printed out in ten copies like a bestseller for all to read and reflect on. It was totally uncool.

The real turning point, though, was when Teddy called a meeting via video call. Everyone was there, including Guy and Monica. Teddy was great at pouring balm on troubled waters, and in true Stanhope style, he concluded with a moral message about the lessons to be learnt. It was a masterpiece that left everyone feeling much calmer. But the real surprise came when he added, "Of course, this all means that the estate is quite a bit more valuable as a going concern than we first thought, and upon advice received, we believe we now need to see what Mr Willington can achieve before reviewing the estate accounts again and having a revaluation. So, in the first instance, Laura, you will need to extract us from our contract with the selling agents. Naturally, we will lose our deposit, but that's just small beer. After that, the estate is no longer for sale, until further notice."

It was a strange note on which to end the week, and Laura went to bed on her own, once again feeling despondent about the way things kept turning out. She still thought that the thing with Peasley had been awesome, though – maybe Margaret was rubbing some butter into his back right now? She only wished she had been brave enough to give him a slap for all he'd done over the years in lowering the quality of her life.

CHAPTER NINETEEN

SOLO-MAN

It was September, a month reminiscent of the start of a new academic year, and it had that kind of a feel to it right now for Laura. The fun of the summer had passed, and it was time to focus and move on with the business of life. A glorious Indian summer prevailed over the UK – autumnal shades abounded, but temperatures as high as 18 degrees C. made it feel like it was still summer. Laura sat in the sun with a glass mug of fruit tea in her hand and pondered her life.

The estate was now stable again. Chris Willington had moved into Keeper's Cottage, and Teddy was flying home to spend a couple of weeks with him, as part an induction process. Naturally, there was no handover period with Peasley, and that was a good thing. Mr Willington needed to be free from any influences of the past – the more pleasant estate customs that had endured over the centuries, notwithstanding.

Although Laura was due for a work restart at Hauptman Vyse, her main focus was on Guy and moving ahead with their relationship. However, this was proving difficult, after all the Peasley upset. Right now, she could normally expect to see Guy either lingering around looking for sex, or carrying a coil of steel wire over his shoulder. The latter was winding down anyway, as Guy had now sold all his creations and wasn't starting any new projects. In many ways, she could sense an uncomfortable nervousness about him.

Monica, by comparison, was living a life of tranquillity. Her house now finished, she seemed to be spending all of her time in the garden, planting shrubs and hedges. Her Pigs were long gone, and she'd typically be found doing yoga or reading a book. Her new love interest, Cavan, whom she met at The Torture Garden, was now a regular occasional visitor. Guy had spent some time down there recently, as well, enthusiastic about helping her to make clever plant selections for the garden.

****

Laura had always locked the interconnecting door between her part of the house and Guy's, but over the last few days, she had left it unlocked, in the hope that it might encourage him to misbehave, but no such luck.

There was a beautiful sunset that evening, and it made her feel wistful about her life. She took the unusual step of wandering into Guy's part of the house. "Yoo-hoo. Anyone home?" There was an indistinguishable male-sounding reply which she followed to the large study where she found Guy looking at books and maps. He was pleased to see her and was very affectionate, but her intuition sensed there was a massive wall between them.

Sitting him down on the sofa, she asked how he was feeling about their relationship.

"Laura, you know I love you." Actually, she didn't. He had never used those exact words before, so this immediately came as a shock. "And don't worry about all that Peasley stuff," he said, holding her hand. "This weirdness has zero to do with you. Zero to do with your lovely parents, whom I adore. It's just the stink of the estate and my position here, and I'm blaming nobody, not even poor Gordon. It's just a shit-show, and we need to just weather it out."

There appeared to be a massive 'but' brewing, and it was making Laura nervous. Really nervous. So, she pushed on, trying to purge it, and it didn't take long to come out.

"Laura, I've told you on many occasions how underutilised I feel here. It's in no way a complaint – for many, this is a dream job. But I don't want to be a ponce; I want to achieve something with my life, just like you have, and I want to get my master's degree, as well."

So far, so good.

"And you know, I've been applying for other jobs, and now I've found one. One that has a master's degree built into it. It would only be a temporary secondment, so it's not like I'm trying to run away, or anything."

Laura hardly dared ask, but she had to. "Where and for how long?"

"The Solomon Islands. Two years, but before you panic, I do get to come home occasionally, or you are more than welcome to come with me."

"Oh, okay. Look, I'm starving. I haven't eaten all day," replied Laura.

Her response elated Guy. "Great! Cool." He leapt up and started to prepare dinner and drinks whilst rambling on about his new job. This wasn't something Laura could possibly begin to quantify in such a short space of time. It would most likely take several days of asking one-line questions and then doing research before asking another question and then visualising how it would all look and work in reality, before she had any idea how she felt about what he'd just said.

"Do you fancy some wine? Red or white?" asked Guy. Laura had no preference. "Okay, so, wait for it... It's a UN inter-agency task force project designed to help the islands 'graduate' from being an LDC – that stands for a Least Developed Country." Guy went on and on, and Laura tried her hardest to be attentive and ask all the right questions.

Whilst Guy cooked and rambled on about his new life, pretty much with no mention of Laura being in it, she took out her phone and looked at her diary for the next day. There were a couple of short video calls booked early a.m. She could cope with them, but her big meeting with Chris Willington, in the afternoon, as important as it was, was going to have to get shifted. This was Laura's life, and she needed at least one day off to digest the impact of having this paving slab dropped on her.

"What are you doing tomorrow evening, Guy?" She knew that by tomorrow evening she would have a billion more questions to ask him, so she needed to make sure he wasn't going to be out doing some self-indulgent nonsense.

After dinner, the last thing she wanted was sex, so she feigned a Margaret-Peasley-style migraine.

****

Okay, ground zero. Where even were the Solomon Islands?

Laura was sat up in bed with her laptop and her morning cup of coffee.

So, they were not even in the northern hemisphere. They were literally at the ends of the earth. Next. How long does it take to get there?

"Holy mother of Mary. What? Flight time '1d 21h duration'?" Even worse: "No way! Four different flights: via Dubai, Singapore and Brisbane?" It sounded like the journey from hell.

Sinking back into her pillow, Laura began the equally long and tortuous journey of unravelling this new paradigm that had been imposed on her. Obviously, there was no way of talking him out of it. The one big concern for her was the deafening ticking of her biological clock. The whole wretched issue of what two years could do to her fertility. Momentarily, she wondered if she might be able to ask Guy to get her pregnant before he left? But on reflection, that just sounded desperate and just wrong in every way.

She drank the last of her coffee and then pondered the possibility of going with him. He had seemed to be really enthusiastic about that. So, she looked it up on the net. The first couple of tourist pictures looked great, almost like the Caribbean, but then there was all the talk about crocodiles, coral snakes and bull sharks. Laura was English. The UK had no sea-beasts or deadly snakes. She browsed a few more videos and websites and decided that living there wouldn't be for her, not in a million years. Even for a holiday, the proposition didn't fill her with much joy. A round trip would involve almost a week of exhausting travel, and the first Trip Advisor review she looked at mentioned that the hotel had been overrun with feral cats and Chinese prostitutes.

Laura was now feeling a degree of resentment for the way Guy had placed her in a situation where it was clear she was not his primary consideration. Maybe, if he was prepared to roll the dice, she would as well? Maybe she should keep her love options open? But the thought of dating again filled her with even greater horror. It was all so sad, and she just wanted things back the way they had been. The worst thing was that she knew it could be like that again, if he were to just drop the Solomon idea. What would have been great, would have been if Guy had taken Peasley's job. Teddy had suggested it, but Guy detested schmoosing with the 'Toads' and that was a big part of the job.

****

As the day of Guy's departure drew nearer, Laura became more and more upset and agitated. It was a nightmare thinking of him being there, everything normal, one minute, and then gone in the next – almost like he had just died.

She had to decide where she would see him off. Would it be at home, or at the airport? It was like planning a funeral. Monica was being fully supportive about everything, and said she would be available to help her 'pick up the pieces' and 'plan a way forwards'. Monica's friendship was all Laura had to cling to. Besties are an absolute godsend at times like this.

****

Bang! That was it. Suddenly he was gone.

He was now 37,000 feet up in oblivion and heading away from her at about 530 mph. Laura missed him already. All she wanted to do was go out on her horse and hunt him down and tease him and make love with him. She wanted to have great meals together, to dance naked in front of him with music playing. She wanted to go paddleboarding, wander into town with him, along the riverbank on a summer's Saturday evening, to be with friends. Have evenings with Garth and Gren playing Marquandy. She wanted to sit in front of the fire with him and plan skiing trips and think about weddings and babies. All these things were gone. They were so precious – no wonder they were so hard to get.

And now that was it. Back to square one. But at least she had Monica, and she was with her now, and they were already on their second bottle of Prosecco.

****

Guy couldn't believe it. He was headed to the Solomons. He had only ever travelled to Europe before and once, briefly, to Peru to do Machu Pichu when he first graduated. The Solomons were crazy. They were right out there. Ever since he was a kid, he had wanted to travel to amazing places. He absolutely hated tourism and, even worse, package holidays, but he longed to go to rare places with scientific people. Unexpected pleasures. Getting involved, discovering things and sitting around a table at night, in shorts and T-shirts, with colleagues, looking over the data and swigging a beer. The camaraderie, the in-jokes, the combined sense of purpose. Crazy characters. Eating interesting food out of an aluminium mess tin. Days off, poking around.

It seemed crazy to be leaving Laura, though. Guy sat in his plane seat, and at that moment, as he looked out of the window at the blanket of white cloud below, he had no doubt that he loved Laura. She was delicious and wholesome, and he knew it would hurt if she dropped him, and there was every likelihood that she would do that. He could only hope. Hope and rely on luck and good looks to carry him through.

After what really felt like a journey to the ends of the earth, Guy arrived at Honiara International Airport at Guadalcanal. Walking out of the terminal building with just a forces' kitbag over his shoulder, he began to absorb the much anticipated 'culture shock'. Welcome to the Hapi Islands read the first sign. This was somewhat contrasted by another sign warning of Prohibited Activities. It read:

Prohibited Activities.	Fine
Use and consumption of alcohol	$100
Illegal marketing	$100
Prostitution	$100
Smoking	$ 50

Chewing and spitting betelnut	$ 50
Littering	$ 20

Without any doubt, a major priority would be to get some betelnut and see what he was missing out on. Bored with airline food, Guy headed straight for the well-known Honiara Central Market. He knew it would almost exclusively sell fresh produce. Somewhat ironically though, all he could think about, right then, was how much he'd love a good chicken stir-fry. Looking past stalls selling palm-frond broomsticks, jewellery, coconut oil and hair tonics, he saw one selling the ultimate fast food: bananas. Guy bought three, not knowing when he might eat next.

Guadalcanal was great, but he needed to get to the island of San Cristobal, where the UN camp was based, that afternoon, so he hopped on the boat that would take him there. The vessel gathered speed as it left Honiara harbour. Guy had decided to take the boat, so he could get a rest from air travel, and he was not disappointed, because after about twenty minutes he saw some flying fish. He'd never seen them before.

Programme Leader Dr Caroline Dickson was waiting at Kirakira harbour to meet him. It was a great welcome, as he had just been expecting a taxi, or for one of the interns to collect him, and it presented an ideal opportunity to begin his introduction.

At the base, Caroline showed Guy to his quarters and told him to make himself at home and then come along to the evening briefing. Being a socially confident individual, Guy thought he would take a wander round and maybe chat with a few people. Straightaway, he bumped into a very chatty couple from South Africa, called Rik and Peta, who were very much into scuba-diving. He gleaned lots of advanced tips from them.

Some people were relaxing and sunbathing in the park area, and it was kind of on the way to the meeting hall. There was a woman standing there with her back to him, just ending a conversation with two women who looked like they were leaving. She had big red hair which made Guy freeze for a split second, in a confused déjà vu moment where time moved really slowly. She turned towards him as she left the other couple. He couldn't believe what he was seeing, and he could feel his anxiety levels soaring.

"Oh, hello. Fancy meeting you here," she said. "Small world, isn't it?" It seemed such a ridiculous understatement. She was doing all the talking. "Look, sorry if there was any bad feeling back at Harrogate. It was totally my fault. Shall we start again? Welcome to the Hapi Islands," said Mariette, holding out her hand.

Guy asked her how come she wasn't in charge, given her advanced qualifications.

"Well, it's kind of a long story, but I had a bit of a disagreement with a female couple, and they filed some allegations against me. It's all rather complicated, and I'm still fighting it, but for now, let's just say I'm 'resting', so I'm currently officially barred from heading up projects, but that's just a paper formality.

"Yep, this project is all my work. Caroline is the public face of things... but I'm still very much the one in charge," said Professor Kreutzmann.

Read on for a preview of the next book in the Chalkewood Series...

A REQUEST TO REVIEW ON THE MARKET

I really hope you enjoyed reading **On The Market** and are eager to find out more about Laura and he crew with the next instalment from the **Chalkewood Tales, Wonderlust (preview on next page).**

Before you move on and download Moving On, my Free Gift to You, I'd like to make a small request first.

I would be most grateful if you would leave a review for On The Market on Amazon. To make life easier, I have provided the links to go directly to the Amazon review page for USA amazon.com and UK amazon.co.uk:

Reviews On The Market USA - Amazon.com

https://Amazon.com/review/create-review?&asin=
B0BGNDD2ZR

 Reviews On The Market UK - Amazon.co.uk

http://Amazon.com/review/create-review?&asin=
B0BGNDD2ZR

PREVIEW BOOK 2 THE CHALKEWOOD TALES - WONDERLUST

Things haven't turned out as planned and Laura is at a loose end now! She's realised she is in love with Guy and thought she had found 'the one' but he's moved to the other side of the world now.

Laura needs time for herself and a feeling of wonderlust takes hold. At times like these, a girl needs friends and family to provide distraction. It's a big world out there after all and Laura's life is anything but boring and settling for second best isn't her style. An invitation to a hen party in Paris provides her with the perfect distraction and antidote to making decisions.

Ordinary won't do and understanding if her feelings for Guy are real and getting back her passion for life is now her main focus. Laura's up for anything that come's her way and she's out to grab life by the balls.

Guy's living in paradise but why isn't it working out for him?

Laura's still in touch with Guy remotely, but her intuition senses that things are not quite right. He's out of her life now but she needs to find out what's going on and whether what went before was just lust or real love.

Wonderlust is the 2nd novel in the Chalkewood Tales series. Lose yourself in Saphel Rose's imagination for the esoteric, comedic and sometimes absurd situations that life draws us into.

A laugh out loud, romantic comedy, Wonderlust carries on the theme of hilarious feel-good moments.

DOWNLOAD WONDERLUST EXCLUSIVELY AT AMAZON USA HERE:

https://www.amazon.com/gp/product/B0BGQG5B2P

DOWNLOAD WONDERLUST EXCLUSIVELY AT AMAZON UK HERE:

https://www.amazon.co.uk/dp/B0BGQG5B2P

WONDERLUST CHAPTER 1 - THE POWER OF LOVE

You've been invited to a Weekend Hen Party! How do you react?

It could be a lot of hassle... but what if it was amazing, like once-in-a-lifetime type amazing...? And you had chosen not to go? Maybe you felt like you were too busy? Maybe all your best clothes were all too tight? You couldn't exactly go in your comfortable fleece and leggings that you work from home in, now, could you? Such are the worries of the average hen-party storm trooper.

Martha Bush, soon to be Martha de Beers, was the captain in charge of this weekend's flight of adventure. Being the doyenne of partying within the Diplomatic Service, expectations were high, but so too were the stakes. Ever since her enlightening experience when she first met Monica at a BDSM party some years ago, Martha loved anything edgy, anything where there was some risk or jeopardy, so she had talked the group into going to Paris to test out a new extreme escape game, called 'Abduction'.

At some point during the weekend, the girls were going to get abducted by a team of super-fit looking guys and taken to a converted, redundant cold-war bunker, now a dungeonesque maze of rooms and passages that had been made to look like a film set. They would need to work collaboratively to escape. Dress code? Comfortable fleece and leggings.

****

For Laura, though, it would be a bitter-sweet experience. Martha would be celebrating the very thing that Laura had just lost when Guy, her potential life-partner, had left her to take up an 'amazing' job in the Solomon Islands for two years – a place so far away it took two or more days to get there. Laura knew Guy loved her. He had said so, hadn't he? But the separation was unbearable, and Laura was now keeping an open mind about life. Right now, this weekend was exactly what she needed.

It was a warm but grey September morning when she wheeled her bag onto the Eurostar concourse at the iconic St. Pancras station in all its gleaming, refurbished glory – with contemporary statue of Sir John Betjeman looking up at the vast single-span arched roof of wrought iron and glass that he himself had fought to save from closure.

Downstairs, at platform level, an old plinky-plonk upright piano had imaginatively been installed, so that anyone could just go up and play it. Sitting there now was an elderly gentleman, and he was playing Jennifer Rush's 'The Power of Love'. Adjacent to this was the departure board. Train 9018 10.22 to Paris Gare du Nord, the 'diplomat special', but it wasn't boarding just yet. Then, from behind her, there came a voice.

"Is it too early for alcohol, do you think?"

It was Martha! They hadn't seen each other in five years and their warm embrace reflected that.

****

Martha had booked two adjacent Premier Class tables on the train and the girls were in their seats now, chatting noisily. Nobody cared. The people in the seats behind were two families with very whiney kids, so they were in no position to complain. The train dispatcher blew her whistle, and the train began to move. But one seat was still vacant. Beth, where was she? It was only a brief moment of sadness, though, because just then she came bursting through the interconnecting door, having just managed to board and walk through from the back of the train.

Laura loved hen parties. The cheaper and dirtier the better. A bunch of mates in a hot tub, all drinking tequilas through penis straws – perfect.

Martha was in a different league though, not for her the spray string and the foam, or the 'L' plates, or sex-shop novelty toys. She craved something that would be remembered forever. Originally, she had thought maybe a high society bachelorette party, in the style of the old days of the debutantes, but nobody was doing that sort of stuff anymore.

The meal had just been served and talk now turned to the 'Abduction' theme. Nobody wanted to be the first to ask about it. But Beth was the most nervous, so she tackled the elephant in the carriage. "So, what exactly are these men going to do to us?"

Martha was so tempted to tell her a few fibs, but she decided to play it straight.

"Right, we are pretty much the first to try this, so there could be the odd glitch. It's run by Didier Defois. He's a close friend of one of the diplomats I work with, so be assured, we are all in good, safe hands. The guys themselves are either Sorbonne graduates who work out, or are ex Chippendale-type actors or models and that sort of thing, and basically, they abduct you. Hahaha," laughed Martha.

More questions followed. "It sounds like it could be a bit spicy. I like all that, but I've got a boyfriend and we're pretty serious," said Hannah.

Martha spoke up. "Okay, pay attention, this is how it works. Listen very carefully, I will say this only once. Don't wear the wrong badge. You have to decide what level of experience you want at the start, and that is communicated by the colour of the badge that you choose to wear." Martha spelt it out nice and slow. "White means you want to play it straight, just get herded around a bit – you'll focus more on trying to solve the escape game. Yellow means they get a bit more hands-on with you. Orange means you get touched up, hands down your bra and knickers and all that. Red is even better. Purple means pain, and you get interrogated and whipped, etc. Black... yeah, well, just don't. It's pretty much all the above, plus they take you out the back and bang you."

Everyone was looking very contemplative now and much discussion over badge colour was taking place. Just then, their train entered the Channel Tunnel at Folkestone for its thirty-three-mile journey under the sea. The kids in the seats behind were getting very excited. "Mummy, will we be able to see the fish?" said the little boy, holding his teddy bear's face to the window. Awww, sooo cute! The little boy's remarks brought on a flush of maternal instinct. And that was what this was all about. The transition, at least for Martha, from being conspicuously single, through to having a brand-new human being crawl out of your front bottom. A daunting prospect, so this weekend would have to be outrageously fun for Martha, of that she was determined.

****

The train began to slow down as it left the rolling French countryside. It was now slowly weaving its way through the suburbs and squealing and swaying as it crossed all of the junctions on the approach to Paris Gare du Nord station. Nobody in the hen party was in a hurry to get up, so they let the other passengers off first.

Getting up to leave, Martha noticed the little boy who had been sitting behind them had left his teddy bear on the seat and the family had gone now. Before she could say a word about it, someone lurched past her.

"Woah, quick, out of the way." Laura grabbed the bear and ran to the exit. Pushing past anyone in her way, she ran along the platform, but the family was nowhere to be seen. How had they managed to get away so quickly? How sad. Laura walked back towards the carriage, feeling somewhat despondent.

Just then, she noticed the family had walked the other way down the platform, so the boy could watch the trains. Boy and bear were joyfully reunited. Unfortunately, it was now Laura who was an item of lost property, as all of her friends had vanished without a trace. But hey, you're never lost so long as you have your phone... and that was the real problem. Laura's battery was flat, which was a bit like having her arms and legs cut off. Rummaging through her bag, she dug beneath her flat reserve power pack and found a phone charger, French adapter and lead, and plugged it all into a socket at the base of a nearby pillar.

Thanks to modern technology, Laura and friends were soon reunited. In the station booking hall stood a man holding a card with the name 'Bush' on it. He escorted the girls through to a small luxury coach parked on the station forecourt for the twenty-minute journey to the 14th arrondissement of Paris.

****

Arriving, they stepped out into the Paris evening. People wax lyrical about Paris in the spring, but Martha loved the city more in autumn. Warm, grey, moody. Neon lights coming on as the daylight faded. Old buildings, the gentle slow rumble of traffic along boulevards lined with plane trees. A homeless Syrian family sitting on a dirty old mattress inside a lovely cardboard box beneath a majestic concrete underpass.

There were a lot of items still left in the party's travel hamper, and Martha went over to the cardboard home to offer it to the family. The head of the household looked quite cultured, possibly a doctor or something. Martha handed him the bag.

He spoke perfect English, and he thanked her for her gift of leftovers.

"You look like you are here on a hen party, or something," said Akbul. "Well, welcome to Paris, have a lovely time." Maratha was a bit old-fashioned, so she still carried cash. She took a 50 euro bill out of her purse and handed it to Akbul. "Super, thank you very much indeed," he said. Taking out an old business card, he showed it to Martha. He used to be a city architect. "If ever you come to Syria, please come and visit us. We own a rather nice six-bedroom, detached pile of rubble and an acre of dust."

"Martha, for crying out loud, will you get over here?" The girls were getting restless now.

Their accommodation, L'Hotel Mystique, was hidden behind a beautiful garden. They had been given two interconnected suites on the first floor, each suite containing two double beds. Didier Defois had booked it for them, and he would meet them in the evening to explain the itinerary for the weekend.

Wonderlust is currently available exclusively on Amazon Kindle and Kindle Unlimited.

Buy Now Amazon USA For Only $4.99 – Go To Amazon Link HERE:
https://www.amazon.com/gp/product/B0BGQG5B2P

Buy Now Amazon UK For Only
£4.99 – Go To Amazon Link HERE:
https://www.amazon.co.uk/dp/B0BGQG5B2P

Moving On (The Prequel) - Free Book

Making the most of her secondment from London with management consultants Hauptmann Vyse, Laura Stanhope wants to make the most of her time living and working in New York.

Laura's connections see her at the forefront of organising a charity dinner for the company, with the great and good of New York society attending. Following its success, she is looking for some excitement outside of work. Meeting friends and influencing people is Laura's style and she soon makes new friends at work and in her neighbourhood.

Her family have pedigree, owning Chalkewood, a country estate in England. Chalkewood has been in the family for generations and Laura as Lady Of The Manor in waiting has decisions to make.

Will she make a go of her career and new friendships in America or go back to England to support her family, who want to move on and sell the estate. Laura needs to make the right decisions as she's looking for love.

'Moving On' is the first instalment of this laugh out loud, romantic comedy series and is the Prequel to the first book, 'On The Market' in 'The Chalkewood Tales' series.

Preview Your Free Book - Moving On (The Prequel)

Preview Moving On Here

https://saphelrose.com/book/moving-on

Download Moving On Here – FREE BOOK

https://saphelrose.com/download-moving-on/

About Author

SAPHEL ROSE

Raised in Hertfordshire, England in the United Kingdom, Saphel has led an interesting life. They say that 'curiosity killed the cat' and so it nearly did on a number of occasions whilst Saphel pursued a life exploring the curious. From the back streets of London, to the closed areas of rural China, or the snow-covered peaks of Europe, Saphel could never resist the lure of knowing what lay, just around the next corner.

Whether it was people or places, Saphel always wanted to know how and why things worked. Most of the characters, or events in Saphel's books are either real or are based on true stories.

Saphel is the ultimate storyteller and will take you into the lives of some fascinating people and their unusual ways. Many of these people are Saphel's women friends and Saphel feels proud to have known them for all their quirks and unusual ways. Although the stories are designed to entertain, they do still address the wants, ambitions and issues that are common to many people.

These days, Saphel is to be found living in Salisbury, England. The home of the Russian Novichok poisonings, but also the home of a Cathedral with a 123 metre spire ...as any good Russian agent will tell you.

Having strenuously resisted every call to write a book, Saphel has finally given in and agreed to lay bare the stories of an extranormal life.

MORE ABOUT SAPHEL ROSE

FOR LATEST UPDATES AND TO JOIN MY
NEWSLETTER GO TO:
SIGN UP NOW:
https://saphelrose.com/sign-up/

website: https://saphelrose.com/

Or Visit My Facebook Page

https://www.facebook.com/saphelroseauthor

Made in the USA
Las Vegas, NV
29 November 2022

60652092R00225